# GETTING REEL

# ROSEVILLE ROMANCES

Book One: Picture Imperfect
Book Two: Finding Harmony
Book Three: Curtain Call
Book Four: Getting Reel

# GETTING REEL

by

Alyssa Roat and Hope Bolinger

Getting Reel
Published by Mountain Brook Ink
White Salmon, WA U.S.A.



The website addresses shown in this book are not intended in any way to be or imply an endorsement on the part of Mountain Brook Ink, nor do we vouch for their content.

This story is a work of fiction. All characters and events are the product of the authors' imaginations. Any resemblance to any person, living or dead, is coincidental.

Scripture taken from the Holy Bible, NEW INTERNATIONAL VERSION®, NIV® Copyright © 1973, 1978, 1984, 2011 by Biblica, Inc.® Used by permission. All rights reserved worldwide.

© 2023 Alyssa Roat and Hope Bolinger
Published in association with Cyle Young of Cyle Young Literary Elite.
ISBN 9781953957-37-5

The Team: Miralee Ferrell, Kristen Johnson, Tim Pietz, Cindy Jackson
Cover Design: Indie Cover Design, Lynnette Bonner Designer

*Mountain Brook Ink is an inspirational publisher offering fiction you can believe in.*
Printed in the United States of America

# HOPE'S ACKNOWLEDGMENTS

There is so much about this whole publication process that makes us feel out of control. But God, you are in complete control. You open doors when it's time for them to be opened, and You shut them when it's time for them to be shut. Thank You for being in control of this series, as we hope it blesses the hearts of readers.

To my coauthor, who has dealt with me in all my want to control the process, and who has been there for me when so many things went wrong throughout this process. It has been an absolute delight to coauthor seven books with you. I do hope that there are ways we can collaborate down the road. This feels so bittersweet, writing the final acknowledgements for this series.

To Miralee, who believed in us and gave us the chance to do this. We've loved how you have fallen in love with each of the characters. And to the MBI team who has graciously helped us put this together. To the editors, cover designers, formatters, publicists, and everyone else. Y'all are amazing.

To my friends and family, who are beautiful blessings in this process. To Grace, Daniel, Mom, Dad, Libby, Ian, Grandma, Grandpa, James, Carlee, Ellen, Jess, Tyler, Sonya, and so many others. To Trey, who I met halfway through the writing process of this. You helped ground me after I dealt with a lot of interpersonal things. To my ridiculous cats Odin and Freya who impede my writing progress.

To all the ridiculous group chats who cheer us on—The Cyle chat, the Pizza Squad, the PWR chat, the Goon Squad, amongst others.

To the cover sharers, reviewers, launch team members, bloggers, and everyone who got the word out about these books. We are so grateful and indebted to you.

And to our readers. Thank you for finishing this series strong with us, and for cheering on our characters as they face their deepest fears and enjoy the beautiful blessings that life has to offer.

# ALYSSA'S ACKNOWLEDGMENTS

And with that, we reach our fourth season, and with it, the fourth and final romance.

Hope, we did it. Seven books together, how does it feel? I would never have even thought to attempt writing sweet romance without you. We make quite the team, and it's been an honor.

To Miralee and the team at MBI, from Tim and Kristen to editors, proofreaders, formatters, our lovely cover designer, and our talented audio narrator, thank you. What an amazing home for these books.

To my family—my ever-supportive parents, my sister, grandparents, aunts and uncles and cousins and all of you who are my biggest fans. To Kookoo and Zibby, who can't read but do scream for food and walk on the keyboard to remind me that they love me.

To my friends—Nikki and Juli, the Goose family, the Indy peeps, the Skittles, all of you who cheer me on and come along for the ride. I would lose my sanity without you.

To the prowrites, the Cyle chat, my favorite librarian, and all those who have been with me in the process, but I haven't yet named here. I haven't forgotten you, and your support means so much.

To our readers, reviewers, bloggers, and everyone who helps share about our books, thank you. We couldn't do this without you.

I hope you enjoy this final book, dear readers, and may you delight in the adventure of pursuing God's calling, wherever He leads.

# HOPE'S DEDICATION

*To Nikki, who fought so hard to see this book being brought to light. We've loved all your film expertise—albeit a ton of that expertise coming from horror films. Most of the content that will not end up in a sweet romance. We love you!!*

# ALYSSA'S DEDICATION

*Also to Nikki. Bet you thought we were kidding about these dedications, but we were NOT! Also bet you didn't realize those years ago that Miralee's new publicist (and said publicist's co-author) were going to claim you as part of our batty trio, but now you're stuck with us. Love you ;)*

# Chapter One

ZINNIA PRESTON FROWNED AT PETER PARKER, the spider plant. The spiky-leaved greenery in a hand-sized adobe pot sat right square in the middle of her camera shot.

Her living room, littered with spider plants of all kinds—named after famous spiders in literature—left her little space to film. Auditions for movies tended to require a blank wall, so the casting directors could view the actors in their full glory.

Now twenty-seven, and well past the age of most starlets who broke into Hollywood, Zinnia's window to break into film had thinned over the years.

When would she run out of chances?

She cradled Peter Parker in her palms, acrylic nails tapping against the drawings on the pot. Pink flowers decorated this one. Last week, Zinnia allowed the neighbor's children to paint designs on her various "pets."

Since work prevented her from the chance to come home and take a dog for a walk, she made the most of her vegetation friends.

"Come here, Peter." She set him beside the mama spider plant, Shelob, that spawned all the little spider children. "Come join Mama Shelob over here. She'll be so happy to see you."

With two fingers, Zinnia patted the tips of Peter's leaves. Then she rose and returned to the camera, through which she'd just filmed her latest take.

A long breath passed her lips. With a quick glance, she flicked her gaze outside.

Golden light washed the room. Outside the screen door to her condo, tips of leaves on the trees in her backyard bled red and orange at their ends. Reaching the end of September, nature would soon watercolor every piece of green outdoors.

It was getting pretty late.

She chewed on her lip. "Too bad Clark didn't let me out early."

Zinnia skipped lunch today in the hopes that that extra hour could give her plenty of time to audition. With her coworker Caroline getting swamped with new picture book projects, her boss Clark Knox sent more of Caroline's copy work to Zinnia.

Which meant she spent an extra hour today at the nonprofit where she worked, Helping Hope, instead of filming at home.

On the camera, she tapped the latest "take" and watched the video.

"Hello." A woman with blonde hair and thin eyebrows smiled. Sure enough, Peter Parker's leaves formed shadows at the corner of the screen. "My name is Zinnia Preston, and I will be auditioning for the role of 'Woman on Park Bench'."

Zinnia winced at how her voice sounded through the camera, all tinny. Certainly not what the audition listing had mentioned. She glanced at the link to the audition again on a Facebook page for film actors.

Call for Auditions for a Netflix series, to be filmed in Grand Rapids this Saturday, September 24. Roles needed to be filled listed below. Please send a video introducing yourself and read the sides provided at the link below. Email the audition to laurel@silverspotlightcasting.com by no later than 7 P.M. tonight, September 22.

**Roles Needed:**
**Woman on Park Bench (ages 20-30):** Speaks in a low voice, any ethnicity, any height, but under 5'8" is preferred.
**Mysterious Man (ages 30-40):** Any ethnicity, preferred height 6'0" or taller.

Zinnia hit pause on the camera and sighed. Because her plant got in the way, she'd have to retake this, wouldn't she?

A buzz muffled into the carpet. She picked up her phone that she'd put down a second ago and squinted at the device.

Clark's name blipped on the screen. Even though it was near seven in the evening, he'd blitzed her phone with nonstop texts since she'd left the office at five.

Her stomach squeezed as she tapped on the text.

**Clark:** REad eMail

Clark Knox was good at many things—hunting safaris in Africa, creating resources for at-risk kids in the Roseville, Michigan area...yelling at his staff.

But Clark Knox did not have skills in a certain area—texting. Thick thumbs did the man a major disservice whenever he typed a message to his workers.

Zinnia collapsed onto her carpet.

Long carpet strings tickled her neck as she clicked onto her email inbox. She'd left this on mute on her phone, in the hopes that she could create some workspace boundaries between Clark and herself. But that didn't seem to work, now did it?

Dryness filled her eyes as she read the email. How much sleep had she gotten last night?

*Zinnia,*

*Caroline is swamped with the latest picture book project. She and her illustrator Andy are going to do a book for our spring catalog, and we've rushed the deadline for this.*

*She was unable to get to some of the copy assignments I sent her way. I've attached them. Turn them in to me sometime this evening.*

*Clark Knox*

Six attachments rested at the bottom of the email. Ugh, that would take her hours to complete.

With a groan, she sat up and glanced up at her camera.

"We're going to have to go with that audition take, aren't we, Peter?"

The spider plant didn't reply. Zinnia lifted herself and plucked the camera off the tripod. She clicked off the ring light that highlighted a blank spot on the living room wall with a wash of beams.

With hasty speed, she uploaded the file to her computer and crafted her email to the casting director. Craning her neck to the left, on her couch, she soaked in the dark orange that filled the sky.

"Please, God. Please let this be the one."

Every part of her wanted to reshoot. Take a little extra time on this audition and give the casting directors something perfect. But a voice of her late grandma rang in her head.

"If you try to control every situation, to make it perfect, you'll end up controlling nothing. Everything will slip through your fists like sand."

*Okay, Grandma, I won't try to control this one.*

A shaky finger tapped the send button.

She shut her laptop and shoved the computer into its case. Heaven knew she'd marked off her house as a sacred space away from work, so she'd have to complete the tasks for Clark at the favorite coffee hotspot in Roseville—She Brews.

Wisps of smoke from a cinnamon-scented candle spiraled as she blew out the flame. She looped her purse strap over her shoulder and headed toward the front door. Right as she turned the knob, her phone buzzed in her bag.

Digging the device out, she expected to spy another message from Clark. Instead, one from her younger sister Georgia blinked.

Georgia? Even though the two sisters lived about twenty minutes apart, Zinnia counted her lucky stars if they met twice a year. She opened the message.

**Georgia:** Hey, girlie! Have some downtime on Saturday. But only between one to three. And I may have even less than that. Matt—the adorable husband that he is—needs me for something in the evening. Shall we go to that teahouse in Roseville that you love? Can you reserve that for us? I have no time on my hands. Ha ha, gotta love married life.

*Georgia* loved that teahouse, *not* Zinnia. But Zinnia's younger sister always had a way of twisting words like pretzels. She knew that somehow Georgia would find a way to spin a former message from Zinnia to make it seem like Zinnia loved the tea place called, "Spill the Tea."

She also knew how Georgia would never let Zinnia forget it if Zinnia dropped a possible time for the two of them to hang out.

*What happens if I get cast in the film on Saturday?*

Georgia dropped heavy hints in their last outing together about how she didn't foresee Zinnia making it into film.

A headache pounded Zinnia's temples. She'd have to worry about that later.

Casting directors tended to make quick decisions, so she'd cross that bridge when it appeared.

After all, she couldn't control any of that now.

She threw a wave at her neighbor Joy, and the three kids, all decorating the sidewalk with their latest chalk creations, then locked her front door and slid into her car seat.

Joy had always seemed like the older sister Zinnia hoped for, but never had the luck of receiving.

Zinnia plugged the key into the ignition and the engine puttered to life.

Yikes, she'd need to take this in for an oil change soon. Maybe she could squeeze that in between her morning workout and shower tomorrow.

If Clark didn't send any other tasks that needed to get done in the morning. He did that sometimes.

Gold sunlight glinted on car windows as she zoomed to the coffee shop. Bees buzzed in her brain as they seemed to say *buzz,* assignments from Clark, *buzz,* spending time with Georgia, *buzz,* would she fail another film audition?

Tires screeched as she made a quick turn into the parking lot. Rows of cars filled the spaces.

Oh boy, she'd forgotten how when students went back to school for the fall that they'd swarm the local joint in the evenings to catch up on assignments. At the farthest corner of the lot, she spotted an open space.

Bingo!

Her car sped toward the spot. Two headlights blinked into view, bright blue ones. The kind of lights that car dealers attached to the latest and most expensive vehicles.

Why did that sleek, silver car look familiar? Had she spotted the vehicle in the theater parking lot once? During that play where she'd helped out her friend Griffith?

A name popped into her head—Ryan.

Griffith's other friend, the one who almost ruined the play last year by changing up the light cues in the booth.

"Ugh, Ryan. Let me have that spot."

Both of their cars' noses faced each other, like some Western high-noon fight.

Ryan's engine revved.

"Seriously?" She shoved her palm against the car horn. "I was here first, sir."

Even though she couldn't peer through his tinted windows, she imagined he shot her some sort of dirty look. Everything about that man screamed diva. Zinnia would know. Georgia often called Zinnia that over text messages.

Zinnia's phone buzzed in her purse, stationed on the passenger seat next to her.

"I don't have time for this, Ryan. I need to get some work done."

Her engine growled as she yanked her wheel to the left and

wedged herself into the spot. Through her rearview mirror, she watched Ryan's car. It sat there, for a few seconds, as if stunned.

Then the vehicle skidded forward, roaring.

She slackened herself against her seat and let out a long sigh. Guilt gnawed at her insides, but she'd have to address that later.

"Let's just hope"—she unbuckled her seatbelt—"that we don't have any more Ryan encounters in the foreseeable future."

Ryan Torino stared at the car that had just zoomed in front of him and stolen his parking spot.

He gripped the stick shift and jerked to life, heading to make another loop around the parking lot of his favorite coffee joint, She Brews.

"That's fine, no one else needs a parking spot besides you," he grumbled to the other driver as he passed. "It's not like getting this thing in and out of gear is hard or anything. Please, be my guest. Zoom in front of me."

Maybe if he wasn't in such a foul mood to begin with, he would recognize the other car did get there a *few* nanoseconds ahead of him. It wasn't *their* fault he liked the extra control afforded by a manual drive, which led to situations like this where his engine revving probably came off a bit aggressive, even if accidental.

After the engagement photo session he'd just had, he needed one of his friend Griffith's coffee concoctions and to go home and pet his dog. And cat, if Buttercup would deign to acknowledge his existence today.

On his second circle of the parking lot, a car pulled out, leaving an opening not far from the vehicle that had stolen his original spot. He pulled in and shut off the engine in time to see the owner of the thieving vehicle enter the coffee shop.

Swishing golden hair, stylish clothing, a confident stride—none other than Zinnia, one of Griffith's other friends…who also happened to scare the living daylights out of Ryan.

He gulped. Great. She already looked down her nose at him. Now she probably thought he was a jerk, as well.

He debated turning around right then and heading home, avoiding the scary stage manager altogether. When she pointed a finger at him and threatened to throw him out of the light booth last winter if he kept adjusting the light cues during the play—he'd just been making some slight improvements—he'd gotten the impression she meant literally.

She had just *honked* at him. One did not *honk* at others in the great state of Michigan.

He blew out a breath, now more annoyed than intimidated, and unbuckled his seatbelt. "I can be civil. In fact, I can be *polite*." He could turn this situation around. He didn't like leaving conflicts unresolved, and there was always a way to fix things.

He headed into the coffee shop, a breeze with a hint of fall coolness ruffling his hair. He pushed up his glasses as he stepped inside, the tinkling bell chiming with the rippling voices of students, couples, Bible study partners…wow, was half of Roseville at She Brews this evening?

At the bar, his playwright pal Griffith handed Zinnia a cup. Griffith had a full-time job at the theater now, thanks to the play both Ryan and Zinnia had helped with last winter, but the playwright still occasionally came in to help at the coffee shop when they needed it. Another creative outlet, this one for wacky brews. Zinnia flashed a smile, and they exchanged a few words before she turned toward the rest of the room to find a seat.

Her gaze met Ryan's, and the smile slipped from her face, replaced by pursed red lips and a wrinkled nose. She immediately looked away and headed toward the other side of the room.

*Great.* He joined the short line, trying not to look like he was watching as she set up with a laptop in a corner. She seemed engrossed in work. Not today, then. She would probably only be more annoyed if he tried to strike up a conversation now.

*Chicken.*

He tapped his fingers on his leg, replaying the vehicular standoff over and over in his mind until he realized what he was doing. Obsessing. Obsessing over a situation it was too late to change.

He forced his mind to other things, but his brain apparently had it out for him today. Instead, he found himself remembering the photo shoot from earlier.

The couple had requested a sunset shoot, and he had readily agreed. Though the lighting would be difficult, he would love getting those colors on camera, and he had plenty of ideas for silhouette shots, angles, maybe even getting the light reflecting off the engagement ring…

But the pair had shown up fifteen minutes late, wasting valuable daylight, and when he had suggested silhouette shots against the sunset, the bride-to-be argued that she wanted their faces to show up clearly. Even once Ryan explained they would get some of both.

He tried to direct them into candid poses, but they wouldn't stop posing stiffly. They wanted straight-on shots rather than angles that might interest the eye. Plus, due to their lateness, he didn't have time to fiddle with that perfect, sunset-reflecting ring shot.

A wash. A complete wash for any sort of artistic expression, and they seemed the sort who would complain later about the photos, despite not listening to his advice. Thank goodness for photo editing software. That should help with the too-dark pictures.

"Hey. What can I get for you?"

Ryan gave his head a small shake, focusing again on the present. He'd reached the front of the line, and Griffith stood on the other side of the counter, a hand towel over his shoulder.

"Hey, Griff." He scanned the menu. "Um, my usual."

"You got it." Griffith rang him up.

Ryan honestly wasn't sure exactly what went into his "usual," but Griffith had made the concoction once, and Ryan had ordered the same thing ever since. Not too sweet, not too bitter, a little bit of spice and cream. Secretly, it was the only "Griffith specialty" Ryan had ever enjoyed—they tended to include strange flavors like lavender or rhubarb—but he wouldn't tell his friend that. Better to let Griffith think he just *especially* loved this one.

Despite the crowd, Ryan received his coffee not long afterward and scanned the room for a seat. Sweat prickled the back of his neck as he spotted the only open space available—a faux leather chair near Zinnia.

Like a man marching to his death, he straightened his shoulders and crossed the room to that empty seat.

He plopped down, not quite making eye contact. *Say something, Ryan.* "Hey-o." His cheeks burned red. *Hey-o? You idiot.* His brain had short-circuited somewhere between "hey" and "hello" and decided on a mashup.

Zinnia lifted one well-shaped eyebrow, nodded to him, and returned her full attention to her computer screen.

So much for a chance to smooth things over. He didn't think he could muster the strength to offer more words for an apology after "hey-o." He fumbled for his phone, anything to keep his hands busy.

A little bubble above his email app displayed four unread messages. How he hated those little bubbles cluttering his pristine screen, every app in its place. They sent a jolt of anxious energy through him, a sense of unfinished business.

He deleted three junk emails and was about to hit "delete" on a fourth from an unfamiliar sender when he noticed the subject line: Roseville Film Festival Thirty Day Filmmaker's Challenge.

*Thirty days?* A quick turnaround, but maybe for a short film, especially if he had a script already written…although, his photography business was booming, taking up most of his time as Roseville's beautiful fall weather approached, perfect for engagement shoots, weddings, and senior pictures.

He clicked.

As he scanned the lines, his eyebrows rose. The project would be demanding, but…his eyes widened as he read the names of the judges and those who would be attending as talent scouts. Names he knew.

Hollywood names.

How long had he been praying for a way to advance his career? His parents had convinced him not to make the risky move to Los Angeles, to "start small," but he had never given up his dream of working on major motion pictures, shooting high-budget sets, directing award-winning actors. Twenty-six was beginning to feel late in the game, but with a chance like this, he might actually catch someone's eye.

As he kept reading, his chest tightened. These requirements …would he have time? Could he execute a quality project on a deadline?

Deadlines had never been his strong suit.

He shoved his phone in his pocket and took his coffee to go. He needed to do some thinking, and sitting next to Zinnia's intimidating presence wasn't going to help.

*Good thing we don't work together.*

Time to hole up with a computer and brainstorm.

# Chapter Two

ZINNIA CLUTCHED THE GIFT BASKET CLOSE to her stomach and peered out of her cubicle at the door that led into the Helping Hope offices.

Still no Caroline.

Perhaps, today, Caroline would at last forgive her for what happened a year and a half ago.

Zinnia spun around in her swivel chair and examined the contents contained within the wicker basket—kale chips, mixed nut packages, chia pudding. If any healthy snack company needed a spokesperson, Zinnia would sign Caroline up for the job.

She observed the color of her outfit today as she set the basket down on her desk.

Blue, every piece of her outfit screamed, "Hello, I am a robin's egg. An innocent, adorable little vessel for a bird. Please don't hate me."

According to some YouTube video Zinnia watched a few months back, cool tones conveyed friendliness and non-aggression. Given her past with Caroline, she could use all the help she could get.

Zinnia once more checked the doors to her cubicle. No Caroline. Zinnia buried the heels of her hands into her forehead.

"What was I thinking last spring? Trying to hijack Carrie's project?" She whispered this to herself. A phone rang in another cubicle nearby.

What had she been thinking?

Well, she thought that Caroline had sprouted some pretty dark circles under her eyes. That her coworker hadn't gotten enough sleep. And by the way that Caroline's hair frizzed and jutted in every direction, coupled with her missing some deadlines, that perhaps she needed a little help.

Zinnia's help, if Zinnia wanted to be precise.

Now, scanning through those memories, Zinnia realized she came across as controlling, manipulative.

It didn't help that control simply came with the territory of Zinnia-land. Even this morning, she timed out every second. Dedicating fifteen minutes in the shower this morning, and cutting short her breakfast smoothie, so she could get her car in for an oil change before work.

Heels muffled against the carpet.

Zinnia sprang from her chair and darted to the wing panel on her cubicle.

Sure enough, a short woman in six-inch pumps that could double as weapons rushed past. Caroline dove into her cubicle and let out a long breath.

*I hear you, sister.*

Workers at Helping Hope got used to the stop-and-go nature of Clark's assignments.

Tremors took over Zinnia's hands as she cradled the gift basket in her fingertips. Okay, here went nothing. Her lips twitched into what she hoped looked like an amiable smile, and she padded toward Caroline's cubicle.

"Knock, knock."

Caroline spun in her chair, breathless. Even a year and a half later, her hair could use some taming. Zinnia trained her focus on some of the other items in Caroline's cubicle, as a distraction from her rapid heartbeat.

Her eyes landed on a photo of Caroline, embraced from behind by a tan man with the easiest smile in the world. Andy. To think that Zinnia had had a crush on that easy-going artist at one point. Feelings for him soon dissolved once Zinnia saw how well Caroline and Andy paired.

*I wonder when they're going to finally get engaged.*

"Hey, Carrie, I had some items in my kitchen that I don't think I can eat anytime soon. Mind taking them off my hands?"

It wasn't entirely a lie. These did live on Zinnia's kitchen countertop for two days, after her Saturday grocery run.

Caroline cocked her head. "Again? This must be the second time this month, Zin."

Yikes, she needed to space out the days between "peace offerings" more. Otherwise, Caroline might start to get suspicious.

"Yeah, ha ha, guess sometimes I can get distracted at the grocery store and grab the wrong items. Anyway, here you are."

Her teeth bit into her front lip hard as Caroline's fingers filtered through the items.

"Oh my goodness, Zinnia." Caroline gasped. "You even have that natural kind of soda in here. The one made with juice and monk fruit, with no added sugars. I've been seeing ads for this everywhere." She clasped a hand to her chest. "Are you absolutely sure you don't want any of these?"

Tension released in Zinnia's gut.

Good. At this rate, maybe Caroline would be open to a friendship sometime in the next few months—after several more peace offerings.

"No, no." Zinnia leaned against the cubicle wing. Two coworkers behind her rushed past, muttering something about free oatmeal packets in the breakroom. "They're all yours. I hope you enjoy."

Heartbeat launching into her throat, Zinnia peeled herself away from the "door" to Caroline's office, to make a quick escape back into hers.

"Oh, Zinnia, while I have you here—"

Zinnia returned to her spot, eyebrows raised. "Yes?"

"—Clark's been having me run around like a beheaded chicken, trying to do off-site work and also stuff for the upcoming picture books. He mentioned that I might be able to offload some of those duties onto you?"

Had he now?

Thanks to Clark, Zinnia had stayed till close at She Brews trying to complete the assignments. He'd butchered the copy on several of them.

Wasn't it weird that Clark asked Zinnia to pick up some of

Caroline's duties?

That felt like an overstep.

Although both Zinnia and Caroline did similar jobs in copy work, Caroline always volunteered for any off-site tasks. Across all of Roseville, Helping Hope had several individual charities and groups that they ran. Caroline always claimed she enjoyed getting out of the office to stretch her legs.

Something also told Zinnia that Caroline enjoyed spending a few extra hours with the at-risk kids at one of the off-site clubs.

"You—you don't have to, Zinnia, if that is asking too much from you. I'll manage to do both. There's a lot going on right now, that's all."

Zinnia stared at her own blue flats. She'd figured heels might come off as more intimidating today.

*After everything that happened last year, I owe it to Caroline, right?*

"Monday, you said? That should be no problem."

Caroline brightened. "Oh wow, thank you, Zinnia. You are amazing. Any chance I could get you a salad at that new shop downtown as a thank you?"

Weakness overtook Zinnia's skull. Hoisted on the wall behind her, a clock told the time as noon. She hadn't eaten at all today, had she?

She couldn't expect Caroline to pay for a salad for her.

"Appreciate it, Carrie. But if you saw my inbox—let's just say that Clark got a little email-happy this morning."

Caroline giggled and fiddled with the petals of a plastic flower in a vase, stationed next to her laptop. "Oh, I get it."

*Might grab one of those oatmeal packets they mentioned, though.*

Zinnia left Caroline's cubicle and marched toward the breakroom.

On the countertop, a wicker basket with a neon index card labeled, "Free," offered several oatmeal packets. She grabbed a cinnamon-spice flavored one, dumped it into a bowl, and poured hot water over the contents.

Steam wisped off her Styrofoam bowl. Spoon stirring the makeshift "brunch," she perched against the countertop and sighed.

*I think that went well?*

Thanks to a rougher upbringing, Zinnia didn't have many skills in the way of making friends.

Anyone who deemed her an acquaintance in high school and college did so because they happened to be in the same sports or clubs together.

She ladled the contents of the bowl into her mouth and sighed as the sweet brown sugar taste danced on her tongue. Most days, she avoided sugar. Perhaps today she could make an exception.

Her pocket to her blue pantsuit buzzed. She set down her bowl, next to a coffee grounds container, and wedged out the device. An unknown number displayed on the screen.

With impressive speed, she ducked into the conference room next door and swiped open the call.

"Hello?"

"Hi, is this Zinnia Preston?" a breathless, deep voice of a woman asked on the other end. Wind whipped through the receiver. Whoever called had to have dialed her from the outdoors.

"This is. May I ask who is calling?"

Scents from Expo markers and whiteboard cleaner filled the office, probably fresh from one of the meetings from this morning.

"Yes, this is Laurel from Silver Spot Productions. I received your audition and wanted to call."

All the oxygen fled Zinnia's lungs. It took her several moments to remind herself how breathing worked. She sank into a chair and tried to keep her voice steady.

"Oh, wonderful! Thanks for calling me."

"Yes, you are one of the actors we would love to consider for—"

A pause, perhaps Laurel needed to scroll something on her phone, the cast list maybe. Dings sounded from the receiver, like a bell to a shop. A coffee grinder screamed in the background.

Oh, Laurel must've gone to pick up her daily cup of joe.

"—for the part of Woman on Park Bench. Can you hear me? It's pretty loud in here."

"Yes, I can." Zinnia's chest seized. She blew out a long breath and forced herself to stay calm. "I'm so grateful to be considered."

"I just wanted to check to make sure you're okay to shoot with us all day Saturday and Monday."

Wait…Monday?

"Oh, I, umm—"

Zinnia promised Caroline to take over some of her off-site tasks for that Monday. Could she go back on that already? Plus, Clark discouraged workers from taking sick days or vacation days. The latter needed several weeks in advance notice.

Georgia texting Zinnia nonstop about reserving them a spot at that teahouse didn't help matters.

"I—" Zinnia regained her voice and blinked moisture away from her eyes. "I thought the listing said it was shooting Saturday."

Most film dates took place during weekdays, during office hours. Clark balked at the idea of someone taking a week in the Carolinas for a beach trip, let alone skipping work to be an extra in a Netflix film. Hence the reason why Zinnia's "film career" didn't kickstart as fast as some of her other peers from college.

"It had originally been for this Saturday, but unfortunately, we reshuffled some of the dates. Is Monday not doable for you?"

Through a blur of tears, Zinnia focused on the drawings on the board. One of their coworkers had a certain talent with replicating cartoon characters. Snoopy, from the *Peanuts* comics, perched on his dog house in red Expo marker.

"I—I'm afraid I will be unable to do Monday."

The receiver muted for a few seconds. Maybe Laurel turned off her voice on the call to place her coffee order. Laurel returned moments later.

"Thank you for letting me know, Zinnia. We wish you the best in all your acting endeavors."

The line went dead.

"Get out of the fridge. You are not a condiment."

Ryan shooed Buttercup out of the way with his foot, replacing the water pitcher before closing the door to the refrigerator. She stalked away, tail flicking, and sat next to her food bowl with a pathetic meow.

He rolled his eyes and chuckled, grabbing the glass of water he'd just poured and carrying it back toward his editing suite, also known as the spare bedroom of his apartment. "I fed you two hours ago. You're fine."

His husky, Balto, trotted beside him, bumping against his legs. Balto suffered from a debilitating need for attention at all times, from which he would clearly perish at any moment if he didn't get pets and love.

Ryan plopped into his spinning office chair and patted his knee. Balto set his chin on Ryan's lap, tail thumping the desk as Ryan scratched behind his gigantic ears. "And *you* are just wasting away, aren't you? Unloved. Uncherished."

Balto gave a small, "Awoo."

Ryan laughed and set down his glass to ruffle the husky's thick coat with both hands. The dog had received a lengthy walk and a long brushing session this morning. Long enough that Ryan had almost missed his usual eight a.m. work start time, but a husky's shedding coat waited for no man, and clumps of hair around the apartment drove Ryan crazy. He already vacuumed every other day.

Balto draped his front half over Ryan's lap, and Ryan accepted his fate as he turned back to his computer, absently patting the dog with one hand while staring at his computer screen, email pulled up front and center, the message about the film contest emblazoned in high definition.

The one-month challenge had plenty of checks in place to prevent preparing ahead. Namely, five elements that had to be included.

"You wanna hear them, bud?" He patted Balto's side. "Of course you do. You want to commiserate with your poor dad."

A knock sounded outside the office. Balto flailed off Ryan's lap and bounded for the front door, barely holding in a tiny "awoo" of excitement. He knew he wasn't supposed to howl inside. Ryan heaved himself to his feet and followed.

Outside, Griffith stood on the welcome mat.

Ryan cocked his head. "You're here early."

"Calm day at the theater—I know that's an oxymoron—so I figured I would come over." He grinned. "A script to write, huh?"

Early was an understatement. Ryan had expected Griffith this evening, not now. His fingers tap-tapped on his thigh. This would throw off his hour count, when he planned to do what, and he hadn't checked the kitchen after cleaning it, and…

*Deep breaths. Stop the runaway train.* His brain might feel like the day was spiraling out of control, but that wasn't the case. He smiled back at Griffith. "I appreciate your help. I know story and production and directing but…writing isn't my strong suit. Your advice will be super helpful."

"I don't get to do enough of it lately. The writing and script side of things, that is." Griffith grinned. "I'm ready to dive in."

He followed Ryan inside, stopping to pet Balto, who sniffed Griffith's shoes for traces of Griffith's dog, Chekhov. The husky danced in a circle, voicing his excitement via "talking," long and short sounds that sometimes almost sounded like words. No howling in the apartment, but Ryan wasn't about to tell a husky not to talk at all.

"Need a drink?" Ryan called over his shoulder. "There's still some coffee in the pot."

"I'm good." Griffith headed for Ryan's editing suite and plopped into the second chair. "What are you working with?"

Ryan sat in his usual seat, wiggling the mouse to wake up the computer screen. "Okay. We have a twenty-minute cap."

Griffith nodded, then grunted as Balto launched into his lap. "I've done plenty of ten-minute plays."

"Cool." Ryan scrolled. "Any genre, so plenty of creative freedom. The hardest part is the five elements you have to include." He turned the screen toward Griffith so they could both read.

**Theme:** Honesty
**Setting:** Must use at least three unique settings
**Must Include:**
- A blue prop that is important to the plot
- At least one moving shot
- Someone wearing a plain white t-shirt
- The word "plethora" included in one of the lines
- At least one use of practical or special effects

Griffith whistled. "All right. That's a lot to keep in mind, but doable."

Ryan tapped his fingers on the desk. "A lot of the elements suggest they're trying to make sure the production team knows as much about the technical side of things as the storytelling side. Camera shots, settings, special effects. We really need to stand out." His fingers drummed faster.

Griffith waited. "Er, were you going to add to that?"

"Oh." He'd accidentally allowed a dramatic pause, something his mother always complained about. *"Just get to the point, Ryan."* In truth, he liked to weigh his words before continuing, but Mom always made comments about how maybe he should shoot for Broadway instead of Hollywood with his theatrics. "I was thinking, you know what you don't see very often in a film festival?" He snapped his fingers. "Humor. And what's funnier than zombies?"

Griffith blinked. "Well. Um, I'm sure zombies can be funny. I don't know if I would say they're the funniest topic I could think of…"

He hesitated. "We can work with that. We may want to keep spit balling ideas though, just to have options."

"Sure." Ryan spun a pencil between his fingers. "You don't see a lot of fantasy or sci-fi either, since the special effects can be hard to pull off well."

"You have one month, Ryan."

"Right." He stared at the computer screen. He needed an idea that would blow the judges away. Something new, fresh, something they had never seen before.

His heart started beating faster, anxiety creeping through his veins. Could he really pull anything off this fast? Or would he only embarrass himself? Even with Griffith's help… "You know what." He sat up straight. "I don't think I should do this. I appreciate it, Griff. But I don't think I have time."

Griffith slid Balto off his lap and crossed his large arms, more intimidating than he probably intended. "Ryan. I've watched you working toward this for years. What's the worst that can happen?"

Ryan just stared at him. The worst that could happen?

So many things. Maybe the film would be awful and someone there would see it and bar him from Hollywood forever. Maybe his family would come to the festival and feel justified in not believing in him. Maybe he would let down his entire cast and crew, waste all of their time. He had hoped to think this over longer before talking to Griffith, but his schedule had been messed up, and…

Deep breaths. He inhaled, held the breath, exhaled. "Sorry, man. I guess I'm in my head."

"Listen, you helped me pursue my dreams last winter with the play."

True. Ryan had helped with the play that gained Griffith his current job as a director, but he had just been the lights guy.

"Now it's my turn to repay the favor. Let me help you brainstorm. I can even think of some people who might be interested in auditioning."

Ryan tapped the pencil on his knee. "Okay." A thought struck him. "Hey. How would you like to be a co-writer on this project with me?"

Griffith perked up like Balto when Ryan held up a doggy treat. "Really?"

"Sure. I write pretty slow." Ryan rubbed the back of his neck. Was this a bad idea? He hated giving over the artistic reins. Last time he'd shared responsibility with someone, there had been disastrous consequences…

*Not the time to think about that.* As co-writers, they would have equal input, right? And besides, he would be directing and editing everything. It would be fine. "I'm not great at actually…completing a project. I could really use your help, and two brains are better than one, right?"

Griffith slapped his hand in an enthusiastic and mildly bone-crushing handshake. "You've got yourself a deal. Let's write a movie."

# Chapter Three

Zinnia tapped the Bluetooth button on her call. Joy's tinny voice filtered through the speakers.

"Can you hear me, Zin?"

Zinnia flipped up the turn signal in the right turn lane. Ahead, a row of brightly painted shops glittered. They seemed out of place on the brink of autumn, what with their pastels feeling as if they belonged sometime in spring or early summer.

Out of place. Much like how Zinnia felt whenever she and Georgia got together. Like they would today at the teahouse.

"Zinnia?"

Zinnia shook herself away from her thoughts as her car skidded into the intersection. "I can hear you, Joy."

Although Zinnia prided herself on her multitasking, when it came to manning a wheel, she could never bring herself to read a device whilst driving. Hence her need for the Bluetooth today.

At least the call from her neighbor, Joy, could soothe her nerves this Saturday afternoon. And perhaps could fill the hole in her stomach from the fact that she gave up a day of filming with Netflix for this.

White fluffy clouds shielded the sky, allowing for pockets of blue to shine through the cracks.

"Okay, I'm glad you can hear me." Joy's breathy sigh crackled in the car speakers.

In the background, someone screamed. Most likely, Zinnia assumed, Joy's child who'd just entered his terrible twos. She considered Joy a superhero for handling the three kids so well.

"Zinnia, are you absolutely sure you're fine with babysitting them tomorrow? I promise I shouldn't be at service for long."

As Zinnia whizzed past a sign advertising the Roseville

Oktoberfest, she grinned.

*Typical Joy.*

The neighbor always apologized whenever she needed an extra hand with the kids.

"Joy, really, it's no problem. I'll be at the earlier service at The Vine, anyway. Also, I have off work." She flicked on her blinker again. Cars behind her swerved into the right-hand lane as she waited for a break in traffic to pull into the parking lot.

"Okay, well although you can probably hear Justice screaming behind me—"

A wail broke through the speakers, as if on cue.

"—he tends to be really good with babysitters. Just decides to misbehave the moment Mom and Dad get home." Zinnia could almost hear Joy's playful eye roll in the background. Justice did implement some impish attributes whenever the parental units arrived. "The other two are really good, especially if you put on *Bluey* or play princess with Verity and Honor."

"Yes, yes, Joy, I know. You had me babysit them last month. They're good kids. You're doing a wonderful job with them."

Zinnia's tires screeched as she located a break in traffic.

Heartbeat thundered in her ears as she flew into the parking lot and pulled into a spot near the bright-pink door to the teahouse. In curly font, a pink sign—likely neon at night—advertised the name for the place, "Spill the Tea."

Zinnia clocked the time. Georgia wouldn't arrive for at least seven more minutes.

Always she arrived somewhere between five to fifteen minutes early to locations—in case she ran into an accident mid-route or needed a breather before charging into an awkward social situation.

When she flipped down the overhead mirror to check her makeup, Joy's voice piped up again. No doubt she'd gone on mute to wrangle one of the kids.

"Thanks, Zin. That means a lot. Sometimes moms can get caught in the parent-comparison-trap."

On one occasion, Zinnia spotted Joy sighing as she scrolled through social media. Mothers on Instagram made potty training, discipline, even cleaning dirty dishes appear so effortless.

Coldness spiked Zinnia's veins as she watched the lot for her sister's Lexus.

*That makes two of us with the comparison snare, Joy.*

"Well." Zinnia cleared her throat and dabbed more gloss on her upper lip. "*I* think you're doing an excellent job. Now, can I get you and Ben any pastries while I'm here?"

Ben, her husband, had few flaws, according to Joy.

Except for one…an incurable sweet tooth.

"Oh, seriously, you don't have to—"

"I insist. You like the macarons they have on the display up front, right?"

Silence overtook the car for a few moments. Perhaps Joy once again clicked the mute button.

Her voice returned. "We'd love the tiramisu and raspberry flavored ones. But I'll pay you back—"

"I'll hear nothing of the kind." Zinnia's index finger wiped away some of the eyeliner fallout that smudged on the corner of her eye. "See you tomorrow. With some *complimentary* treats."

Zinnia hung up before Joy could launch any more protests.

Unbelting herself, she slammed the overhead mirror closed and exited her car. Might as well busy her brain with the dessert display case, instead of waiting for her younger sister to strut across the parking lot.

Flats sizzled against the warmed pavement. Even in late September, Michigan hoped to eke out some unbearable days before dipping into permanent cool temperatures.

Bright pink umbrellas decorated tables outside the teahouse.

She swung open the door and a bell tinkled. A woman in a black monogrammed shirt smiled at her from the hostess stand.

"Reservation?"

Zinnia nodded. "Should be under 'Georgia.' My party isn't all here yet, though." She gestured at a glass display case that featured various pastries and French-style sweets. "Mind if I peruse?"

"Not at all, ma'am." With a rose-colored pen, the hostess scribbled something on a sheet of paper. Perhaps to note that Zinnia had arrived.

Swiveling on her heel, Zinnia glimpsed the treats. Madeleines, cream puffs, and—of course—macarons glittered in the white display lights. Someone had sprinkled some edible glitter on some of the pastries to make them catch the beams even more.

Zinnia grinned at the cashier, a young woman with her hair pressed into a tight bun. "Six macarons, please. Three tiramisu, three raspberry."

With a nod, the woman rang up the total at the register. Just as she did so, the bell at the entrance tinkled, a breeze whisking inside.

The tall figure at the door sashayed in.

"Zinnia, sissy, you've done something to your hair. It looks…interesting." Georgia's large lips puckered.

No, Zinnia had not, in fact, changed her hairstyle in years. Not after Georgia teased her mercilessly when, two years back, Zinnia attempted a dark brown shade and bangs.

But Georgia had, it appeared, made some alterations to her own tresses. Platinum blonde covered her once honey-blonde hair. Those lips looked larger too, and that chest area. Zinnia averted her eyes back to the chocolate-dipped madeleines in the display case. Had her husband, Matt, paid for all of those "adjustments" with Grandma's inheritance?

Or did Georgia's bouts as a model on the runways and in photoshoots mean she'd have to "fix" her appearance?

She forced her eyes back to her sister—before Georgia could comment, as she always did, on Zinnia's lack of eye contact. Today, Georgia styled herself in a black crop top and expensive-looking cigarette pants.

Zinnia tugged at her own pantsuit, hoping Georgia wouldn't take notice of the sheer amount of wrinkles on the legs.

Georgia's eyes went right to Zinnia's hands, and back up at her, eyelids closing in a sneer.

"Did you put our names in, sissy dear?" She collapsed into Zinnia in an awkward hug, and as soon as her arms embraced, Georgia released. As though Zinnia's skin had somehow singed her. "Why haven't we been seated yet, then?"

"I did, but I figured since both of us weren't here yet—"

Georgia clicked her tongue against her brilliant white teeth, another new addition. "I can't go anywhere with you." She paired this with a laugh, something Georgia enjoyed doing whenever she delivered a zinger. That way, if Zinnia complained, she'd scoff and reply, "Oh come on, sissy, it was a joke. Learn to get some thicker skin."

The hostess returned and led them to a clothed table.

In the far corner of the room, a group of young girls in princess dresses held up their teacups, pinkies raised. On a small table beside theirs, two ladies in red hats dinged small spoons in their cups, after they ladled two sugar cubes into the fruity mixture. Everything smelled of fruit tones and caffeine.

"I put us both down for a shared afternoon tea, sissy." Georgia patted her nonexistent stomach. "Have to watch my weight for the runway tomorrow, you know. I know you have no problem saying yes to some of the sweets, so splitting afternoon tea seemed only fair."

Laughter followed this. Zinnia focused on the soft piano music that played on a speaker nearby, as her hand, by reflex, reached her stomach. Unlike Georgia, she'd grown a muffin top there, which seemed to scream out about its existence any time the two of them took a photo together. Somehow Georgia knew the perfect angle to make herself look beautiful, and Zinnia—well, less beautiful.

*Listen to the classical tune, Zin. If you retaliate, Georgia's going to act like a victim.*

Grimacing, Zinnia shielded her face with the menu and read the description for shared afternoon tea.

**Shared Afternoon Tea**
Enjoy three tiers of delectable sandwiches and pastries, perfect for two.

**Top Tier**
Macaron & Pastry of the Week

**Middle Tier**
Scone with Clotted Cream and Jam, Mousse Cup, Tea Biscuit

**Bottom Tier**
Three Tea Sandwiches—Cucumber with Chive Cream Cheese, Chicken Salad, Shredded Egg with Garlic Spread

"Sissy, dear."

Zinnia placed the menu down in time to watch Georgia run her finger around the rim of her teacup. Blue Devon cottage patterns decorated the exterior.

"I just heard of this new Korean skincare routine, Zinnia. One of the models at my most recent shoot told me all about it. Of course, I have a rigorous routine already, so I don't need it. I figured you may want to give it a try."

Zinnia fought the itching in her fingers to touch her nose. Blackheads sprouted there this morning. "Why would you say that?"

Georgia shrugged and flapped open her menu. "It never hurts to have a good one. Especially with all those film things you've been auditioning for." A flicker of a sneer crossed her face.

The hostess arrived at their table seconds later to take their tea orders. Zinnia, a chai, and Georgia, a hibiscus-flavored blend. Georgia asked the hostess three times to make sure it "was low fat" and "had no caffeine."

Then the hostess collected their menus. There was nothing left to hide behind.

"Can't do caffeine personally, sissy. Does horrors to the complexion. Speaking of—we'll circle back to that skin routine later."

Of course they would. Georgia never let anything rest until Zinnia gave her what she deemed a satisfactory answer.

"Anyway, how have film auditions been?"

Shame bloomed in Zinnia's cheeks. As she opened her mouth to stumble through some explanation about Clark keeping her busy at work, her bag buzzed. She unzipped the top and spotted Griffith's name on the Caller I.D.

"Sorry, Georgia." She breathed a sigh of relief. "Need to take this. Won't be long."

Her chair skidded against the waxed floors as she bolted from her seat and out the doors. Shade from a pink umbrella gave her reprieve from the bright sun outside as she answered the call.

"You could not have been more timely, Griff."

"Oh yeah? Then I think you're going to like this message."

She doubted it. Griffith tended to recruit her for theater projects. Much as she loved giving back to the community theater space, it chewed up almost as much of her schedule as Clark's constant emails did.

If she wanted any hope of making it into film…

"Yeah, Griff? What's that?"

"I have a close friend who is planning on entering a film festival. It's one of those crazy ones where you have to pull it together in a month—"

Yep, been there, did that, last year with a winter play with Griffith.

*Would really like to not repeat history.*

"—I guess some Hollywood bigwigs are going to be at it. The winning movie could get optioned, original actors likely to be cast in the feature-length film."

*Then again…repeating history sounds really nice.*

She swallowed. "What are you saying?"

"I'm saying that I've been tasked with helping to write the script. Let's just say there's a character who is perfect for you. I'll send you the audition info later today or early tomorrow, all right?"

Her pulse spiked.

Could this be…it? After all these years?

She thought back to the Netflix audition, spirit wilting in her chest. "I don't know about scheduling. Most film things happen during the work week."

"Our director's schedule actually works really well with yours. He does wedding and engagement photography on the side, so that takes up most of his time during the 9 to 5 hours. Now, Zin." She could hear him wagging a finger at the phone. "You better audition for this, or so help me—"

"I'll audition. I'll audition." She giggled. "Thank you."

After they hung up, it felt as if someone had filled her chest with helium. She returned to her table in time for the hostess to set down a three-tiered silver tray. Georgia pilfered the cucumber sandwich from the bottom before Zinnia could grab it.

"So." Georgia nibbled on the sandwich corner. "More work stuff? Clark's been working you senseless."

*True, but at least I'm working. Unlike* some people *who can coast on their husband's hefty salary.*

Zinnia shooed away the thought as she placed the shredded egg sandwich on her flowery plate. Georgia had hoped to run a dance studio, up until she married Matt. But dreams changed. Georgia claimed she enjoyed a stress-free life, so she could do more modeling gigs.

*And you don't need to work to have purpose.*

"Actually." Zinnia brushed her now-eggy fingertips onto her cloth napkin. "It was something really promising for film. Georgia." She couldn't help the lift in her voice or the genuine smile stretched across her face, instead of the taut grin she tended to wear around her younger sister. "I'm so excited for this. Maybe this is the Lord finally opening a door."

Georgia's expression remained stony.

Perhaps it was Zinnia's imagination, but something scarlet bloomed in Georgia's high cheekbones for a fleeting moment.

"Well, that's great, sissy. *If* it works out." She raised a perfectly plucked eyebrow. "And *if* it does, someone needs to hear about that new skin routine."

Zinnia sank into her chair and went onto autopilot for the next hour.

Ryan rubbed his eyes and fought off a yawn. He readjusted his glasses, squinting at the blue light of his computer screen. He shouldn't have stayed up so late last night, but he couldn't stop thinking about the film competition.

Buttercup stalked across the keyboard and flicked her tail in his face. "Hi, girl," he mumbled, absently stroking the cat's long fur.

She tolerated the affection for a moment before she began to gnaw on his arm. "No." He sighed, scooping up the cat and depositing her on the floor. "We've talked about this. You lose privileges when you chomp."

He returned his attention to the document on the screen, shared between himself and Griffith. Notes filled nearly two pages, thoughts on plot, characters, settings, theme…but as of yet, no actual script.

They had settled on a contemporary, real-world setting yesterday—no zombies, no Greeks, no spaceships. Ryan patted the Darth Vader bobblehead next to his monitor. "Someday, buddy."

They had exactly one character description finished—the female lead, "Self-Assured Woman (20-30)." Griffith had said he had an actress in mind, but Ryan would still post a casting call later, once they finalized the character list.

He checked the time in the bottom right corner of his computer screen. Thirty minutes until he needed to leave for a wedding photography gig. Since a lot of people couldn't do photoshoots during normal workdays and work hours—and weddings were almost always on weekends—he'd long ago decided that he would work Saturdays and take off Sunday and Monday instead. As a bonus, not many people tended to be running errands on Mondays. He liked grocery stores and post offices as empty as possible.

Of course, sometimes certain things had to happen on Sundays or Mondays, and he made exceptions. But after he'd overworked himself a couple of years ago and landed in the hospital, he made sure to take a different day off in the week to recover.

Speaking of. He slid his inhaler into the camera bag sitting on his desk, then stood and stretched. Balto's tail thumped in excitement. "Sorry, buddy. Just getting ready to leave. You went on a walk half an hour ago."

The dog mumbled his complaint.

Ryan checked his camera bag and supplies for the third time. Everything in place. Time to make himself presentable.

He headed for his bedroom and the formal wedding attire he'd laid out. Hopefully Buttercup hadn't rolled on his black pants in the few hours he'd left them out. He practically needed a lint roller in every room of the apartment thanks to his fluffy pals.

His pocket vibrated, and he fished out his phone, his heart sinking at the name on the caller ID. He accepted the call and hit speakerphone, forcing friendliness into his tone. "Hi, Mom."

"So he is alive." She laughed as if she didn't make the same joke every time he went a week or so without calling.

"What's up?" He set his phone on his bedside table and began changing into the wedding clothes, miraculously untouched by Buttercup. "Just to let you know, I do have to head out soon, but I can talk until then."

"Oh, where are you going?"

He stifled a sigh, knowing what would come next. He shouldn't have mentioned needing to leave until the last minute when she wouldn't have time to question him. "I'm shooting a wedding."

"Working on the weekend again?" Her tone turned fretful. "Are you tight on cash? We can send you—"

"I'm fine, Mom. I work Tuesday through Saturday, remember?" He scooped up his phone and headed for the bathroom to check his appearance.

"Okay. I worry about you, you know."

He certainly did. She reminded him every time they spoke.

"Dad said they're looking for a new management position…"

"Mom."

To put things delicately, the Torinos weren't hurting for money. Ryan's father owned a lucrative chain of businesses, and both of his parents never failed to remind him that he could come work for his dad any time he decided film wasn't working out. When Ryan refused that…Mom freaked out and started throwing money at him.

He ran a comb through his hair.

"I know, honey, you can make it on your own, but I just wanted to remind you there's a spot if you want it."

Ryan set down the comb and turned off the bathroom light. Stared at the switch for a few moments to remind himself that he'd done so. Then he turned to exit. "I know. Thanks. What are you up to this weekend?"

While Mom chattered about church and lunch with some of her friends, Ryan continued his sweep of the apartment. Bedroom lights off. Door closed. Retrieve camera from editing suite. Make sure the monitors were logged out and sleeping. Door closed. Unplug the toaster. Unplug the coffee pot. Stare at the toaster and coffee pot to remind himself they *really were* unplugged.

Then he returned to stare at the doors again. Stare at his pets. Cat and dog, both in the living room, not accidentally shut away.

"Ryan?"

He tuned back in to the conversation. "Yes? Sorry, missed that last part."

"I asked how your OCD is doing."

He pressed his mouth into a thin line. "Well managed."

In high school, as stress had piled up on him, the effects of Obsessive Compulsive Disorder he'd faced all his life cropped up with a vengeance. His repetitive compulsions—the checking, the overwhelming thoughts, the need for everything to be perfect—had taken up hours of his day, until Mom and Dad noticed and sent him to a therapist.

Eventually, he had learned enough skills for managing his OCD to only visit a psychiatrist every few months for check-ins. But Mom still treated him like he might crack at any moment.

"Are you sure? It seems like you answered that a little quickly."

He grabbed his keys, smothering a sigh. Any slight inflection, any hesitation, and she assumed he was hiding something.

Sure, he hadn't told his family about the hospital incident two years ago until they heard through the grapevine, but…

He shut the apartment door behind him and locked it. "I'm really sure, Mom. I'm a little distracted because I'm heading out the door."

"Okay. Don't be afraid to ask for help if you need it."

Wait, did he unplug the coffee pot? He had been distracted by Mom. *Yes. You did. You stared at it to remember that.*

The anxiety monster inside him calmed.

"I'll remember that." He paused. "By the way, I'm entering a film competition. It seems like a great opportunity."

He filled her in on some of the details on his way to his car, connecting his phone wirelessly before driving away. Maybe if she heard about the things he had going on, she would realize he was doing *fine*. A grown adult, not her sickly, asthmatic son with anxiety who needed coddling.

"Well, that does sound interesting," Mom said. "It's good to keep your expectations in check, of course. There will be plenty of competition, but if you have time, I suppose it's worth a shot."

"Yeah." His hands tightened around the steering wheel. "I know better than to expect to win."

"That's good. Best not to get your hopes up too high with these things."

Similar logic to when she'd told him not to go to L.A. Not to throw everything into film. He knew she was right—with so many variables, no one had any control over whether they would succeed in the business—but it still stung that she didn't believe he could do it.

"Well, I should probably let you go and focus on the road. I love you, Mom."

"Love you too, Ryan. I'm proud of you."

She wasn't. He knew she wasn't.

But maybe, if he could win this competition, someday, she would be.

# Chapter Four

ZINNIA WAS EITHER AN EVIL QUEEN or a dragon. Verity hadn't decided which yet.

Verity, along with her sister Honor, spun in circles in their princess dresses in the playroom. Meanwhile, the two-year-old Justice sat in the corner and smashed two toy trains together. Every once in a while, he'd look up at Zinnia to make sure she'd paid attention to the crash—whether he just got away with something he didn't often do when his parents were home, or he hoped he'd find a fellow destruction junkie, she wasn't quite sure.

"Okay, be careful, Honor." Zinnia sprawled her arms out toward the girl in a pink princess dress and coiled curls for hair. "You're going to trip over the puzzle we just did."

Babysitting Joy's children often involved hopping from activity to activity every five minutes or so. Even though Joy—leading worship at The Vine today—promised she wouldn't be gone longer than an hour and a half, they'd already completed—

Blowing bubbles outside, drawing chalk figurines on the sidewalk, watering Joy's plants, coloring in coloring books, singing to the latest Disney princess songs and having a dance party, watching three episodes of *Bluey,* reading over some picture books, *re*-reading over the same picture books because Justice loved the part about the mouse wanting a cookie, and completing a puzzle.

Whew, man, how did Joy do this on a regular basis? That woman must've had the stamina of a marathon runner.

Honor's feet—toes bedecked in pink sparkles from when they briefly painted their nails today after the bubble blowing—tripped over the puzzle as she landed into Zinnia's arms. Zinnia picked her up and placed her on a squishy chair in the playroom.

"Okay, now before we continue in our game, am I an evil queen or a dragon? I really need to—you know—get into character." Zinnia spouted off an evil laugh and then pretended to spew fire.

This set all three kids giggling.

Justice chucked a train at a stuffed animal dinosaur.

"Hmm." Verity, bedecked in her Cinderella blue princess dress, screwed up her face in deep contemplation. "Dragon!"

"Dragon," Honor agreed.

"Dragon, dragon, dragon." They chanted this while spinning circles around Zinnia. Puzzle pieces flew from underneath their feet.

"Okay, okay, a dragon it is." Zinnia grabbed the dinosaur, injured by the train, and placed it on her head. "Rawr! I like eating princesses."

Honor and Verity shrieked. Hand in hand, they fled to the opposite end of the room and clasped each other's arms in a mini huddle. A mixture of sadness and warmth swirled in Zinnia's gut.

She and Georgia used to play games like this all the time. Before Mom left the picture…and before Grandma enlisted them in pageants, dance classes, and etiquette lessons. Grandma had a very staunch idea of what a young girl should get involved in, and none of that involved prancing around in bare feet and princess dresses in playrooms.

*I miss you, Georgia. The you that you used to be.*

A door squeaked from far off. The princesses and the train destroyer broke from their stupor and raced toward the entrance to the house.

"Hey, guys." Joy's bubbly voice sounded as Zinnia heaved herself onto her feet. Her knees cracked. Aw man, she was starting to get old, wasn't she?

Zinnia found Joy in the kitchen, bubbled by her children. As Joy placed some plastic bags on the island counter, with some label for a Greek restaurant, she pulled out a Tupperware container and popped off the lid. Scents of pita bread drifted toward Zinnia.

Her stomach growled. With going to the early service at The Vine, and foregoing her morning workout and breakfast, Zinnia's schedule had been thrown way off.

"Hey, Zin." Joy ladled yellow-tinted rice onto plates. "Can I interest you in any of this? They gave me an extra serving of baklava for free." She waggled her eyebrows. "And since the sugar-addict husband of mine is stuck at church for a men's Bible study, I figured that a certain wonderful babysitter could pilfer it from him."

Zinnia's lips twitched.

"I'd hate to take your food from you, Joy."

"Nonsense." Some mixture full of mushrooms, cucumbers, and tomatoes steamed on the plates. With Joy's other hand, she drizzled milk into a sippy cup, featuring dinosaurs. Zinnia went to help her with the pour. "Thanks, now eat with us."

Joy and Zinnia helped the younger children into their highchairs, and with setting up the placemats and food bibs.

At last, Zinnia dug into her garlic smothered meal, savoring the combination of the creamy sauce against the romaine lettuce. The mouthfuls of rice mixed so well with the cucumber-tomato salad.

Thoughts drifted back to yesterday. After Georgia went on and on about skincare routines, she told Zinnia about the importance of cutting back on carbs. Never mind that Georgia forced Zinnia to eat the scone and most of the sandwiches because Georgia, "Couldn't risk it with the runway tomorrow."

*Why would she even ask me to tea in the first place if she couldn't eat three-quarters of what was on the table?*

Had she done it to humiliate Zinnia? To brag about her perfect life to her older sister?

"You look really angry at the mushrooms, Zin—"

Joy had lifted herself from her seat to wipe off some grapes Justice knocked over from his highchair. The kids, instead of consuming the Greek food, dove into some leftover mac and cheese Joy had heated up.

"—and don't get me wrong, when mushrooms are cooked the wrong way, I too, experience an insatiable rage."

Zinnia snickered into her rice. "I'm not mad at the fungi on my plate."

"What then?"

With a heavy sigh, Zinnia unloaded what happened the previous day at the teahouse. Her story got interrupted a few times by Verity who wanted to show her freshest scabs from the fall on the walk she and her family took the other day around the neighborhood.

"Hmm." Joy smudged a napkin on Honor's hair when Zinnia had finished. The girl, Honor, had a unique talent of hiding food in her curls, probably for some snacks for later. "Now tell me, Zinnia, does Georgia have a job of any kind?"

Zinnia frowned over her piece of baklava.

One bite into the treat, and a mixture of walnuts and honey stuck to the inside of her teeth. But oh, how the cavities were well worth it.

She swallowed. "No. She did want to run a dance studio at one point, but she seems pretty content with the unpaid modeling gigs. Says that Matt makes a ton and would rather see his wife unstressed and doing the things she loves."

Georgia *did* like modeling, right?

The younger sister never appeared to complain about the frequent photoshoots and days spent on the runway.

But during their etiquette classes, Georgia did stick her tongue out at the instructor whenever the severe-looking woman turned her back. Georgia had never been a fan of when the woman would tell them what to do or how to behave.

*Modeling basically is that, right? Following instructions, looking how someone else wants you to look.*

Perhaps her sister had changed. She did prance around yesterday in six-inch heels, as if the parking lot and teahouse had transformed into a makeshift runway.

Plus, who wouldn't want to claim they *modeled*? Movie stars married beautiful women like that.

Zinnia's cheeks burned at Georgia's remarks from the other day about skin care routines. Had her face truly grown as "leathery" as Georgia claimed? Would any movie director or star ever deem her beautiful as she had been in her younger twenties?

"Uh huh, and"—Joy, at last, returned to her place and dug her silverware into her no-doubt-now-cold food—"do Georgia and Matt ever plan on having any kids?"

Fork in hand, Zinnia poked at the remainder of her yellow rice.

"Georgia had been obsessed with kids in college. Her face would look super pitiful anytime she heard a baby cry. She even signed up at a local church to help out with the children's ministry, despite having a full credit load."

Then what happened?

Zinnia's memories blurred together. Georgia met Matt late into college, that much she knew. He'd popped into the picture after Georgia experienced a really bad breakup with a not-so-good guy. And Grandma died, leaving Georgia with the majority of the inheritance. She *definitely* remembered that part.

Hadn't Georgia mentioned, during her one-year anniversary, something about Matt not wanting kids?

Did Georgia agree with him now?

"I guess Matt doesn't want them. Maybe Georgia decided that married life is busy enough and left that dream behind."

Joy's face didn't betray an expression. She answered with one word. "Interesting."

"Why do you ask?"

Joy crumpled a napkin onto her plate and began to collect the other empty ones around the table. "I suppose it's none of my business."

Buzzing erupted from Zinnia's bag. She dug out her phone and spotted an email from Griffith. Tapping on the message, she read.

*Hey, Zinnia!*

*Okay, so I have all the materials for the audition for you. My director friend is planning on posting the details on audition pages on Facebook soon, so the earlier you get in your audition, the better. Before we get swamped with submissions.*

*You'll find the sides and all other information in the attachment below. Best of luck! I'll be praying. It does help that I know the director pretty well ;) I'll make sure to put in a good word for you.*

*He does make the final call, though. And can be pretty picky, if I do say so myself. But if anyone can blow his socks off, it's gonna be you.*

*Griffith*

With a breathy sigh, she dropped her phone back into her bag. "Sorry, Joy, need to go take care of something."

"I've held you here for longer than the call of duty"—a wail from Justice interrupted Joy—"plus, this little one may be due for his nap soon. Didn't get much sleep last night, with all the excitement of Miss Zinnia coming over here. At the very least, this stinky boy needs a diaper change." She grinned at Zinnia. "Thanks for the macarons, by the way. I suppose I should eat my portion before Ben gets home. That man turns into a whole other person around sweets."

Zinnia thought back to the playroom and imagined a dragon munching on some French pastries.

As she slipped on her shoes by the door, she spotted Joy carrying Justice up the stairs. Joy swung around and held herself steady on the railing.

"Zinnia, I—" She paused and blew some hair off her forehead. "—I wouldn't let Georgia's words get to you. I feel like something deeper may be going on."

Before Zinnia could ask what, Joy ascended the steps and disappeared into the upstairs hallway.

"Well, Griff, this is a very…positive story."

Griffith sat on the other end of Ryan's couch, digging into buffalo chicken dip, their favorite snack for bro nights. "Yeah, the outline felt a little bleak."

Ryan balanced his laptop on his knees, his feet propped on the coffee table, and scrolled through the document. When he'd laid out the scene basics for Griffith and given his friend free rein with the dialogue, he'd first of all expected Griffith to take longer than a day. Could he really do a good job in that short of a time?

He'd also expected Griffith to write something that adhered more closely to Ryan's own vision.

Ryan removed his glasses and rubbed the bridge of his nose, trying to figure out how to say what he wanted to convey. Griffith had done him an enormous favor helping to write this script, and he was grateful. But some of the choices…

"It looks great, Griff. Thank you. I'll just make a couple of tweaks, but it looks awesome."

A lot of tweaks. Griffith didn't need to know that, though.

"No problem, dude. It was fun." Griffith grabbed the TV remote and turned on the flat screen in preparation for tonight's movie, also part of bro night tradition.

Okay, bro night was just eating snacks and watching movies once a week. But "movie night" didn't sound as cool. Especially after Balto knocked over Ryan's projector this spring and Buttercup tore the sheet he used as a screen, watching on a normal TV also felt a little lamer.

After that fateful day of projector disaster, Ryan had moved his collection of old cameras to the editing suite, where he could keep an eye on them if Balto's thumping tail and Buttercup's claws were around.

Ryan reached over and dunked a chip in dip, popping the flavorful combo in his mouth with a crunch. "Did you pick a movie from the list I sent?"

"Yeah, I'm thinking *Die Hard*. I feel like I should at least see it once because of the pop culture significance."

Ryan shot forward in his seat, staring at Griffith. "You…you've never seen *Die Hard*?"

Griffith shrugged. "Not really standard movie fare for a missionary compound, you know?"

Griffith had grown up as a missionary kid in the Dominican

Republic, about as opposite from Ryan's upbringing as the son of a wealthy businessman could be. Yet, they'd hit it off over their love of film and the stage, ultimately not that different of mediums in many ways. Griffith had brought Ryan to plenty of plays, and Ryan had made it his mission to introduce Griffith to all the great film classics.

"The usual disclaimers," Ryan said, sitting back. "It had a big impact on the film world—and rocks as an action flick—but falls victim to a lot of the shortcomings of its time as far as the depiction of—"

"Let me guess," Griffith broke in with a small smile. "A movie from the eighties falls short in depicting women and minorities appropriately? Displays some toxic masculinity? And"—his smile grew—"drips with a good helping of eighties cheese?"

Ryan blew out a dramatic breath. "Yes. But you didn't have to steal my thunder like that."

He chuckled and flipped to the right streaming service. "Speaking of casting and directing failures—"

"Not *failures*, just cultural blind spots—"

"—have you put out the casting call?"

Ryan needed another big mouthful of buffalo chicken dip for this. He crunched for a moment before responding. "Yeah. I put out the call, but I don't think I can run the whole set by myself. I also need a crew." He sighed. "Back in college, we always had…" He snapped his fingers. "That's it! College. I've done a ton of favors for the alma mater when it comes to filming and shooting events. I bet if I asked, they would let me use their resources, and maybe some of the undergrads want to be on set to boost their resumes."

"I'm sure the film program would be happy to let you use their space, if only because it will be good for those undergrads to get experience." Griffith swigged a bright purple drink that apparently contained decaf coffee. Ryan didn't ask too many questions about the coffee concoctions. "If someone came asking for help for a play festival when I was in college, I would have jumped on it."

Ryan hesitated, glancing at his laptop. "Mind if I…"

"Go for it. We can start this testament to Bruce Willis after you send an email."

"Thanks, man."

Ryan tried to be quick with bro night on hold. Yet he found himself writing and rewriting the email five times, trying to get the wording just right. He was asking for a lot, and he didn't want to come off as demanding or entitled, but he also wanted to mention how much pro bono work he'd done for the college…

Glancing sideways, Ryan saw it appeared Griffith had exhausted his Facebook feed and had begun playing a ball-bouncing game on his phone. Which meant Ryan was taking *way* too long.

How had Griffith written all the dialogue for a script so quickly when it took Ryan this much time to craft one email? Ryan would definitely need to rework that script. He would leave Griffith's name on the credits as a co-writer of course, but…

Oops. He'd gotten distracted. He re-read the email one more time, double-checked the email address, and hit send.

"Okay." He shut his laptop and slid it onto the coffee table. "Thanks. Now I'm ready."

As the movie began, Ryan's mind wandered.

For the film competition, he and Griffith had decided to be "meta" in the vein of *La La Land* or *Tick Tick Boom*, putting together a story about a struggling wannabe screenwriter trying to make her way in Hollywood—minus the musical numbers. They figured the judges would relate.

But in Griffith's ending, the main character's screenplay was picked up to be made into a major motion picture. That didn't feel realistic.

*That's okay. I'll just change it.* His co-writer wouldn't mind, right?

His stomach clenched, remembering someone in college who had messed with his work and taken the credit. Steve, his ill-fated film partner. His fists clenched along with his stomach. When Steve had stolen Ryan's hard work…

No, he wasn't being a Steve. Steve was a thief. Ryan would still give Griffith full co-writer credit. Griffith wasn't even that invested anyway.

Griffith's chuckle snapped him back to the movie. "This limo driver is my favorite character so far."

"There's a reason this movie is a Christmas classic."

Griffith snorted, draining the last of his purple drink. "It is *not* a Christmas movie."

"Come on." Ryan reached for his own drink, a cream soda, his special treat for one night a week. "John McClane is as iconic as Santa Claus."

"I'll tell Hadassah that when I dress up as Bruce Willis instead of Santa Claus for her younger siblings this Christmas."

Ryan let out a guffaw at the image of Griffith explaining that costume to his shy, quiet girlfriend. The two of them made a perfect pair—a director and an actress, two of the kindest and most supportive people Ryan knew.

A hole grew in his stomach that he didn't think more buffalo chicken dip could fill. What was that about? Did his belly think it would be nice to have something like what Griffith and Hadassah had?

Why did his thoughts drift to Zinnia of all people? Zinnia, who hated him?

He shoved away those strange thoughts. *Eyes on the prize, Ryan. Win this film festival, and you'll have something to show for yourself.*

Not just to his mother. But to everyone.

# Chapter Five

ZINNIA WOULD PAY FOR CAROLINE'S SALAD if it killed her.

After their morning session at the first off-site task—playing a variation of Duck, Duck, Goose with the kids at the charity run through Helping Hope—Caroline suggested hitting the local salad place in Roseville.

Monikered "It's a Toss Up," the restaurant boasted of a Chipotle-style menu. Variations of lettuces and salad toppings displayed in silvered containers.

When Zinnia had reached the end of the salad prep station, a worker in a hairnet held up a tiny ladle of chipotle-ranch sauce. "Full-ladle or half-ladle?"

Most of the times Zinnia stopped by this place, she'd order a quarter of a ladle. Otherwise, thoughts of Georgia and her warnings about "growing a gut from using too much salad dressing" would swarm her brain.

But on a Monday like this—a day she could've dedicated to filming for a certain Netflix special—

"It's a full ladle kind of day."

The worker nodded, drizzled the orange sauce over the ingredients to Zinnia's southwest salad, and used tongs to mix them in the large silver bowl.

She eyed the heaps of bacon added to the mixture. Oh well, chastisements from Georgia aside—bacon cured all.

When she reached the register, a girl with a nose ring gestured at a number of snacks that came complimentary with the meal. Zinnia asked for the cup of butternut squash soup and glanced back at the line.

Caroline had just begun her order.

"Hey, umm." Zinnia lowered her voice as the checkout girl spun around to scoop soup into a cylinder container. "Is there any way I can pay for the person behind me? And any way you can make sure she doesn't know who paid for it?"

The girl nodded and clapped a plastic covering onto the soup bowl.

"We get loads of people here—around the winter holidays—'paying it forward.' You're a little early to the season, but I'll think of something."

A twinkle ignited in the girl's eye. She set Zinnia's meal onto a tray and rang up the final total. Zinnia slipped her a twenty, in case Caroline felt like splurging on some of the cookies they had featured in a glass display case.

Paper fall leaves decorated the windows and walls. On a bulletin board nearby, advertisements for a haunted corn maze blared in creepy font, on orange cardstock paper. No thank you. Zinnia would stick to the less frightening fall activities this year—like apple picking, pumpkin patch scavenging, and eating cinnamon-cider donuts.

Once seated in a booth, she watched Caroline's reaction.

The woman's blonde brows narrowed on the bridge of her nose in clear bewilderment. Then Caroline clasped a hand to her heart. A good sign, Zinnia thought.

Laden with her tray, Caroline ambled to the table. A bounce overtook her steps. Sometimes a free meal could do just that.

*It's still not enough to compensate for last year, though.*

"So." Caroline clacked her tray onto the table and slid into her seat. Two recycled-paper napkins went onto her lap. "Strangest thing. They said I was the one-hundredth customer of the day, so my meal was free."

Zinnia averted eye contact. "Wow. That's great, Caroline."

"Why I say strange is that this restaurant only opened twenty minutes ago, and it's hard to believe that one hundred people have already checked out."

Surveying the sparse line that wound around a stanchion, Zinnia couldn't help but agree.

How could she be more cautious while also making up some ground for all the past wrongs she'd committed?

Time for another subject change. "Those kids at the Helping Hope club adored you, Caroline." Blowing on her soup, Zinnia shoved the mixture into her mouth. Her stomach concaved at the delicious taste of sweet, salty, and a pinch of brown sugar. Man, oh man, she wished butternut squash could be an all-year type of flavor.

Her spoon stirred in the toasted sunflower seeds.

"Do you really think so?" Caroline stabbed a piece of kale with her fork. "I'm sure it helps that Andy and I include them in our books. They're probably really biased. I think they really warmed up to you too."

No doubt, they chose her for the variation of the "goose" in their Duck, Duck, Goose game several times. Probably because she couldn't run all that fast in a pencil skirt.

"Speaking of Andy." Steam wisped off of Zinnia's next spoonful. "Didn't you say that you needed me to do *all* of your off-site tasks today, because of book planning?"

*Instead of, you know, preventing me from getting to film with a certain major movie company today?*

The anger sizzling in Zinnia's neck cooled. How could she get mad at Caroline for something Caroline didn't even know about? Besides, even if Zinnia had Monday free, she would've had to jump through a million hoops to convince Georgia to cancel their tea date.

Rose bloomed in Caroline's cheeks.

Now she took a turn in avoiding eye contact. Instead, her gaze rested on a woman in runner's clothing. Athletes frequented this place during the lunch and dinner hours.

"I"—Caroline cleared her throat—"do need you to take the reins on the college campus tour happening at twelve thirty, but—"

She sighed and tipped back her bottle of sparkling water.

Then her pitiful eyes met Zinnia's.

"I'm sorry. It's just the control freak in me—needing to be at all the off-site tasks. Andy had something come up, so we don't need to meet until late afternoon."

'It's just the control freak in me.'

*You and me both, sister.*

Perhaps she and Caroline held far more in common than at first glance. When Caroline had first stepped foot in Helping Hope, years ago, Zinnia thought a tornado had swept up the woman. Her hair would fly in all directions, and sentences would come out in such a rapid stream that Zinnia would have to replay all the words in her mind to understand what Caroline had said.

Now?

"No worries, Caroline." Zinnia's lips twitched. She cracked open the plastic lid on her salad bowl. "Happens to the best of us. Mind walking me through what I need to do at the college campus?"

Five minutes later, Caroline had explained it all. Zinnia was to meet up with the tour guide at a building called "Ferrell," and attend the tour with the Helping Hope kids who had received full ride scholarships to that school through the nonprofit. There, she would evaluate the tour and return to Clark with any improvements she suggested.

In another five minutes, they'd finished their meals and bid one another adieu.

When Zinnia arrived at the college campus, it took her forever to find the visitor parking. Signs, dilapidated from years and inclement weather, didn't help all that much. Finally, some freshmen boys in cargo shorts took pity on her and pointed her to the right lot.

Thank goodness she always budgeted some extra time in between commutes.

Still, when she locked her car, she amped up her walking pace. Reminiscent of how fast Caroline tended to traverse the pathways into Helping Hope.

*Not so different indeed.*

Following a campus map Caroline gave her, she located the

building called Ferrell at the edge of the academic buildings. Rose bushes, wilting from the September temperatures, lined the mulch. Trees bordered the bricks, leaves sprouting tips of orange.

There she spied a cluster of students and parents. A few of the high school seniors sported bright orange Helping Hope t-shirts. She nodded to them and spotted a girl with a clipboard in hand.

*Ah, the tour guide.*

Zinnia approached her and extended a hand. "Hey, I'm the rep from Helping Hope."

"Mariana." The girl shook Zinnia's hand, then fiddled with a dangle earring. Zinnia looked with envy at the girl's effortless, beautiful wavy brown hair. With a skin complexion like that, Mariana would never hear any type of skincare routine lecture from a certain Georgia anytime soon.

Although if the girl lacked something, it was eye contact and a bold, confident voice.

Mariana clasped her own elbow, once she set free the earring.

"Nervous?" Zinnia glanced down at her own footwear to make sure she hadn't donned heels today. Even with her flats, Zinnia had, on more than one occasion, been told she intimidated the "living daylights" out of people.

"Yeah." Mariana bit her lip. "First tour."

"You're gonna do great, okay?" Maybe getting the girl's mind off the hour ahead could ease her nerves. "What's your major?"

"Film."

Zinnia's heart warmed at this. She and the girl had something in common.

"Are you enjoying it so far?"

Mariana's shoulders eased, and her eyes sparkled. "Yeah. I was actually just asked to be part of a film for this huge festival thing, so I'm excited. They don't usually ask freshmen to help with the bigger projects."

Huh, Zinnia wondered if it was the same project Griffith had her audition for. She'd re-taped the thing ten times before she deemed a perfect enough shot to send the email to admin@torinofilms.com.

Before Zinnia could ask more, a bell tower chimed in the distance. Mariana snapped to attention as a male student on a longboard sailed past their group on the sidewalk.

"Hi, everyone! I want to welcome you to today's campus tour. Now to start us off, let's do an icebreaker."

Mariana walked backwards on the sidewalk and gestured behind her at a vertical-shaped clock tower.

"Question—how many bells are in that tower?"

The group ventured guesses as the chimes within the tall building gonged. Anything from four to one hundred ranged in the answers.

"Trick question." Mariana lifted a finger. "The answer is none. It's all electrical, no real bells are being used."

Zinnia had to hand it to this girl, she already had the group hooked. With her easy smile and bubbly voice, Zinnia wondered how in the world Mariana even struggled with confidence.

She thought back to some of her younger days. Hadn't Grandma stamped out most of her self-worth through the pageants? It took Zinnia spraining an ankle just to get out of those and the rigorous pointe classes and competitions.

Mariana led them across the snaking sidewalks. Brisk breezes skirted around Zinnia's ankles. September, at last, decided to dip into the cooler temperatures. She probably shouldn't have opted for the pencil skirt today.

As goosebumps erupted on her legs, she spotted a familiar figure exiting from the film and media building.

Blocky glasses that could give Clark Kent a run for his money, scrunched shoulders, deep eyes that could be deemed attractive if they didn't belong to…Ryan.

Memories reeled.

To the lot outside of She Brews…hadn't that jerk revved his engine at her when she took that parking spot? She'd dealt with plenty of guys like that in college, who would threaten to run over students in the street, engines growling at the poor freshmen. To think that a guy she worked with in the play would put someone's life at risk, just because someone took a spot they wanted.

The sheer audacity of that man to even tell her "Hi," in the shop after doing that to her. Perhaps he didn't recognize her vehicle at the time.

*Let's refresh his memory, shall we?*

It helped that their group beelined his way, as they would begin the inside-the-buildings portion of the tour.

Ryan's shoulders hiked to his ears when he spotted her. Oh ho, he *definitely* remembered.

As Mariana talked about the film and communications programs, Ryan nodded to her.

"Zinnia."

"Ryan," she said this through gritted teeth.

"Wow, surprised I can hear you. You know, with how loud you honked your horn in that lot. Can you hear me too, or did your horn blow out your eardrums as well?"

She snickered. Did it take him several days to come up with that one?

Had to hand it to him, though, he always looked like he saw a ghost whenever he hung around her. Must've mustered some courage to say that.

"Yeah, well." She quirked a brow. "At least I'm not destroying my car engine with how loud a certain someone was revving his. Especially a rich boy car like yours."

He flinched at "rich boy."

Oooh, Grandma taught her and Georgia early on how to inflict the most damage with words. She'd found a weak spot, time for another one.

"Usually most gentlemen can acquiesce when a woman rightfully gets a spot first but—" She eyed him up and down. "—who ever said you were a gentleman?"

With that, she flounced behind the other group into the building, pulse spiking in her eardrums. Guilt gnawed her gut seconds later. Why had she done that? Sounded just like Georgia in those moments?

As Mariana called for a bathroom break, she pulled Zinnia aside to some couches, stationed next to the lobby that led into a theater. "I didn't know you knew him."

"Knew who?"

"Ryan. He's the guy who recruited me to be on that film with him. Here, I'll pull up the listing."

Mariana scrolled on her phone. This couldn't be good.

"Ah, here it is." Mariana lifted the screen, so Zinnia could peer at the listing.

Sure enough, the screenshot was for an audition for the same film festival Griffith had mentioned. And the email contact for Ryan? Admin@torinofilms.com.

Ice filled her veins.

She'd just insulted the guy directing that movie, AKA, her last chance to make it into the film world.

Why had he said that?

Ryan stomped back into the film building, trying to wrestle his anger under control. Zinnia always brought out the worst in him.

Today had proved frustrating enough before Zinnia came along. The college's film program had indeed been eager to partner with him, so he'd driven over early this morning to check out what equipment they had, talk with a couple of professors about which students needed internship hours, and scope out possible shooting locations.

Professional filming equipment cost tens or hundreds of thousands of dollars, which meant Ryan didn't own a lot of it personally. Instead, he would need to rent the equipment or use what the college provided.

In good news, the college had two RED cameras—older models, but still worth more than his car.

In bad news, the grant that provided the cameras seemed to have run out after that. A lot of their lighting equipment was old and rickety, and Ryan might need to purchase a few mic covers and other odds and ends for the sound equipment.

He'd been able to acquire a few undergrads to be part of his crew, so at least that worked out well. A student named Mariana seemed especially promising. But when Griffith arrived later to scope out possible shooting locations with Ryan, they realized they had a problem.

Michigan looked nothing like Los Angeles.

The two of them had scoured the campus for sets that could work, rustled through the film department's collection of props and backgrounds, even taken a peek at what the theater had to offer—Griffith had friends there—but none of it screamed Hollywood the way Ryan wanted it to.

He should know by now. Every time he set out to shoot anything, whether a short film or engagement photos, nothing ever lived up to his vision. But with the stakes so high this time…

"Whoa, what happened? Did the snacks attack?"

Ryan blinked, focusing on Griffith where he sat on one of the hard couches in the lobby of the film building, laptop open.

"Snacks," Ryan repeated. "Right." He'd set off to grab some food for them while they took a break from scouting to look at audition tapes. After running into Zinnia, he'd completely forgotten and turned right around. "I'll be right back."

Griffith shot him a puzzled expression, but Ryan was gone before his friend could say anything else.

A brisk walk through leaves just starting to turn began to soothe Ryan's ragged nerves as he headed for the snack selection in the college's student center. Maybe he would get Griffith a weird coffee. The playwright deserved it after all his help today looking for sets and props—and for what he was about to do, sifting through audition tapes with Ryan. Ryan liked having a second opinion when making decisions, and Griffith enjoyed watching auditions.

"Well. When I don't have to deliver the final verdict," the playwright had amended. "When people's hopes and dreams are pinned on me…" He grimaced.

Ryan understood the feeling. Usually he would do anything to avoid hurting or disappointing anyone.

Which was why his earlier behavior with Zinnia shocked him.

At the first glimpse of Zinnia, his heart had sped up and his shoulders had tensed, as usual. Before he could even muster a polite smile, she'd given him a look like he was one of Balto's little gifts left behind on a walk.

He had still tried to give her a polite nod and greeting, but when her lip curled…he'd blurted a jab about their ridiculous parking lot encounter. Not even a well-worded or clever jab. But if she held him in such disdain, she should know that she wasn't exactly innocent either.

She had instantly gained the upper hand, of course. Every barb she flung hit its mark like a needle popping a balloon. He *had* revved his engine—accidentally—and yes, he had a nice car, one he'd purchased secondhand at a significant discount from Dad once his father moved on to the next biggest and best thing. He sometimes wished he'd just bought an older vehicle instead of accepting Dad's deal, if only so people like Zinnia didn't make assumptions. "Rich boy." Those two words carried so many connotations—lazy, entitled, underqualified. He winced again just thinking about it.

He purchased an assortment of healthy and not-so-healthy snacks, bagged them up, and grabbed two drinks from the small coffee joint within the student center before heading back for the film building.

*"But who ever said you were a gentleman?"* Perhaps the barb that hurt the most.

As the youngest of three, Ryan had been subject to plenty of teasing from his two older brothers about everything from his asthma, to his smaller stature than theirs, to his taste for film and the arts rather than sports and the bar scene.

He'd grown up seeing all the ways his manliness didn't stack up against his brothers—but he'd also learned some ways he *didn't* want to be like them. Crass. Brash. The way they talked about women and treated other people like tools to be used. If he couldn't be a manly man, he would at least be a gentleman, the way his mother had always taught him to be.

Apparently, to Zinnia, he wasn't even that.

He opened the doors to the film and media center and took a deep breath. What Zinnia thought didn't matter. She was just one person, and they hardly ever interacted with each other anyway.

He crossed the foyer and plopped beside Griffith on the couch, setting the bag of snacks between them and the coffees on the low table in front of them. "I've got the goods. Let's get this party started."

Ryan set up his laptop on the table next to the coffees and navigated to the auditions. He'd gotten more responses than he expected in such a short time—actors must be desperate.

Griffith ripped open a bag of chips. "I was thinking about the script again."

"Yeah?" Ryan grabbed a headphone splitter so they could both listen without disturbing the occasional students and faculty passing through the building on their way to various classes.

"Are we sure we want to set it in L.A.? We're having a hard time finding sets that will look realistic." He nodded toward the large windows overlooking the atrium. "The leaves are starting to turn. It's a beautiful time for Michigan. Maybe you could capture some of that nature magic."

Ryan drummed his fingertips on the table. "An aspiring screenwriter in Michigan. Shot by an aspiring filmmaker in Michigan. Do you think that's too on the nose?"

Griffith shrugged. "Our breakout performance last winter at the theater was a play about a director directing a play. Play-ception. I think people like it when you get a little 'meta.'"

He could be right. Besides, Michigan *was* beautiful in the fall, and if he could work in those colors, the charm of Roseville…contrasted with the plight of a starving artist…

"Yeah. I think you're onto something. Let's talk more after we check out these auditions."

Over the next few hours, they pored over the clips and resumes. Ryan made notes on his phone while Griffith scribbled comments on a pad of paper.

For minor roles, he didn't have to be overly picky. But for the female lead, the actress needed to be perfect. Needed to embody the drive, yet desperation, a commitment to realism while also not being honest with herself…

"Hold on." Ryan sat forward, staring at the laptop screen.

While he'd been pondering, Griffith had pulled up the next audition tape—revealing a familiar blonde-haired woman with eyes that could cut through steel. Although, when that gaze wasn't pointed at *him*, it could almost be…elegant. Beautiful.

Ryan shook his head so vigorously his glasses slipped down his nose. "No, we don't want to work with her."

Griffith's eyebrows shot up. "Dude. I reached out to Zinnia personally."

Ryan's brain seemed to short circuit for a moment. When Griffith had mentioned he thought he knew someone who would be good for the lead… "The person you thought of was Zinnia?"

"Yeah. She works hard, she was an amazing stage manager, and she knows a lot about acting. I thought she could be great for the role." He shrugged. "Assuming the audition tape looks good, of course. She's our last one."

Ryan suppressed a sigh. Griffith and Zinnia were friends. He couldn't say anything too bad about Zinnia. Well, no harm in watching the tape. He was sure he could pick apart some things that he could use to make an excuse for not casting her.

He hit play.

As the audition rolled, Ryan froze, staring.

She wasn't just great for the role.

She was *perfect.* Like he and Griffith had written the character specifically for her.

Once the recording finished, Ryan slumped back on the couch, staring up at the high ceiling. He *couldn't* cast Zinnia. She hated his guts. But none of the other auditions had come even close.

He sighed, sitting up. "We can open casting for an extra day."

"Dude." Griffith fixed him with a harder look than usual. With Griffith's size, it almost could have been intimidating if Ryan didn't know his friend wouldn't hurt a fly. "You're running out of time. That audition was amazing. What do you have against Zinnia?"

Ryan took off his glasses and rubbed between his eyes. If Zinnia had auditioned, she must know they would have to work together and had decided it was worth it. If she could handle it, shouldn't he be able to as well?

"I don't think she likes me," he said finally.

Griffith's lips twitched in a smile Ryan didn't quite understand. "You two bump heads, but you might have more in common than you think." He took out his headphones and stood to stretch. "Think about it. Especially on a rapid call in the Midwest, you don't find an actress like Zinnia every day."

You didn't find a *person* like Zinnia every day, Ryan wanted to say.

Instead, he responded, "Let's talk about the supporting roles and circle back."

Maybe, in the meantime, he could come up with a reasonable argument not to cast the person who seemed to hate him most in this world.

# Chapter Six



*"DEAR COURAGEOUS, MAGNIFICENT, AND OUTSTANDING MOVIE DIRECTOR,"*

Zinnia hit backspace on the email. What a terrible opener. Ryan could probably read through the desperation. Once she cleared the words, she started afresh.

*"Hey, Ryan?*
*What's up?"*

Nope, too casual. Even though she and Ryan worked together on a play once, actors and directors had to keep things professional on email communications—backspace, backspace.

*"Look, I know I'm kind of the worst, but if you just give me this chance, I'll work harder than any actor you've ever—"*

Absolutely not, that would never work.

She shut her laptop and perched the back of her neck against the couch. Dressed in leggings and an oversized sweatshirt, Zinnia had also tied up her hair into the messiest of buns this Monday evening. Her evaluation of the college tour took way too long to get to Clark when she'd stopped by She Brews. Probably because her thoughts reeled the scene over and over again of her exchange with Ryan outside of the media building.

Which she'd *hoped* to remedy with an email. Try as she might, though, she couldn't force herself to manipulate her way into the film. It felt wrong.

*Okay, Zinnia, relax. You can't control this situation.*

Georgia, in this scenario, would probably craft an email inflating Ryan's ego until she could force him to forget any faux pas she committed.

After all, she'd done that plenty when Zinnia and she grew up. She reminisced about some of those exchanges Georgia once had with her.

"'Zinnia, you'd look so much more beautiful without that hairclip. And since you look so stunning now without it, I think you should give it to me, so it won't go to waste.'"

"'Zinnia, I know you want a full-sized bed, but I hear a twin-sized bed makes you have better posture. Why don't you trade your bed for mine? My posture is pretty straight and can handle it.'"

"'Zinnia, you deserve a much better guy than him. I know you two wanted to go on a date, but I don't think he realizes what a gem you are. My thoughts? End it now.'"

Yes, Junior year of college Georgia snatched up that same Matt, who she claimed a year before Zinnia wouldn't click well with. Although Zinnia attempted not to hold any ill will about the situation, she always wondered if Georgia had cooked up lies…

Just so she could manipulate her way into Matt's heart.

Zinnia sighed and dug a spoon into a tub of safe-to-eat chocolate chip cookie dough. She stared at the spider plants lining the wall.

"What should I do, Peter Parker?"

In the darkness of the room, the spider plant didn't answer.

Chocolate chips crunched in her teeth, and she patted her content tummy. Zinnia didn't know many truths about life, but chocolate chip cookie dough could soothe any pain at any time.

"Well, Lord." She placed the tub on her coffee table and adjusted her fuzzy socks. They'd begun to slip down to her ankles. "Maybe the exchange outside of the media building today was You telling me that it's time to give up the whole film thing."

A lump formed in her throat.

It had taken her years to accept this. *Had* she accepted this?

Her phone buzzed. She knew that distinct vibration. The moment she bought the device, she made it a habit to learn the different types of notification dings and sorted them in her mind based on priority.

A little buzz? That meant a text message.

A longer *hmmm* noise? That meant an email, most likely from Clark, AKA top priority.

Her phone had just made a vibration of the longer sort. So that entailed an email message.

"Ugh, Clark." She groaned into her oversized sleeves that covered her hands. "It's ten o'clock at night."

Despite herself, and her rules for "no working at home," she flipped up the lid of her computer. Otherwise, the impending notification would bother her the whole night.

Sure enough, an email sat in boldface font at the top of her inbox. But it hadn't come from Clark. Instead, Ryan's name jumped out at her on the screen. Anxiety tingled in her fingertips as she clicked on the message.

*Dear Zinnia,*

*I would like to offer you the part for "Phoebe" in our short film production, title pending. As I'm sure you remember from the audition listing, we begin filming right away, as we have less than a month to pull this project together.*

*I apologize for the rapid timeline. With that being said, I will need you to respond within the next twelve hours if you are willing to accept this part.*

*I have attached a schedule. Please also confirm that you are able to make all the dates and times included in the calendar. As I'm sure you remember, the same schedule had been posted on the audition listing on the Facebook pages.*

*I look forward to hearing your response and hopefully collaborating on this project with you.*

*Sincerely,*
*Ryan Torino*

Her pulse roared in her ears. It took her several minutes to soothe her heartbeat through breathing exercises she'd learned in a college yoga class.

He offered her a part? Really?

*Man, I apparently should insult men more often.*

Her spirit drooped against her bones a moment later. What about the schedule? Griffith had mentioned that her and Ryan's calendars matched pretty well, but he never sent over the production calendar. What if he had been mistaken?

What if the Netflix situation repeated itself here?

Tapping the attachment, all tension released in her gut. She could make all those times—they took place right after work at Helping Hope. Maybe she could convince Ryan, between takes, to let her grab dinner on campus, since she'd have to rush from her job. But other than that, it worked out well.

She hit reply and sent her message. Once it delivered, she proofread it. Yikes, she used so many exclamation points in that email back to Ryan.

But she didn't care.

At long last, she would act in a film—a movie that could perhaps change her prospects forever.

"Oh, Peter." She jumped from the couch, bounded to the shelf, and lifted the tiny plant into the air. "Mama's gonna be in a movie! Can you believe it?" She spun the plant around and set him beside Mother Shelob again.

Then a little buzz sounded from the couch.

A text.

Loping back over to the loveseat, Zinnia swiped open the notification from…Aunt Millie?

Aside from Grandma's funeral, Zinnia had few interactions with her aunt throughout her life. All she knew was that Millie had a habit of sending back dishes in restaurants several times before the food would meet her satisfaction standards.

The message blinked on the screen.

**Aunt Millie:** Hey, girls.

Zinnia opened the notification and realized Aunt Millie had looped her and Georgia into a group message.

**Aunt Millie:** I'm downsizing and would like for you two to sort through your grandmother's things that I took after the funeral. I know the two of you were grieving heavily at the time, so I went ahead and stored unclaimed items here. But now that my new house will have no room, many of these knick-knacks need to find a good home. Any chance you two could swing by on Wednesday?

A day with Georgia sorting through Grandma's stuff? No, thank you. Zinnia had enough energy for one Georgia interaction per week maximum. After the "fun times" at the teahouse, she would've rather let another date with her little "sissy" wait for another time.

Three dots appeared on the screen, followed by a message from Georgia.

**Georgia:** Oh wow. I miss her so much.

Georgia accompanied this text with three crying emojis, and then another message.

**Georgia:** I know Zinnia works a lot. So Zin, if it's all right with you, I'll take whatever home with me. I'm sure Matt will absolutely ADORE some of those photo books in the TV cabinet. I'm assuming you're giving those up to a good home, right, Millie?

Anger sizzled underneath Zinnia's fingertips as she reread the message. Grandma had already given Georgia most of the inheritance. Claimed that after Georgia faced a terrible breakup in college, that the girl had "mentally not been right," and that the extra money from her will could get the poor thing on her feet.

Zinnia, on the other hand, got one thing from dear Grandma. Spider plants.

She'd vowed to make them multiply, proving to her grandma that she wouldn't squander any wealth given to her.

Now…

Now, Georgia planned to take even more away from Zinnia. Grandma spent years compiling those photobooks, full of grainy film memories of Zinnia's dance recitals, speech and debate championships, and graduation pictures.

*I'm not letting you manipulate the situation, Georgia.*

Sucking in a deep breath, Zinnia's fingers shook as she typed. She reread over the message five times, to make sure that Georgia couldn't twist anything. Georgia had a tendency to latch onto one word, in entire paragraphs, just to start spats with whomever she could.

**Zinnia:** I'm free Wednesday—

And she was. She double checked the calendar Ryan sent. They didn't shoot on that day.

**Zinnia:** I would love to go through the stuff with Georgia :) What time?

As three dots materialized—no doubt, Aunt Millie explaining her schedule for the day—Zinnia placed the device, screen-down, on the couch and returned to her cookie dough.

*You can't take everything, Georgia. Not this time.*

Not this time.

In the end, Ryan couldn't come up with a good reason *not* to cast Zinnia.

"Believe me, I tried," he told Balto, patting the dog's head. Sticky notes littered Ryan's desk and monitor. In front of him, a three-ring binder filled with page protectors awaited the creation of his production bible, the definitive collection of all of the actors, crew members, shots, characters and backstories, scripts, locations, expenditures, and more that the project would require.

Sure, Ryan could digitize all of it, but he liked the comfort of a binder in his hands while he directed on set.

He tapped a pencil against the edge of the desk, staring at the list of names in front of him, actors on one side, crew on the other. At the top of the "actors" side, Zinnia Preston's name stood out in bold.

She had responded last night and accepted the role, in an email that employed several exclamation points. Part of him wondered if her excitement stemmed from the anticipation of watching him with a judging stare. *No. That's not fair to her.*

Next to his crew, he began to write out their roles. From her portfolio, Mariana seemed the most competent, so he would give her the role of first AC, assistant camera, to film when he was busy. Hopefully that wouldn't be too often. He continued down his list of three college students, then began writing out sets, scenes, and shots.

Hours later, he held a binder full of carefully typed up and organized instructions, character sheets, and several copies of the script. He would need to buy more ink for his printer soon.

*Show time.*

As he made his usual check of the apartment before heading out, confidence buoyed his steps. He had a plan for everything, almost down to the minute. This first meeting of the cast and crew had no choice but to go perfectly.

A short time later, an autumn breeze ruffled his hair as he strode toward the college's film and media building. He spotted a guy with short-cropped curly hair and a pair of headphones around his neck heading in the same direction. Ryan waved. "Hey, Martell."

"Hey, director." The college student's steps bounced to a beat Ryan couldn't hear as he quickened his pace to catch up with Ryan. "Excited for our first day."

"Me too." Although nerves had begun to climb up his throat. Should he have gone over his production bible again?

Ryan pulled open the door and they both entered. Before he could say anything else, he spotted Mariana and a gangly dude with shaggy hair waiting on the couches. "Wow, thank you guys for showing up early."

"We got out of class not too long ago just down the hall, so we figured we'd hang around." Mariana shyly fiddled with a string bracelet on her wrist.

Ryan had been hoping to get things set up beforehand, but these students had shown initiative, so he couldn't complain. "Okay, I think we have Room 105 reserved for the evening." He hesitated a moment, then started walking in that direction.

What would Griffith have done? Would he have made small talk? Maybe Ryan should have done that. Small talk wasn't his forte though—he didn't want to make things awkward.

The three college students followed Ryan to the classroom like shuffling goslings behind a mother goose. The guy with shaggy hair, Tristan, muttered something to Mariana, who giggled, and Martell snorted. Good, the three were already friends. Hopefully that would help prevent the drama that sometimes plagued sets.

As Ryan opened the door to the classroom and flicked on the light, allowing the students to file in, he heard footsteps on tile and turned to see Zinnia striding toward him.

She nodded to him. "Ryan."

"Zinnia." Should he say more? But what?

Instead, he stepped aside to let her pass. She didn't seem to want to engage in much conversation either and went to take a seat in one of the folding chairs Tristan and Martell had begun setting up. The black chairs blended in with the ceiling, walls, and floor of the room, which had been painted all black, a blank slate for filming and lighting.

Once the three other actors had arrived, Ryan propped his production bible on a music stand and faced the group, clearing his throat. "Hey, everyone. Thank you all so much for coming out, especially our actors. You won't need to show up every time, but I wanted us to all come together in the beginning to make sure we're all on the same page."

He proceeded to outline the schedule, the concept of the film, on-set protocol, and every one of the bullet points he'd written down on his list for day one.

Once he finished, he looked up. Seven pairs of eyes stared back at him, most a little glazed. He pushed his glasses back up the bridge of his nose. "Ahem. So, with that said, I guess we'll start with roles and introductions. Martell, I hear you're the guy when it comes to sound and lighting. I'd love for you to be our combo sound mixer and gaffer."

Martell snapped out of his stupor and offered a wide smile. "Oh yeah."

"Great. Mariana, I've loved your camera work. Would you be the first AC?"

Her cheeks pinked at the compliment. "I'd love to."

"Awesome." Ryan turned his attention to the final student. "And Tristan, I've heard you're a jack of all trades sort of guy, good at everything. Would you be our combo PA/PD?" PAs, or production assistants, ended up juggling a lot of random tasks on set. As for PDs, or production designers, Ryan wouldn't need someone constantly working on sets, so being a PA as well would help Tristan not to be standing around very often.

"Dude, yeah, PD?" Tristan leaned forward. "Do I get to do any pyrotechnics?"

Martell gave Tristan a playful shove while Mariana covered a smile.

"Hopefully not. Any pyrotechnics we end up with will be a bad sign something went very wrong. So I guess you could say you're part of the *anti*-pyrotechnics team."

Tristan grinned. "Cool. I'm adding that to my IMDb."

Ryan hoped he was joking. "Okay, now that we've assigned roles for the crew, let's meet our cast."

One of the actresses raised a hand. "Could some of the crew not make it today?"

"No, that's the full crew." A sinking feeling began in his gut. "Why do you ask?"

"Oh." She shifted in her seat. "I was just wondering if the DP and AD couldn't make it."

Zinnia raised an eyebrow, then turned her gaze to Ryan.

*No, Zinnia, we don't have a director of photography or an assistant director. Sorry we aren't making a Netflix special.* He took a deep breath, forcing himself not to say anything defensive. "We're working with a small crew, so I guess you could consider me the producer, director, DP, and AD all rolled into one." He tried for a lighthearted smile.

The actress's brow furrowed, but she nodded.

"All right." He flipped to a new page in the binder. "I'm going to pass out the scripts, and then I think we'll try our first scene."

While the actors pored over the script, Ryan and the crew worked to set up the simple scene. In it, Zinnia as "Phoebe" would be auditioning for a role. The scene would only be a few seconds long, so Ryan thought it would be a good one to start with. For that purpose, he'd made sure the props they needed would be in the room already.

Tristan set up the backdrop while Martell fiddled with the lights and Mariana adjusted the camera. Zinnia already wore clothes that would work for the scene.

Ryan cringed as Mariana positioned the camera too close to the backdrop. Then Martell used an extra light. Tristan's backdrop was wrinkled…

None of this would do.

For the next fifteen minutes, Ryan adjusted their work. "It looks great, guys. Just a few tweaks."

"Hey, Ryan." Zinnia approached, holding her copy of the script. "Should I get in position?"

"Er, yes. That would be good. Let's see how the light looks with you in the scene."

As the first scene in the entire process, Ryan wanted this to be perfect. He adjusted one of the lights. "Zinnia, could you push your hair behind your left ear? It's casting a shadow."

She did so, but now too deep of a shadow rested on her neck and shoulder. Ryan tweaked the light again, then checked through the camera lens. Too saturated.

It took another ten minutes to get the shot positioned just right. He could hear the crew and cast getting antsy behind him, feet shuffling, but they only had one shot at this film festival. It needed to be perfect.

"Okay, Zinnia. While we finish this, would you mind delivering your first line?"

"Of course." She looked to the right of the camera, as if facing judges offscreen. "Hello, my name is Phoebe Holloway, and—"

"Sorry to interrupt." Ryan popped up from behind the camera. Finally, she looked right with the lighting. "Try not to enunciate quite so much. The camera and mic are close to you, so you don't have to project how you would on stage."

Someone yawned behind him. His ears heated. *I'm sorry it's taking so long, everyone, but getting everything right will be worth it.*

Zinnia lifted a brow. "Got it."

Maybe if he moved on a bit and got the camera rolling, the crew would feel less agitated and everyone would fall into a flow. "Okay, why don't we try filming the scene?" He motioned Martell and Mariana forward. "Let's get a sound check going."

The two glanced at each other but did as they were told.

A few minutes later, Ryan heard himself calling "cut" for the third time as Zinnia shot him a murderous glare. This might be a longer evening than anticipated.

And if they couldn't even shoot one scene, how did they ever expect to win?

# Chapter Seven

"IF I COMMIT MURDER, I WILL need your help in hiding the body, Joy."

Joy's voice chuckled in the receiver of Zinnia's car speakers.

"All right, Zinnia. Tell me how bad the director was at filming the other day."

Zinnia unleashed the story about how Ryan accomplished next to nothing because he kept making corrections and scrapping certain takes. It didn't help that the other main actress—nice as she was—implied upon Zinnia's first meeting with her that Zinnia was…no longer young.

Her exact words?

"'Oh, that's cool you're trying to get into the film scene now. I know most of our alums from this place made it big when they were in their early twenties, but late twenties is neat, too, I guess.'"

Zinnia finished the story for Joy as she swerved around two kids on their bicycles in her aunt's neighborhood. Leaves scattered in the bikes' tires. "If I hear the phrase, 'Watch over-enunciating, Zinnia,' one more time, I am going to strangle that boy."

True, Zinnia hadn't gotten as used to the mics used for film sets as opposed to being on stage.

In theater, Zinnia would have to over-dictate words and make her *inside* voice, well, an *outside* voice. Apparently in film, anything above a whisper would draw a "cut" from Ryan.

Zinnia's car twisted into her aunt's long driveway as Joy spoke up again.

"I'm sure it'll get better. As you know, I used to be a choir teacher, so I've definitely been guilty of getting nitpicky."

"Sure, but did you make people sing the same measure of a song *twenty-three* times?" The amount of takes it took for Zinnia to get her first line out. Much as Zinnia would voice her opinions to any zealous director, she'd started off on the wrong foot with Ryan. No use in telling him to relinquish control until they'd established a better rapport.

Therefore, she stayed silent yesterday, allowing the anger to sizzle in her ribcage.

"Actually, Zinnia, yes, I have. Twenty-seven times was my record, in fact."

Zinnia pulled up next to a Lexus in the circle drive. Of course, Georgia arrived before she did, probably to make up for arriving later to the teahouse. Whenever the two of them would drive back from college, they would never carpool. Instead, Georgia insisted on racing Zinnia home, claiming she beat her by her copious use of the cruise control.

A sprawling mansion sat before her car. Zinnia imagined "downsizing" for Aunt Millie meant buying a $800k home, instead of one in the millions.

"I should go, Joy. Georgia's going to comment about how much I scroll on my phone in the car otherwise."

Sometimes, before going into Georgia's house, Zinnia would take a breather by tapping through text messages. Until, one time, her sister commented about how Zinnia spent "too much time on Instagram."

"Sounds good, Zin. Oh, are you able to help me with the children's ministry this Sunday?"

"This Sunday?" Had Joy asked her before? In the buzz of getting ready for the first day of filming, Zinnia must've forgotten to read her texts from Joy carefully.

"Yes, I noticed last time that they have two teens running a classroom by themselves. Apparently, they've been doing that for a good three years. They could use some relief."

Many people at The Vine balked when it came to caring for the kiddos. Most parents, tired out from the week of chasing and corralling their own children, hoped the single people, youngsters, and childless couples in the congregation could teach the children for an hour and a half on Sundays. And said singles, couples, and youngsters tended not to enjoy the company of kids and opted out.

Unlike them, Zinnia didn't mind. Her heart yearned for adoption and fostering.

Perhaps, like her grandmother, she could adopt two young ones in need of a good home someday.

*Elementary aged. Everyone goes for the babies. Older children need shelter and care too.*

"Sure thing, Joy." The large front door swung open. Out stepped Aunt Millie, an older woman in a flowy long-sleeved shirt. "Gotta go. Talk soon."

Speaking of adoption, maybe Joy would adopt Zinnia as her younger sister if she asked. Zinnia spent so much of her life protecting Georgia from hurts and ills that it would've been nice to be on the receiving end of such love.

Zinnia popped open her door and pasted on a smile. "Good to see you, Aunt Millie."

The woman tugged at a large, chunky silver necklace she'd bought at a friend's jewelry party, one of those sales groups that frequented the church. She'd often invited Zinnia to attend one of those with her, but Zinnia couldn't ever find the free time. "Better get in quick. Georgia's already boxed up half the goodies."

Had she now?

That answered the question as to how early Georgia arrived before Zinnia this time around.

Zinnia dug her acrylic nails into her palms and attempted not to betray any sort of expression.

"Hopefully there's plenty of it to go around. Mind showing me in, Aunt Millie?"

On a large Persian rug inside, Zinnia slid off her flats by the front door. Cool, slick hardwood met her bare feet. A winding staircase disappeared into the upstairs floors, and everything carried the scent of a lemon-fresh cleaner.

Zinnia often wondered why her mom elected Grandma as Zinnia and her sister Georgia's godmother, when her never-married aunt had a sprawling home like this. Grandma, unlike her, owned a split-level squat home, buried in the middle of a not-so-nice neighborhood.

Then again, like the singles in Zinnia's church, Aunt Millie never had a preference toward nurturing kids. Likely, she would've just thrown money at Zinnia and Georgia.

Down carpeted steps, Zinnia descended into the largest basement known to man. Her condo could've fit into this space alone. On a stage—yes, a literal stage which Zinnia and Georgia used to practice their dance moves—surrounded by mirrors, Georgia pilfered through cardboard boxes.

Deep breath in, and out. "Hey, Georgia."

Her younger sister sat up, bedecked today in a tight-fitting dress. Georgia's face blanched, perhaps unready for Zinnia to arrive so early. She smirked. "Hey, sissy. Tons of memories. I feel like I'm getting swallowed up in them."

Zinnia noted the wreath in Georgia's clutches. Purple flowers wound their way around the fake ivy leaves, one of Grandma's favorite household decorations. When springtime arrived back in the day, Zinnia always begged to be the one to put it on the hook on the front door.

*That one belongs to me, Georgia.*

"Hey, Georgia." Zinnia approached with cautious steps, thinking that perhaps if she charged at her younger sister, Georgia would bolt like a Michigander deer. "Would you mind if I took that one? My door's been looking really barren in the springtime."

"Oh." Georgia tucked a long strand of hair behind her ear. At the teahouse, Zinnia hadn't noticed that the icy blonde locks went all the way down to Georgia's hips. Were those extensions? Another one of Matt's alterations? "I thought the little flowers you put up were just precious."

With some command strips, Zinnia pasted some flower clips to the door each spring. Much as she desired to get one of the wreaths from a craft store, they started at a baseline of seventy dollars. Something Matt and Georgia could afford, but not her.

"Yeah, but I was hoping to mix it up a little." Zinnia's voice shot up. She could never use the real tone around Georgia. Her eyes roved to a picture of Aunt Millie on the wall, cloaked in a sepia filter.

Filters. She had to disguise herself in a million of those around Georgia. Because if her sister saw the *true* her, she would tear it to pieces.

"Oh, really? Well, Zinnia, would you have room to store it?"

"I mean, maybe if I shuffled around a few of the plants."

"*Plants*. It would take moving an actual *living* thing to store a *fake* wreath. I'd hate to see you kill off any of your little spiderlings for the sake of this dusty thing. You don't have room, you said it yourself—"

Georgia latched onto one word, as she always did.

"But I think, sissy, this would be just divine in that extension Matt built for the house. I think I'll take it, if you don't mind."

Zinnia's imagination could've played tricks today, but a certain bite accompanied the word "extension." Did Georgia not like the additions Matt built? Yes, it involved some of Grandma's inheritance, because Matt's funds had been tied up in investments, but Georgia raved about it at her last holiday gathering with the family.

Either case, Zinnia wouldn't win this battle.

"Sure thing, Georgia. It's yours."

Georgia pursed her lips and placed the wreath into a laundry basket, stationed by her hip. Feet growing tired from standing, Zinnia parked herself next to another box. She dug through the dusty contents and pulled out a pair of pointe slippers, tied together with satin strings.

"Oh." Georgia gasped and clasped her hands onto her heart. Genuine moisture filled her waterline. "Grandma's ballet shoes. Do you mind if I—?"

"Of course."

Zinnia handed her the shoes. Cradling them, Georgia swiped a finger underneath her eyes. She'd applied a healthy dose of mascara today, and likely wanted to prevent an ashy river from flowing down her cheeks.

Now Zinnia could earn some of Georgia's favor back again. "You should take them, Georgia. Grandma absolutely loved how you danced on stage. Said that when you did ballet, something beautiful took you over, and you seemed right at home."

Georgia's features slackened.

"I feel right at home in modeling and with Matt, you know. Not just when I did with dance."

Why did Georgia's voice turn so icy now?

Again, one word, "dance," and Zinnia had set her younger sister off.

Zinnia's tongue stuck to the roof of her mouth, fumbling over the next few words. "Oh, of course. You're talented in so many areas, Georgia. Not just dance. You're an absolute treasure to the modeling world and to Matt."

This appeared to abate the redness that surfaced on Georgia's neck.

Georgia tossed the shoes at Zinnia. "I changed my mind. These would be a great addition to your house. Maybe you can hang those on the door in spring, by the satin strings."

To celebrate the "Sugar Plum Fairies" perhaps, that appeared in that season? Or wasn't that winter?

*Not worth an argument, Zinnia.* She cupped the shoes in her hands, thumbs rubbing up and down the dirtied soles.

Silence cloaked them for the next few minutes until Georgia gasped again.

She held up a photobook.

Zinnia's eyes locked onto the leathery binding. If all else failed, she would go home with this treasured item. Based on how Georgia's nails pressed into the front cover, though, she would have to put up quite the fight for this item.

Time for a tactic switch.

"Hey, Georgia, why don't we look at some of those photos together? For memories' sake?"

This appeared to catch Georgia off guard. She sucked in a breath through her brilliant white teeth, then let it out.

"Sure. I have time. Do you, though, with how much Clark makes you work?"

Zinnia let the insult roll down her back like a raindrop. "Not tonight. Here, I'll sit by you."

She did so.

Art paper pages flickered through Georgia's fingertips. Something melted Georgia's shoulders and her expression, as she glimpsed the photos. Fuzziness filled Zinnia's stomach as they giggled over pictures of the two of them in silly Halloween costumes and blowing bubbles from wands.

*This* was the Georgia she remembered, that she missed.

"Georgia, look, you in that pageant where you said, 'world peace is for losers' and made all the judges gawk."

Georgia laughed at the photo of her in a ruffled, sparkly blue dress. "Yeah, that was a good day. Grandma never let me hear the end of it. Oh, and look at you for the debate team. You made a boy cry that day."

Zinnia shrugged. "His fault for not doing his research on the library bill that we debated. His team did *not* see me coming. Oh, and check out this one—"

Zinnia's finger tapped a picture of the two of them in Girl Scout uniforms, herding a group of Daisies in blue vests.

"That was the year that their troop leader had to go on medical leave, so we took over, just fifth graders. Remember that?"

Granted, some parents did help. But like the children's ministry at The Vine, two youngsters spearheaded most of everything.

"Georgia, you were so good with kids. An absolute natural. They were so sad when the leader returned the next year."

Stoniness filled Georgia's expression again. She snapped the book shut and hugged it against her chest, like it was a newborn in need of protection against an apex predator.

"I'm good with *more* than children, you know, Zin. Some people become obsessed with them and forget how to be their own people. By the time they want to have any sort of dream happen, it's too late."

Fury rose in Zinnia. She thought about all the stay-at-home moms she knew, such as Joy. That woman had given up dreams for her children, yes, but she hadn't lost herself in the lives of her kids.

*Easy, there, Zin. Not your battle to fight for Joy.*

She'd accidentally snapped a nerve in Georgia, time for reparations. "Georgia, that's not what I meant—"

"I wouldn't expect you to get it. You make work your *baby*, anyway. I don't know who Zinnia is anymore because you seem to make your whole identity Helping Hope. It's no wonder you're having a tough time with all those film auditions. Those directors probably can't figure out who you are, either."

*What is she talking about?*

Words stung Zinnia like nettles. This seemed to come out of nowhere. Maybe Georgia had bottled up these feelings for some time.

Did Georgia mean it? That because Zinnia put so much time into Helping Hope that she could kiss goodbye any dreams?

"Georgia, I—"

"I would like to take these photobooks home."

Zinnia's jaw dropped. What could she say now? She wanted those memories so badly, but after she appeared to insult Georgia to the highest degree—without knowing how she did it…

"I—Georgia—umm."

Fire flashed in Georgia's pupils. For the sake of mending whatever just went down, Zinnia acquiesced.

"Georgia, it's yours. It'll look great in your TV cabinet."

Brightness filled Georgia's cheeks. Had she put on an act to get this item? Or had Zinnia truly pushed one of Georgia's buttons without knowing?

"Now." Georgia's arm rummaged through a cardboard box. "Come look through this one with me, sissy. I think I saw some of Grandma's knitted socks calling your name."

Something about the script wasn't quite right.

Ryan sat on the couch, laptop on his lap, and stared at the screen. Buttercup stalked along the back of the couch like a jungle cat and kneaded the cushion a few times before draping herself on Ryan's head.

"Thanks, girl. Maybe that will warm up my thinking muscles."

Balto's tail thumped beside him, and the dog placed his head on Ryan's knee as if to say, *Human, I am here too. Remember me?*

Ryan scratched Balto's big ears while he thought. The opening scene they had shot yesterday—well, started to shoot—didn't pack enough of a punch. Would the judges get bored before the film even began?

*Bzzt. Bzzt.*

On the coffee table, Ryan's phone screen lit up. He leaned forward to grab it, dislodging Buttercup, who flicked her tail and stalked away to watch birds out the window.

He hit the accept button. "Hey, Andy, what's up?"

"Hey, dude." Ryan could hear his friend Andy Jackson's easy smile through the phone. "Haven't seen you on the court lately."

Ryan snorted, leaning back into his seat with a teasing grin. "I figured we would give you a break after wiping the floor with you last time."

"Hey now, we were down a man. Elijah had a church thing."

The two exchanged a bit of good-natured bickering about their games of pickup basketball. Andy and Elijah were regulars, but Ryan and Griffith joined as well from time to time, especially in the spring.

Eventually, Andy sobered, his tone taking on an unusual note of nerves. "Anyway, I wanted to ask…you do engagement photography, don't you?"

"You know I do." Ryan chuckled. "Congrats, man. Did you pop the question?"

"Not yet. I was hoping I could coordinate that with you. I want it to be a surprise for Caroline, and she'll love having candid pictures."

Candids, hiding in bushes for the perfect shot…Ryan enjoyed these sorts of shoots more than he liked to admit. Unless things went wrong, and the girlfriend said no. That had happened once or twice. But knowing Andy and Caroline, he couldn't imagine anything but genuine joy and excitement—his favorite emotions to capture.

"Would you be free sometime on a weekend in the next few weeks?" Andy continued. "I would ask Caroline to take a day off during the week, but then she would definitely know something's up."

Ryan wiggled the mouse on his laptop and pulled up his calendar. Filming and prior bookings would take up so much of his time the next few weeks, but he did have a few openings. "How about October eighth? That's a Saturday."

"You rock, man. That would be great."

As he and Andy finished hammering out the details, Balto sat up straight, ears angled toward the front door. A few seconds later, a knock sounded—a loud, many-tap knock.

*Oh no.* His gut sank.

Ryan slid the laptop off his knees. He would have to add the engagement shoot to his calendar later. "Hey, man, I hate to do this, but I've got someone at my door."

"All good, I think we're all set. Thanks again, dude."

"No problem." He set his laptop on the table and stood. "See you that Saturday."

Ryan hung up and shoved his phone in his pocket, heading for the door. That obnoxious knock could only mean one thing.

A knock sounded again, a little different this time, but just as loud. He held in a groan. Or maybe it could mean *two* things.

Balto gave Ryan a look and trotted away to the bedroom.

*I agree, bud.* He swung the door open, revealing two tall, broad-shouldered guys in dress shirts and slacks with matching smirks and faces that looked so much like his.

"Little bro!" Travis swung out an arm, thumping Ryan on the back. "What's up, little man?"

"Hey, guys." Ryan forced a smile that might have looked more like he was baring his teeth. "What are you doing here?"

The slightly taller of the two stepped forward. "Visiting our favorite youngest brother, of course." Ryan attempted to dodge his older brother's hand, but Paul clapped him on the shoulder. "How are you?"

"Uh, I'm fine, but kinda busy…"

Travis barged past him, tromping into the apartment. "Nice place, little man. Still just you? No girl?"

Ryan turned, rolling his eyes. "Like I told you last time you were here—"

The sound of the door shutting interrupted him as Paul closed the front door and strolled inside as if he owned the place, like one of the many businesses he ran for Dad. "Ah. You still have a cat, I see." Paul looked down his nose at Buttercup, sprawled in the window.

The cat gave him a dirty look and began cleaning her fur.

Ryan took a deep breath in through his nose and forced himself to exhale slowly. "It's great to see you guys. It's been about a year since you were last here, if I remember right. What brings you to town?"

Travis yanked open the refrigerator and stuck his head inside. "Man. You don't have *anything* good in here. Dude, is that hummus?"

"Ryan has to take extra good care of his health, you know. He needs to stay out of the hospital." Paul leaned against the wall, arms crossed loosely. "As for why we're here, we had some business in the area, and our meetings ended early today, so we decided to stop by. We figured you'd be home."

Sure, he was home. Working. *Work from home is still real work.*

Travis settled on grabbing a bag of chips from the cabinet and ripping it open. The bag of chips Ryan had been intending to use for man night with Griffith this week. *Well, how much can he really eat? We don't need a whole bag for just the two of us.*

Travis shoved a massive handful in his mouth and reached for another.

*Ah. That answers that.*

Paul strode past him and began opening cupboards until he found a glass, which he filled from the Brita pitcher in the refrigerator before putting the pitcher back…without refilling it. "We're doing some expansion in the area, Ryan. In a couple months, we could probably get you a job with a local branch." He leaned against the kitchen counter. "You wouldn't even have to move."

Ryan gritted his teeth. *Stay cool.* "Appreciate it, but I'm doing well enough with my current job. In fact, I'm working on a film right now that could really get me in front of some big Hollywood names."

As soon as the words left his mouth, he cringed. Why had he brought that up?

Travis snorted and spoke through a mouthful of chips. "Are they vacationing in Michigan?"

Paul picked up an apple from the fruit bowl on the counter, inspected it, and took a bite. "When I was your age, I was the head of four county branches. Do you think maybe it's time to stop playing photographer?"

*A position that* Dad *gave you. Not something you worked for and achieved.* Ryan kept his thoughts to himself. "As long as it keeps paying the bills, I'm happy to keep doing what I love."

"Aw." Travis slung an arm around Ryan's shoulders. "Cute. There are a lot of things *I* love doing that this job really helps out with. Especially with all the traveling." He winked.

Ryan ducked out from beneath his brother's arm as casually as he could. "How's your wife doing, Travis?"

He shrugged, grinning. "No complaints from her."

Paul glanced at his Rolex. "We should get going, Trav." He nodded to Ryan. "Next time we see Mom, we'll tell her we stopped by to see you."

Ryan barely kept from rolling his eyes. So that's what this was? A way to appear like good older brothers in front of their parents? "Great. Tell her I said hi."

"Mama's boy." Travis patted him on the head then sauntered toward the door, tossing the empty chip bag on the counter. He gave Ryan a cocky salute. "See you later, little bro."

Paul picked up a banana from the fruit bowl—the last banana—and stuck it in his pocket. "Let me know if you change your mind about that job." Then he followed Travis.

As his brothers left, Ryan stared at the door that had closed behind them, the apartment somehow feeling much smaller after having housed their larger-than-life presence and confident personalities…including the confidence of knowing that Mom and Dad were proud of their two older sons.

Maybe they were the picture of masculine success that he, the sickly youngest child, could never quite live up to. But if so, he wasn't sure he wanted to fulfil that standard.

A wet nose nudged his fingers, and he patted Balto's head. "We'll win that competition, buddy. The right way. We'll show them all our own definition of success."

# Chapter Eight

Zinnia *hated* knitted socks.

Their itchy fabric scratched at her ankles, and she fought the urge to ask Ryan to "cut" the scene so she could tear them off. Hot lights blazed on her cheeks, causing sweat to brim on her upper lip—thanks to the warm socks on her feet. But she vowed she would wear them every day in the fall and winter. In between washes, of course. Zinnia would take *itchy* feet, not *smelly* feet.

This way, she could prove that she made use of the *one* item Georgia let her take home from Aunt Millie's house. Georgia had also offered her some moldy bath mats she found in one of the cardboard boxes, but Zinnia declined.

Like the spider plants, Zinnia would prove that she wouldn't squander any resources given to her, as Georgia had.

Unlike Georgia, Zinnia received no monetary inheritance.

*Plus, Grandma* had *been a fan of the parable of talents.*

One of the parables in the Gospels warned readers to make the most of the gifts given to them, to cause those gifts to multiply.

*I've done that, Grandma, with the spider plants. Why didn't you trust me with more than that? Why'd you throw the "talent" away with Georgia?*

"Zinnia."

Ryan's voice cut through her thoughts. She gazed up at the camera, wincing. "Yes?"

"You missed your line…again."

"Oh." She folded her hands in her lap, fingers brushing up and down the long skirt. "Sorry, what was it again?"

"It's 'I don't know.'"

That sounded about right—a general summary of Zinnia's life in those three words. Any interaction with Georgia left her frazzled and questioning everything. Could she have used a nicer tone? If she encouraged Georgia more, would her little sister stop insulting her? Was Georgia right when she said she needed to give Zinnia "tough love" because at times Zinnia was "difficult to love"?

*Maybe I deserve to be treated the way she treats me.*

"Zinnia, I—" Ryan's voice cracked.

He shoved his glasses up the bridge of his nose and tapped his fingertips onto the camera. A wince overtook his face. Perhaps Zinnia's imagination had played tricks again, but she swore his expression resembled pity.

"Hey, everyone, we've been at this for a good hour. Why don't we take a break and grab some food in the student center?" Ryan nodded at Zinnia. "I want to try that new smoothie place."

He'd read her mind.

The other student workers and actors didn't need to be told twice. They looped their backpacks onto their shoulders and raced out of the set. Ryan tarried behind, clearly waiting for a certain someone who also loved smoothies.

Had she misread him?

From all of their interactions, it seemed that Ryan wanted to dodge her at all costs.

She grabbed her purse from where all the actors left their personal belongings by the door and followed him into the hallway.

Silence hovered between the two of them, until Zinnia at last spoke.

"Smoothies, huh?"

"Yeah, I hear they have some really good wraps at the new place."

"I do love a good wrap." Zinnia chuckled, then paused. What if Ryan interpreted the "wrap" part of that as "rap" music? She could see Georgia calling her out on the structure of that sentence just then. "Wrap as in a sandwich with filling, often including lettuce, a condiment, and some sort of meat. Not the style of music that often involves adding spoken word to beat or rhythm."

Ryan's footsteps squeaked on the tile. He laughed.

"Yes, Zinnia, I suppose that could be the dictionary definition of a wrap. I knew what you meant."

"Oh."

Ryan was such a guy to nitpick on set. Why hadn't he teased her for her wording?

Wind rippled through Zinnia's hair as Ryan held open the door to the outside for her. The air smelled of fall—crisp and full of promises. They meandered toward a building across the street labeled, "Fairweather Student Center." College students called it the FSC for short.

Once inside, conversation held at two-top tables and booths clouded Zinnia's thoughts. They approached a shop with a neon smoothie sign and Zinnia scanned the menu. After she found the right fit, she reached the front counter and asked for a smoothie that contained a healthy amount of passion fruit and chia seeds, and a chicken, bacon, ranch wrap.

Ryan, behind her, listened and ordered the same.

Two minutes later, a worker handed them their bags, and they settled at a high-top table, adjacent to the cast and crew, who had slid themselves into a large booth.

"Zinnia." Ryan tore off the sticker that held together the paper on his wrap. "Are you doing okay? You seem a little spaced out today."

Her shoulders dropped in a sigh as she sucked on the smoothie straw. Chia seeds danced on her tongue. She'd made the right choice by asking for the almond milk instead of the soy today.

"I—"

Should she unload her whole family situation onto a near-stranger? "Stranger" didn't seem like the right word… enemy, perhaps? She and Ryan had worked together before, but they never tended to get along.

She nursed the Styrofoam cup in her hands. "It's my sister. But I don't want to bore you with the details."

"Zin, one of the crew members took ten minutes of my time—when I was setting up—to talk to me about how he's going to get the school newspaper to write an op-ed on why their campus should use two-ply instead of one-ply toilet paper. It doesn't get much drearier than that."

She laughed and stared outside the large windows in the echoing room. Slate clouds filled the skies, in time for a spooky October that fast approached.

"All right, all right, Ryan, I guess it's time to bore you again."

Who knew how much time passed? Certainly, more than the usual ten minutes the group would spend chowing down on their dinner for the night, but she spilled far more than she had intended.

Perhaps it was due to the fact that Ryan didn't interrupt her every two seconds to correct one word she used. Or, like many of her coworkers whenever she would mention Georgia, would get a glassy look in their eyes and say, "Uh-huh, so anyway, what do you think about the meeting we had with Clark this morning?" Instead, Ryan leaned forward, eyes sparked full of interest. Like they were soaking in her every word.

Still, better to clarify everything.

Zinnia found herself stopping to explain, any time she realized a word could be interpreted in more than two ways.

Once Ryan emptied his cup, he placed the smoothie to the side of the table and held up his hand. "Why do you feel like you have to do that?"

She frowned. "What do you mean?"

"You keep trying to explain things to me, like I'm about to attack you or something if you say the wrong word. For instance, you said, 'I want to be very clear that I love Georgia, and maybe I'm going crazy and misinterpreting everything.' From what you've explained, you're not crazy, and Georgia is *very much* understood. She's being a mean person right now."

Her lips twitched as she rubbed her ranch-tainted fingertips onto the napkin on her lap.

"Sorry, force of habit. Georgia often takes things the wrong way."

"Well, I don't. You're understood, not crazy, and doing the best you can in a bad situation."

Ryan scrunched his nose in a way that made Zinnia's gut flutter. She had truly misunderstood *him*. Those deep eyes looked far more attractive now.

"Besides, I do get it." Ryan crinkled his wrapper and tossed it into a bin nearby. Oh right, didn't he play basketball with a group of friends during the winter and spring? He swished that balled trash into the "hoop" like a pro. "Not the specific situation, but sibling troubles."

Ten minutes sailed past as Ryan recounted for her about how his whole family didn't believe he'd make it into film. Zinnia found herself leaning closer and closer to him, over the table.

She'd found a kindred spirit.

Warmth stirred in her insides. Ryan had certainly, after this conversation, moved from the status of enemy to something else.

But was it a friend? That seemed inadequate for the flutters in her stomach.

"—and then Mom keeps trying to force me to take some money to—"

The flutters stopped.

Zinnia had forgotten. Ryan hailed from an affluent family. Even if he and his siblings got into the occasional spat, he would never understand the crippling sensation of getting student loans bills in the mail. Nor could he understand the merit of earning enough after college to purchase a condo, nor car payments on that expensive vehicle of his, nor, nor, nor…

*He's a rich boy, Zin. And that's why you won't be more than friends.*

Because as much as Ryan pretended to relate to Zinnia's plight with Georgia, money played a big factor. Georgia got the inheritance because she couldn't handle a messy breakup. Zinnia received, well, a plant. Something he would never truly understand, if life had handed him everything on a platter.

"What's wrong, Zin?"

She shoved the wads of garbage into her bag and bunched her fist around the empty smoothie cup. "I really think we should get back to filming."

"Okay, true. But are you—?"

"I'm *fine*, Ryan. Let's get back, okay?"

Before he could respond, she tossed her trash into the bin and marched toward the media building without him.

What had he done wrong?

Ryan helped Tristan move a bench from one end of the set to another. He and Zinnia had seemed to be having a good conversation. His blood boiled with how her sister treated her—in some ways, not so differently from how his brothers treated him.

And then her entire demeanor had changed.

That sharp edge returned to her stare, the tightness to the corners of her mouth. The Zinnia who made him want to hide in his sweater had returned.

He readjusted his grip on the heavy piece of furniture. Maybe he'd just caught her at a vulnerable moment. She'd hardly seemed present while they were trying to shoot earlier, so he'd called it for a dinner break. Maybe she just needed someone, anyone, and in a pinch, even Ryan would do.

That shouldn't disappoint him as much as it did.

The bench thumped on the ground as Tristan and Ryan set it down, and Ryan turned to Mariana. "How's it looking?"

From behind the camera, she gave a thumbs up. "Let's get 'Phoebe' and 'Alan' on set."

One of the actresses finished adjusting Zinnia's hair and gave a returning thumbs up. "Phoebe's ready to go."

Zinnia strode into the frame, expression carefully neutral, and perched on the bench. The actor playing Alan joined her.

Ryan walked behind the camera and hesitated. Zinnia needed to turn just a little bit...but would she bite his head off for making a comment?

"Hey, Phoebe, could you angle your shoulders a little to the right?" He looked through the viewer. "And Alan, could you scoot a little closer to her?"

They did so, but the shadow...

"Martell, could you adjust the angle on that reflector?"

He heard Zinnia sigh, and his shoulders tensed. But Martell adjusted. "Sound check?"

Ryan hesitated. "Uh, Tristan, could you move that flower pot a bit to your right? And Mariana, can you man this camera while I set up camera two?"

She looked up from the second camera, where she had been peering through the viewer. "Oh. Um, sure."

Ryan winced. Oops. He should have let her do that herself. Making sure *he* set up all the camera angles showed that he didn't trust her to do a good job.

But that was exactly the problem. With so much on the line, not checking everything himself...he didn't think he could do it.

Cognizant of all eyes on him, he fiddled with the camera. The focus wasn't quite right, the angle...

Martell unsuccessfully covered a yawn.

"Okay." Ryan fidgeted with his glasses. "Go ahead and do the sound check."

"Quiet on set," Martell called.

Everyone froze as he listened carefully to his headphones and captured the ambient noise. When splicing together scenes, it would come in handy. Then he nodded to Ryan.

"Okay, clapper." Ryan glanced around for Tristan.

The student had his head tilted back, downing an energy drink. "Oh." He set the drink down on a nearby table and rushed toward the set. "Sorry."

As he passed, his arm knocked into the drink.

In slow motion, Ryan saw the can tip. Fall.

Bright-colored liquid splashed toward the lighting equipment. One of the actresses gasped and yanked a light out of the way.

Ryan removed his glasses and rubbed the bridge of his nose.

"Sorry." Tristan set the can upright.

"It was an accident." Ryan put his glasses back on. "From now on, no food or drink on set, please. We have some very expensive equipment here, and we can't afford to ruin it with a rogue beverage."

Zinnia muttered, "I'm sure you could just buy a replacement."

He turned and stood for a moment blinking toward Zinnia, stunned. Could this be what had upset her?

Had he mentioned…

His ears heated. They had been speaking so freely, he'd mentioned Mom trying to give him money. Now he felt his cheeks flame as well. He tried not to bring up his family's wealth to avoid anyone making assumptions—assumptions like those Zinnia must have formed.

He understood. After everything she had gone through, no wonder she would be resentful of what she saw as a spoiled rich boy.

*I work hard for this, Zinnia.* Add her to the long list of people he needed to impress with this film.

As they proceeded through the many takes, Ryan's mind wandered to women he had dated.

Not that he and Zinnia were anything close to that. Of course not. She hated his guts. But how people reacted to money…

In college, he hadn't been as careful not to mention his family. When some girls got wind of the Torino business empire, they went a little crazy. Everything he said was suddenly the most hilarious or intelligent thing they had ever heard. He was so handsome. Did he work out? Did he ever vacation in Europe, and could they come too?

Not to mention all of the eligible young ladies Mom tried to send his way, ladies from families that would oh-so-coincidentally make excellent business partners.

So he started trying to make sure no one ever found out. Post-college, living the starving artist lifestyle, he finally began to feel like women might care about him, not just his family's money. Sure, he'd gone on plenty of terrible dates for other reasons, but at least he didn't feel like a prize slab of meat.

Until he started dating Ariana, a talented painter. They had bonded over their love of visual arts while eating ramen and dreaming big dreams.

Eventually, he opened up and started to tell her about his family, and how they pressured him to join the family business, or how Mom tried to get him to accept random cash she tried to throw his way.

Ariana had been angry. Her words still rang in his ears.

"What, did you think it was somehow romantic or glamorous to live the starving artist lifestyle?" She had glared at him. "Some of us are really struggling. We're really trying to make something of ourselves. Is this all a game to you?"

He hadn't known what to say. The next day, Ariana broke up with him over text.

He hadn't made it past a second date with anyone since. At this point, he'd mostly stopped trying.

"Hey, director." Martell shifted on his heels. "It's starting to get dark, and it's messing with the lighting."

Ryan looked up at the sky and sighed. "You're right. I think we better call it a wrap for tonight." Even if they were significantly behind schedule.

As they packed up, he saw Zinnia cast him one final glance of annoyance over her shoulder as she left. Out of the corner of his eye, he caught Martell and Mariana exchanging a frustrated look.

He had a feeling if he didn't pull it together soon, he might have a mutiny on his hands.

# Chapter Nine

"—THAT, FRANCESCA, IS WHY RYAN NEEDS to have someone streamline everything. No one in the crew is willing to speak up, so it's up to me."

In a boardroom, where Clark just held a meeting, Francesca slumped into one of the rolling chairs around a long table. Zinnia had tried out all her ideas this morning on coworkers, only to find that they needed to "make an emergency restroom break" or to "call their wife at home" during business hours.

After the meeting, she pinned Francesca—a coworker who favored pencil skirts and tea over coffee—with a look. Francesca stayed put in her chair as Zinnia ran her through the plan to get Ryan to speed up the filming process.

"Yes, Zinnia." Francesca hid a yawn behind her palm. Then she scooped up her laptop and hugged it to her chest. Today, Francesca sported a lilac ruffled blouse. Frills threatened to swallow the computer. "I'm sure you'll figure it out."

With impressive speed, Francesca's heels clip-clopped out of the room. Carpet muffled the impact of her steps.

Zinnia sighed. Ryan did indeed listen far better to her than anyone else…even if he *had* come from a rich family.

She eyed the whiteboard in the room, scanning up and down the items Clark had squeaked with an expo marker. Everything in the meeting room smelled of those writing utensils, causing her brain to go all fuzzy.

During their meeting, Clark informed them that Caroline's role would change in the coming months.

That meant that the majority of her tasks would be doled out amongst the people in her department. When Clark left the room, coworkers shared grumbles over their morning donut holes—pumpkin spice flavored ones—about how they couldn't squeeze any more tasks into the time allotted for the workday.

"Overtime is going to be a regular thing," Francesca had told a balding man, as she blew off the steam on her coffee cup. "You know how much Caroline gets done in one day."

Clark hadn't mentioned a timeline, but she imagined it would take place right after filming.

That meant she had little luck in any acting endeavors for the foreseeable future, since Helping Hope would take up most of her time.

Maybe she could convince Clark *not* to give her the overtime tasks. Sure, when she first arrived at Helping Hope, she hoped to climb the ladder with impressive speed. However, a few years in, she learned two things.

One, upward movement seldom existed at this company and—

Two, anyone in higher positions could say goodbye to hobbies, families, or any kind of dating life thanks to the generous amounts of overtime they gave the company.

She'd cross that bridge later.

Plucking an eraser, she wiped the board clean and uncapped a green marker.

Today, before her lunch break, she'd commit the list for Ryan to memory on the whiteboard. Then she'd snap a photo with her phone and show him on Saturday. AKA, their longest shooting day. Ryan reserved several extra hours for any weekend shoots.

Although she could send it to him today, on Friday, she needed to bounce ideas off Joy over the phone. And Joy couldn't call until late this evening, thanks to some in-laws visiting her.

The green marker screeched against the slick surface of the board. She wrote. Finished. Then she stepped back to read.

**Ways to Make Ryan More Efficient**

- Show him previous takes and how they probably look better than he imagined them. Ryan is a perfectionist, so he may think they have to seem immaculate.

- Remind him that something called "post" will happen. Editors exist to make anything look pretty and less messy.

- Help him to recall our timeline. Give him a realistic idea of just how much we can get done with the time left, going at the pace we've been going.

- Bring him some bagels as compensation for putting him through the wringer.


Back in school, students would recruit Zinnia for group projects because they knew she did *good* work, but she also did *fast* work. If a cluster of students ever had a perfectionist in the mix, they would invite her to usher in productivity.

"Knock, knock."

Caroline's lips thinned into a line at the door. She must've gotten back from her outing with Andy. Today, Clark sent them on a wild goose chase to a number of fall pop-ups for Helping Hope happening across Roseville.

In Caroline's clutches, she held a store-bought cake. On top of it, scrawled in pretty handwriting, sat a post-it note with the label "Caroline."

Zinnia stopped by Joy's house, after shooting yesterday, to get her to write the name on the card. Caroline knew Zinnia's handwriting well, so they had to take every precaution.

"I found this in my cubicle."

Zinnia feigned surprise. "Oh, Carrie! You didn't tell me it was your birthday."

"It's not."

Caroline frowned and set the cake down onto the table. This pastry sported chocolate drips cascading a backdrop of white frosting. When Zinnia passed Caroline's cubicle, she once spotted Caroline scrolling on Pinterest. No doubt, pinning some ideas for a future wedding with Andy. Caroline had saved photos of drip-style cakes to her "Something Borrowed" board.

"Maybe someone gave it to you to celebrate the one-year anniversary of your book release?" Zinnia cocked her head.

Why had she gotten a cake for Caroline, again? Aside from the fact she needed to make up ground for the events of last year?

Ah yes, when Zinnia went for a grocery run last night, she spotted the pastry in the bakery section. Everything about it screamed, "Caroline is going to love this."

"Nope, that was this past April." Caroline reached into her pocket and pulled out a grocery bag.

Zinnia's veins went cold.

Oh no. In her rush to get back to her cubicle—before Caroline could catch her in the act—Zinnia left behind the plastic bag, didn't she?

Caroline dug her hand into it and pulled out a receipt.

"Umm, Zin, this receipt has your name on it."

"Wow, thank you for alerting me, Caroline. Credit card fraud is no joke. I'll interrogate everyone in this office to find out who stole—"

Caroline held up her free hand. "Zinnia, why did you get me this cake?"

"I'm, umm, terrible at remembering birthdays?"

Lights clicked on in Caroline's eyes. She tugged at a dangle earring in one of her lobes.

"Zinnia did you—are you the one who got me that free meal at the salad place? Are you…trying to make up for what happened last year?"

Caught, Zinnia slumped into one of the rolling chairs and kept her gaze pressed onto her shoes. She'd gone for some nude flats this morning.

"I—er—"

"Oh, Zin." Pity laced Caroline's voice. She rushed over and placed a hand on Zinnia's. "You *do* realize I forgave you for that a long time ago, right?"

No, she hadn't.

In Zinnia's family, forgiveness was earned. Once you slighted someone—Grandma, Georgia, even Aunt Millie—it took months, even years to recover. She'd gotten used to presenting gifts over the years for her many wrongs. For speaking in the wrong tone, for borrowing Georgia's lip gloss, for forgetting birthdays…

Moisture itched Zinnia's eyelids. She reached up a finger to wick away any of the tears.

"No, Caroline, I hadn't realized. I figured you—"

"Listen, Zinnia." Caroline slid herself into a chair. Today, she'd tamed some of those flyaways with the distinct scent of hairspray. "Believe me when I say I've thought *a lot* about those events from last spring. Sometime last summer, Andy encouraged me to see things from your perspective."

She chuckled.

"Let's be honest, I was a 'hot mess.' There's no way around it. I ran into the office every day like a chicken who'd just lost her head. I think I heard the words 'slow down' about five times a day from the other coworkers. Everyone was thinking it, 'She can't do this picture book project on her own.' You were the only one to go ahead and put those thoughts into action."

Zinnia always did that, right? Tried to lighten loads and make productivity happen. Last year, though, she learned a hard lesson about overstepping.

In Zinnia's periphery, she watched Caroline's face soften.

"You were trying to help me, right?" Caroline placed a hand over Zinnia's. "In your own way. Albeit, not the best way. Still, you had the best of intentions."

Quivers overtook Zinnia's bottom lip.

She nodded, worried any words would set off some waterworks.

"Oh, Zin, I didn't mean to make you cry."

"I'm fine, really." Zinnia's hand, underneath Caroline's, flinched. Caroline released her touch, and Zinnia lifted her arm to block Caroline from viewing any tears trailing down her cheeks. "I'm just used to people holding grudges. That's why I got all the g-gifts."

Her teeth bit her bottom lip to stop it from quaking.

"Believe me, Zin, my mom was like that for a while. That's why I'd started suspecting you with all the free stuff I was getting. However"—Caroline squeezed Zinnia's shoulder—"the right people don't hold onto past hurts. They let go. They heal. They move on. Can we do that?"

Weights lifted off of Zinnia's ribcage.

Although she'd never slighted Joy beyond minor offenses, she'd never experienced forgiveness from a friend in this way. A friend. Did Caroline finally consider them to be that?

Zinnia nodded. "I'd love that."

"Great." Caroline lifted herself from her chair. It bumped against the back wall. "Because I need someone to go with me to that salad place regularly. Francesca says she would absolutely not be caught dead in a joint like that."

A watery chuckle sounded from Zinnia. With quaking legs, she stood and held herself up on the board for support. Why did reconciliation take so much out of her body?

Had she held in this guilt for so long that now, as it exited, it caused her to tremble?

"Speaking of that salad place." Caroline reached for her jacket. She must've dropped it on the back of one of the chairs. "Why don't we head there now for an early lunch?"

Zinnia's stomach burned. She could eat.

"This time"—Caroline wagged a finger at Zinnia when she reached the door—"I'm paying."

"Look up here! Do you see the silly little birdie?"

Ryan snapped a picture as the toddler faced the camera. Finally. The five-year-old had blinked, but thanks to Photoshop, Ryan could mesh this photo with one where the little girl was smiling in order to create a perfect family picture, and no one would be the wiser.

A leaf fell from a tree above the family of five, and the oldest reached out to grab it. Ryan snapped a candid. The parents would love this cute photo later.

"Okay, let's do the sisters." He smiled at the kids. "Emery, maybe you could hold Edith's hand?"

Their parents helped Ryan arrange the three little girls in their fall plaid with a cluster of pumpkins. Taking pictures of children could be difficult, but his heart warmed every time the children's loved ones oohed and aahed over their cute kids. He was happy to capture those memories. Especially for an adorable family like this one.

After the shoot, once the family had strolled away to their minivan, arms full of pumpkins with the five-year-old stomping on leaves the entire way, Ryan packed his equipment into his car and then decided to take a moment for a stroll himself.

Pops of orange and gold stood out in the trees in the park, preparing for the height of fall. The sun shone, but a cool breeze rustled the leaves. He could use a short walk before heading home to do more editing. Especially after the disastrous day of filming yesterday.

He began a small loop through the trees, not long enough to properly be called a hiking trail but perfect to enjoy some of the foliage.

Halfway through the loop, he came to an empty bench nestled among the trees. He sat, staring up at the branches above.

"Lord, things aren't going so great with this project." He sighed. "My brothers aren't my favorite people, but they may be right. Getting my hopes up about this is unwise." He'd always felt like God was leading him toward film. But maybe the Lord wanted him right where he was, shooting random photography gigs or filming events.

So why did that make his heart sink?

He pulled out his phone to check social media and see if anyone had tagged his photography account in any pictures. Instead, he saw the face of his most loathsome ex-friend staring back at him.

Steve.

Why had he even shown up in Ryan's feed? Ryan specifically didn't follow him. He checked the caption and realized the post had been made by a mutual college buddy.

*"Great to see the old Steve-inator this week, fresh from Hollywood. Still kinda mind-blown that I'm friends with someone this cool."*

Ryan snorted. "It's not like he's Steven Spielberg or something."

Tightness coiled in his gut. Steve was still doing well for himself, huh? So much for cheaters never prosper.

Despite himself, his mind drifted back to college and his ill-fated friendship.

Steve and Ryan had grown up in the same town, but didn't interact much until college, when they ended up as roommates, both starry-eyed incoming freshmen intent on taking the world of film by storm. From late nights on set to cramming homework in the library to Nintendo nights in the dorm, Steve had been Ryan's constant companion. So it only made sense when they decided to work on their senior project together.

Ryan wrote most of the script, while Steve organized the details. The short film would be a tale of ironic tragedy in the vein of a darker take on *The Necklace* by Guy de Maupassant, with hints of *The Gift of the Magi* by O. Henry. Looking back, maybe Ryan had been trying a little too hard to seem literary, but Steve loved it. Ryan spent hours and hours perfecting the script.

They spent months crafting the perfect ten-minute film together, from writing, to shooting, to meticulous editing.

And then, on one of the final nights of editing, poised to turn in the project nearly a month early, Steve entered their dorm room with a tight jaw and a strange look in his eye. "Bad news."

Ryan put down his textbook. "Yeah?"

"Prof said we need an *original* script." He slumped into his desk chair. "No remakes, no sequels…no modernizations."

Ryan's heart nearly stopped. "I mean…it isn't really a modernization, is it? Sure, we have a few elements from two classic short stories, but—"

"Do you wanna risk it?" Steve ran his hands through his hair. "Do you wanna risk getting a failing grade on our *final project* because we didn't follow the instructions?"

Cold descended over Ryan like a bucket of ice water. Failure? Would it be that drastic? "Can't we talk to the prof? Say we didn't know?"

Steve snatched up a piece of paper and waved it at Ryan. "You think she'll take pity? It's underlined. In bold. We *missed* it."

Sure enough, from what Ryan could see of the paper that looked like part of the syllabus, bold text declared the ban.

"How?" he whispered. "How didn't we know?"

"I don't know." Air whooshed from Steve's lungs. "But we need to film something new. And fast."

In the end, with the help of more energy drinks than Ryan cared to think about, they created a film in three weeks and turned it in right before the deadline. They passed, but Ryan knew the new film was nothing he wanted to be showing his grandchildren someday.

"We did it." At graduation, Ryan clapped Steve on the back. "Can you believe we pulled off that final project, you maniac?"

Steve grinned. "I didn't think it *could* be pulled off. Thanks to you, man."

That was the last time Ryan spoke to Steve in person.

A few months later, he saw Steve's mom post something online about Steve winning a prestigious film award. *Odd that Steve wouldn't tell me.* Ryan flipped to Steve's profile to learn more.

Only to realize…Steve had blocked him.

It must have been an accident. Ryan would let Steve know later and they would laugh about finicky apps. In the meantime, Ryan tracked down the winning film on the film festival's website.

And, slowly, his jaw dropped.

It was the film they made together.

Except, it wasn't. Every line of dialogue remained the same, every camera angle, every prop, every sound effect. But the actors were different, and the scenes were filmed somewhere other than at the school. Steve had copied the film they made shot by shot, line by line.

As he watched, Ryan's blood ran cold. Steve would have had to start working on this project before they graduated in order to submit it in time for judging. Which meant…

His mind went back to how often Steve had been missing those days. He'd said he had a lot of study groups for finals, but…

Ryan's cursor flew as he pulled up the shared Cloud folder in which he and Steve had kept all of the materials for the film.

Empty. Steve had deleted all of the files.

Dizziness overtook Ryan's mind. Steve had stolen all of their hard work, including the script Ryan wrote, and re-made it to cut Ryan out in order to enter the competition and win this award.

And Ryan had no evidence that this was the case.

"You could have asked, Steve." His fist clenched. "Was there actually a ban on modernizations for our final project? Or did you lie about that too?"

Perhaps that was when Ryan's issues with control truly began. His need to read all the fine print, to oversee every aspect of every project.

Steve won awards, moved to Hollywood, worked on actual sets.

And Ryan, because he hadn't looked into things, hadn't backed up files, hadn't checked his own syllabus against the paper Steve waved in his face, remained in Michigan.

A leaf fluttered down and landed in Ryan's lap, bringing him back to the park bench in the present.

Wait. Why *was* Steve back in Michigan? Just visiting family?

Ryan glanced at the clock on his phone. More time had passed than he'd realized. He needed to go home and get to work. Steve didn't deserve any more of his time anyway.

Yet as he headed back toward his car, a feeling of unease lingered in the back of his mind.

# Chapter Ten

"INSIDE THIS BAG…" ZINNIA BEGAN AS she popped her head into the classroom where they would film that day. Ryan had busied himself with some of the set up. "I have an item that will tempt most men beyond reason."

Ryan glanced up from the tripod he'd been adjusting. "Is it the ring of power from *Lord of the Rings*?"

"Nope, bagels."

He frowned and adjusted one of the levels on a tripod leg that had gone wonky. "You know our rule about bringing food and drink onto the set."

Thanks to one of the crew members almost splashing a full can of Red Bull onto the equipment, Zinnia and the cast were told that if they needed a snack, they had to take it outside—in the foyer that led to the theater.

Cinnamon and brown sugar scents wafted from the bag in her hands.

"I know, Ryan, which is why you need to get your butt out here and eat some delicious breakfast pastries."

"Zinnia, I'm busy setting—"

"Get your butt out here, or I'm chucking the cinnamon sugar bagel at Mr. Camera over there."

Zinnia watched as Ryan's shoulders drooped. He marched toward the door and glared at her.

"You better have a blueberry flavored one."

She mock-gasped. "Honestly, Ryan, you assume the worst out of me. How could I leave that shop without Mr. Blueberry?"

"What is with you adding Mr. to everything?"

"I'm sorry, *Ms.* Ryan."

They snickered as they collapsed into cushy seats. Behind them, stairs led up to the theater in the media building. Zinnia cracked open the bag and handed Ryan a blue-speckled bagel in a napkin.

On a coffee table, she set out various cream cheeses. Ryan grabbed a knife and dug into the one with a honey walnut flavor.

"The rest of the crew is going to arrive in about thirty minutes, this fine Saturday." Zinnia bit into a cinnamon crunch bagel. Clusters of brown sugar danced on her tongue. Splurging on sweets came at a price, but a worthy one. "I figured you may want to take a look at this list before they get here—and before they devour the rest of the bagels."

She slapped her "How to Be More Efficient" sheet on the coffee table. Ryan's nose wrinkled as he squinted at the header.

"Zinnia."

"Yes, Ms. Ryan?"

"What is this?"

"It's a piece of paper, you see."

His thumbs rubbed dark spots underneath his eyes. "It's too early in the morning for jokes."

"Very well."

She explained the purpose of the sheet, and the reasoning behind each item on the list. Ryan's expression grew grayer and grayer with each word. Zinnia cut herself short.

"What?"

"I—" Ryan palmed the back of his neck. "I understand why you'd want us to pick up the pace, but I like the way we've been running things. It feels comfortable for me."

Zinnia had anticipated this. Joy warned her, last night, when going over the list, that Ryan may try to argue that he had everything under control.

Brushing her fingertips on a napkin, Zinnia nodded at the stairs. "Take a tour of the theater with me."

"What? I'm not even finished with—"

"Mr. Blueberry can wait. Theater, now."

With a groan, Ryan lifted himself to his feet. The two of them ambled up the staircase into a large, dark theater. Spotlights illuminated the stage. Before them sprawled a magnificent set. Zinnia scanned through her memories to remember a poster board in the theater hallway, advertising the newest production, *Tarzan*.

Vines clung to the stage rafters. Rocks, trees, and paper flowers dotted every crevice and corner of the stage.

"What are we doing in here, Zin?"

"Follow me up onto the stage. That way we can get a finer look at the details."

Their steps galumphed onto the stage platform. Zinnia gestured at the magnificent backdrop behind her.

"It's detailed, right, this set?"

"Correct, *Mr.* Zinnia."

She quirked a brow, and Ryan laughed.

"Right, so Ryan, one of the theater kids, who happens to be on your crew, told me how much time it took to put together this thing, with several stagehands helping. You want to hazard a guess?"

"I'm scared to."

"Several weeks. Now imagine if they had their time cut significantly. Let's say the director told them, 'You have forty-eight hours to put this thing together.'"

Ryan's face went sheet-white at the sheer idea of it.

Dust motes circled Zinnia's head as she lifted a finger to wick sweat off of her upper lip. The wool socks from Grandma did little to help her in these hot stage lights.

"If they had forty-eight hours, what do you think they should focus on?"

He meandered toward stage right and rubbed his fingers on a paper vine. It led up to a tree with fruit hanging off of one of the branches. Zinnia overheard one of the actors had to "spear" one of those apples in a musical number.

"I suppose…" The soles of Ryan's shoes scuffed against the stage floor. "I suppose only the most important set pieces. If you had more time, you could work on the finer details."

He twisted toward her. She reached for her forehead to daub some of the perspiration.

"Do I need to explain the analogy to you?"

"No."

His voice had drained of all color, and she winced.

"Listen, that's what we have Post for. Even if you don't shoot everything perfectly—and from what I've seen whenever you show us a take, you do really well—"

He brightened at this. Did Ryan not receive encouragement often? Back at the FSC, he did mention how his parents and family never supported his dreams. Perhaps like Zinnia, he received compliments like rare jewels.

"—you can fix it later. Let's focus, now, on the essentials."

He shoved his hands into his jean's pockets, and then eyed her. His caterpillar eyebrows furrowed.

"You're sweating a lot."

"Oh, that must be because of these stupid wool socks."

"Wool socks?"

In brief, she explained what Georgia allowed her to take home from Aunt Millie's house. She noticed how Ryan's fists balled when she talked about Georgia and the photobooks.

"I have to wear these socks to prove I make use of any resource given to me. Because unlike Georgia or—" She cut herself off to add 'you.' For all she knew, maybe Ryan didn't have everything handed to him. "I want to be a good steward, that's all."

Ryan blew out a long breath.

His spine straightened. "Is there a costume shop?"

Zinnia pursed her lips. What did this have to do with anything? "Yes. Off stage left and into the hallway."

"Follow me, Mr. Zin, and we'll continue this tour of the theater." Bolting off stage left, Ryan left her behind.

Sponging moisture off of her forehead once more, she took off after him, and landed inside a shop full of z-racks of clothing.

She found Ryan digging through a bin full of some mysterious contents. Zinnia couldn't tell what from her angle.

"What are you—?"

"If I agree to give up control on how I film, I need you to be willing to give up some control on that set, too. Are we agreed?"

Control in what way?

Dizzy, she collapsed on a worn couch in the room. No way she could let him back out of the new plan moving forward on the set.

"Sure, that sounds fine." Her toe nudged several needles on the linoleum floor. Someone needed to vacuum in here.

"Great." Ryan held up a pair of clean white socks from the bin. Actors must've used those for quick changes, or if they forgot to bring foot coverings. "Because you're wearing these on the set from now on."

"I'm what?"

He tossed the bundle at her basketball style, and she caught the socks in both palms.

"Zinnia, you've been sweating like crazy on set, ever since you started wearing those. Under the hot lights, no wonder. Do you know how many times we've had to call 'cut' because you had to retouch your makeup?"

Thanks to the sweat, her foundation melted underneath the lights.

Clutching the socks in her fingertips, her arms shook. She released a shaky breath.

*If he gives up control, you have to too, sister.*

Why did this feel like such a big ask, though? Did Ryan experience the same emotions when she'd told him, on stage, that he had to make some changes?

"What's wrong, Zin?"

Pity overtook Ryan's voice. He parked beside her on the couch, maintaining some space between the two of them.

"I can't shake the feeling that—that Grandma would be wagging her finger at me for not using her socks well. I know it sounds dumb…"

"It doesn't."

Warmth tingled in her stomach. Maybe Ryan *did* get it, even if he hailed from a different financial background than hers. Even on set, with the old borrowed cameras from the school and the lights that tended to flicker from years of use, Ryan made the most of the resources given to him.

"Though, there is such a thing as overkill when it comes to being a good steward."

Back in theater classes, Zinnia had read a play called *The Miser*. In it, a man even reused his mouthwash to save on resources.

Had she turned into the likes of him?

Steadiness overtook her. If Ryan could give up some control, so could she.

She plucked the zipper on the back of her boots and pulled down. After she popped her shoes off, she peeled off the wool socks.

"And I think that's a wrap."

Ryan straightened from behind the camera, stunned. They had…actually finished on time.

When something wasn't exactly perfect with lighting in a shot, he reminded himself that he could fix the saturation in post. When Zinnia's intonation didn't match his precise vision for a line, he took a deep breath and remembered that actors were allowed to bring their own interpretations to film. He even allowed Mariana to set up some of the shots on the secondary camera on her own without hovering.

As they began packing up the set, Ryan thought he even saw Zinnia smile toward him.

"Wow." When they had finished packing, Tristan checked his watch. "Shouldn't have said no to that archery pick-a-date my floor planned for today. I thought we would still be filming too long for me to go."

Ah, pick-a-dates. Ryan remembered those from his college days. Floors or wings of the dorms, and sometimes on-campus clubs, would host a group activity for which each member invited a "date." Activities ranged from pumpkin carving to laser tag to roller skating. He had gone on several pick-a-dates with a few different girls in college as a great way to hang out with someone in a casual group setting and get to know them before attempting anything more formal and serious.

Of course, oftentimes friends would go on pick-a-dates as each other's "date" just for fun, even pairing up for "chick-picks" and "bro-picks." He and Steve did a "bro-pick" once when both of them didn't have time to find a date last minute.

*Steve.* Not something he wanted to think about right now.

Tristan heaved a sigh. "Now I don't even have a date if I wanted to go." He pointed at Martell. "Yo. Dude-pick?"

"Nah, man." Martell slung his backpack over his shoulder. "I had hopes of ending early." He flashed a smile at Ryan. "So I already asked my girlfriend."

"Betrayed by my own floormate." Tristan glanced around, then brightened. "Yo, Mariana. Are you still busy with that thing?"

She rolled her eyes. "Tristan, 'that thing' was filming today. When you asked me on the pick-a-date last week, I told you we *both* were going to be busy."

"Oh, yeah!"

Zinnia placed a hand over her mouth, half-hiding a smile. The other actors had left, but she'd lingered, helping the crew pack up. Meeting her eyes, Ryan held back a laugh. Working with college kids brought back memories of shenanigans he'd participated in, what felt simultaneously like just yesterday and decades ago.

"I just had an amazing idea."

Ryan returned his attention to Tristan, who had looped his arm through Mariana's. "What's that, Tristan?"

He pointed at Ryan, then at Zinnia. "You two. Join us."

Zinnia straightened. "What?"

"Shockingly, that actually *is* an amazing idea." Mariana elbowed Tristan as he grumbled, and they both snickered. "The whole crew will be going. Why not Ryan and Zinnia too?" She hesitated but continued speaking in a softer tone. "I think both of you could use a break for some lighthearted fun."

Ryan glanced at Zinnia, trying to read her expression. She didn't seem to be glowering. In fact, as she glanced toward him, she almost seemed…hopeful?

"I think it could be fun. What about you, Zinnia?" He cleared his throat. "No pressure, of course. Completely understandable if you have places you need to be, or if it isn't really your thing."

She graced him with a rare smile. "You know, I could go for some archery. Maybe I could shoot an apple off your head."

He wasn't sure if she was joking. But, to be honest, if the prospect enticed Zinnia to join them, he wasn't sure he cared.

Twenty minutes later, Ryan climbed out of his car in front of what appeared to be a long, low barn. Vehicles filled the small parking lot, including Zinnia's familiar car. He waved as she stepped out.

From the other direction, Martell approached with a smiling young woman sporting a colorful headscarf, but Ryan's attention diverted from all three of them to the guy standing in front of the barn, waving his arms.

"Yo," Tristan called. "All of you are slow. Come on!"

Inside, a few pairs of college students already stood in a line, sighting down the length of the barn toward targets on the opposite wall and releasing arrows with little accuracy. After Ryan and Zinnia had signed their waivers and admitted they had never participated in archery before, a bearded proprietor led them to one of the few remaining empty lanes.

He held up a bow. "You hold the grip here," he said, revealing a Scottish accent. "Make sure you rest the arrow here, aye, and nock it to the string like so." After he finished demonstrating the rest of the process, he handed the bow and arrow to Zinnia. "Would you like to go first?"

Her eyes sparkled, and she nodded, accepting the weapon. Ryan stepped back to give her space as she spread her feet, nocked the arrow, and sighted along its length toward the target, drawing the string back to her cheek.

Watching her brow furrow in concentration, a bit of blonde hair falling over one eye as her arm flexed but held steady while she pulled back the bowstring…something about it made Ryan's heart give a little thump.

Then she released the string, and the arrow zipped toward the target, hitting the outer ring and sticking there.

Ryan stared. His heart did more than a little thump this time.

"Aye, lass." The bearded man chuckled. "You're a natural. Now teach your fella how it's done."

Zinnia smirked at Ryan as the man ambled away. "Did you catch all of that?"

"I hope so." He accepted the bow she offered and reached for an arrow from the standing quiver on the floor. "Should be like shooting a camera, right?"

She raised a brow. "I guess we'll find out."

It was not, in fact, like shooting a camera.

However, it was arguably just as fun.

With each shot, Zinnia improved, getting closer to the bullseye. Meanwhile, she cheered with Ryan when he finally hit the outer rim of the target. As he lined up his next shot, she said, "I believe in you, Legolas."

He snorted, and the shot went wild. "I don't think they'll be coming to me to play any elves in future *The Lord of the Rings* movies."

"What would you be, then?" She accepted the bow from him.

"Probably a hobbit. I do like the idea of second breakfast."

"You and me both."

Unexpected boldness bolstered his melodramatic challenging stance. "Hey now, there's only room for one hobbit in this town."

She held up the bow and raised an eyebrow, the corner of her mouth tugged up mischievously. "Bold words, medieval cowboy, considering who's holding the bow and arrow." She nocked, drew, and released, and the arrow sailed straight into the bullseye.

Ryan cheered and offered a high five, which she reciprocated with a wide smile. "Okay, I guess I relent. There's enough room for two hobbits."

For the next half hour, they laughed, made archery puns, and tossed movie quotes back and forth. When she didn't look like she wanted to bite him in half, Zinnia could be…a lot of fun.

Still scary, wielding a potentially deadly weapon. Especially when she threatened to use it to assert her dominance as the superior hobbit. But he found his shoulders to be relaxed, his smile easy, and his mind, for once, not spinning with a thousand worries.

*She did that,* he realized. She kept him on track on set, and here, even out of his usual element and surrounded by college students and an alarming number of projectiles, he felt confident standing next to her.

And with that carefree smile shining from her usually pinched expression…he would do just about anything to figure out a way to keep it there.

# Chapter Eleven

Snack time had gotten out of hand.

Zinnia stood as a mediator between two sisters in the Sunday school classroom, who had commenced chucking Goldfish crackers at one another. In the far-off corner, one of the teen volunteers soothed the cries of another girl, who happened to be the victim of a Goldfish-related fall, with a *Dora the Explorer* Band-aid.

"Nessa." Zinnia issued this in a warning tone. "I'm going to need you to hand me your snack, if you're going to keep throwing it at your sister Odessa."

Nessa firmed her jaw and bunched her fists, crunching the crackers underneath her palms. She unfurled her fingertips and a flurry of orange "snow" hit the carpet.

"Ugh." Zinnia groaned through her nostrils.

She lifted herself to her feet to search the back wall for a handheld vacuum. Classrooms 103 and 104 shared one. Because Joy and Zinnia helped in the younger kids' room today, Zinnia hoped the church staff relented and put the cleaning supplies in the room that tended to evoke more messes than the other.

Finding the white handheld vacuum, she slipped her fingertips onto the handle and rotated around—

In time to catch Nessa tripping Odessa.

Odessa face planted and wailed.

Quick as she could muster—still in her stupor from not getting enough sleep last night—Zinnia rushed over to the girl. Last night with Ryan and the crew had been…well, not as bad as she'd anticipated. In fact, call her crazy, but she would label it as good. Free time with that group, especially with Ryan, felt like the relief she needed from all the Georgia drama. Beams of light glimmered in her chest like a disco ball.

*No, Zinnia, focus on the kid.*

"Hey, hey, hey, you're okay."

As Odessa unwound herself from her fetal position, she pierced Zinnia with the most pitiful gray eyes. They reminded Zinnia of Georgia's—that fateful night of the play back in college.

Memories blurred to several years before. The tune from the Sunday school classroom dance instructor—trying desperately to teach the kids some upbeat, catchy song titled, "I Get Down, and He Lifts Me Up"—faded into a popular tune from *Oklahoma!*

Zinnia was in the wings of her college stage with a stage manager headset on. Senior year offered a showstopping performance of the popular play.

On stage, her younger sister, Georgia, flounced around the lead in a gingham-style dress. Her usual vibrant steps lacked luster today, and her shoulders drooped.

Zinnia's features sagged. Something had happened, but what?

"Lighting cue 23 on standby." The headset crackled. The stage manager in the tech booth called out lighting and sound cues for the show up there.

Everything backstage smelled of the bales of hay they had for a later number, "The Farmer and the Cowhand Should Be Friends."

For now, as the lead sang about how she would cycle through several more boyfriends before she said, "I do," Zinnia would have to deal with the mess of straw that tended to litter the black floors. Glow tape lit the way for the actors making entrances on the stage.

A finger tapped her shoulder.

In the dark lighting of backstage, Zinnia turned around and found the finger's owner. A girl playing one of the supporting roles, who appeared later in the show, lifted her thinly plucked eyebrows at Zinnia.

"Your sister's looking a little down today."

"Do you have any idea what—?"

"Bad breakup. Really, really bad."

Zinnia sucked in air through her teeth and let it out in a hiss. As an older sister, instinct kicked in the minute her freshman sister introduced Zinnia to the guy from the frat house. Everything about him reeked of booze and bad behavior. Although she tried to warn Georgia against dating the guy, Georgia would hear nothing of it.

There were two types of people in this world—those who listened, and those who had to find out for themselves.

Georgia always fell into the latter category.

Zinnia could feel lines form on her forehead. She faced the stage and watched her sister do the most pitiful sashay known to man. Teachers of Georgia's dance classes would evaluate her based on this performance. Dance majors had been encouraged to audition for the more choreography-heavy musical.

"Do you think I should cancel my date tonight with—?" Zinnia stopped short.

Matt had returned to the backstage from pushing a set piece on during the number. Tall, with a healthy dose of muscles in the biceps, and easy eyes that were…well, easy on the eyes, Matt had quickly turned into the heartthrob of the backstage crew.

Most English classes on campus offered extra credit to those who would get involved in the crew of the show. He appeared during tech week to help with something known as the deck crew—those who moved the sets on stage.

After the grueling hours and practices that went until two in the morning, he and Zinnia hit it off.

Right before opening night, he plucked enough courage to ask her to go out with him for ice cream after.

She nodded to him as he loped backstage to grab some props for the actors.

Once he'd fled the scene, Zinnia asked the actress the question again.

"Blow Matt off? Are you kidding me? If I didn't have a boyfriend, I would've jumped on the Matt train faster than you can say O-K-L-A-H-O-M-A."

The actors did spell out the name of the play in one of the songs.

A yelp pierced Zinnia's ears. She glanced up in time to spot Georgia hobbling off the stage.

What happened? Had she hurt her ankle in the dance number?

Tears streaked down Georgia's face as she stumbled past Zinnia, out the double doors, and to the left toward the costume shop. Without a moment's hesitation, Zinnia tore off her headset. She thrust the equipment at another stagehand and followed Georgia.

Sobs echoed in the mirrored room that led to the costume shops. Here, actors would smear on heavy foundation and eyeliner for the show.

Georgia, perched on a stool, nursed her ankle.

"Georgia, are you—?"

"Leave me alone, Zinnia."

"Do you need me to get you some ice?"

Her younger sister refused to answer. Instead, she released her grip on her ankle and smudged off the streams of mascara on her cheeks. She then hugged her knees to her chest, ankle no longer appearing to throb in pain.

What a fast recovery.

Wait a second…Georgia had pulled one of these maneuvers before.

During a pageant in seventh grade, Georgia had purpled in fury when Grandma took away her cell phone for failing to do well in the interview round. Unless she could pull herself together for the formal wear part of the competition, she could say goodbye to any technology for a month.

Had it been Zinnia in the situation, Zinnia would've done whatever she could to win over the judges' favor.

But Georgia had never been Zinnia.

During formal wear, in five-inch heels, Georgia "cracked" her ankle and fell on stage. Back in the hotel room, when she nursed a bag of ice against her pinking skin, she whispered to Zinnia that she'd faked the whole thing. In truth, because Grandma stormed off after that, she'd earned herself a little alone time away from that woman. And because Grandma felt bad about Georgia hurting her ankle and all, she relinquished the cell phone back to her goddaughter.

Did Georgia really do the same now, for this performance of *Oklahoma!*?

If Zinnia accused her, Georgia would hold that grudge for weeks.

Better to try a different tactic to comfort her sister and get her back on stage. Who knew how many cues had Zinnia missed, loitering backstage with Georgia?

"How's your ankle feeling?"

Georgia whimpered and hissed through her teeth. Although Georgia was good at dancing, she still had much to learn about the art of acting. She'd grabbed the wrong ankle just now.

Okay, tactic number two…

"Hey, Georgia, how about after this performance, I ditch my date, and we go to that pancake place you love? All I need you to do is go on stage, and just skip the dance numbers. The dancers can adjust. Do you think you can do it?"

"Skip your date?" She frowned. Darkness covered her features. "You have one?"

"I don't need to if my sister's hurting. You're far more important."

Georgia shook her head and blew flyaways off her nose. The copious amounts of hairspray the cast used must've missed this sliver of hair. "I'm not going to ask you to do that." Tears welled in Georgia's waterline.

A door banged open. Matt charged in with a large ice bag in his grip.

"Thanks, Matt." Zinnia retrieved it from him. "I should be backstage soon."

Frost numbed Zinnia's fingertips as she handed the bag to

Georgia, who hadn't peeled her gaze away from the door, long after Matt left.

"Who's that?"

"That's the guy I'm willing to ditch for a pancake date with my sister. Offer's still standing."

A glint filled Georgia's eye. She blinked away the spark.

"No." Georgia's voice no longer came out shaky. This time, it sounded like it had a bite. "Couldn't imagine doing that to you. You two have fun."

Why did that sound like a warning tone?

"Go backstage without me." Georgia waved her off, like bad hairspray fumes. "I'll make a reappearance soon."

Through the thick brick walls, the lead's voice finished a muffled version of the song.

Little did Zinnia know that Georgia wouldn't show up for the rest of the show. Her encore performance would take place when she told Zinnia to dump Matt the next day…

And out of pity for her sister's situation, Zinnia did.

Only to have Georgia ask him out months later. Their first date…a dance held at the college.

Zinnia emerged from the memory to find that Odessa had stopped crying. Instead, the little girl massaged her ankle.

"Does it hurt?"

Odessa bit her lip and shook her head. "It was owwy owwy. But it's not anymore."

"That's the thing about ankles." Zinnia sighed and reached for the handheld vacuum. "They never seem to be down for the count long."

Ryan whistled a jaunty tune while he poured his morning coffee. Balto's ears perked up as the dog danced behind him, responding to Ryan's buoyant mood. The sky had just begun to lighten, and soon he would be able to watch the sunrise while sipping his coffee. The perfect start to a Sunday.

They had finished on time yesterday *and* he and Zinnia had fun together. Two miracles in one day.

In his pocket, his phone vibrated. He pulled it out to read the text on the screen.

**Mom:** You're still planning to come to church with us today, right?

His smile faded. How could he have forgotten?

Mom had been pestering him for weeks to come to his childhood church with them. Ryan reminded her many times that a two-hour drive each way for a one-hour service seemed a bit silly, but she insisted that members of the congregation missed seeing the Torino boys. Finally, he had relented and chosen this Sunday, a day where he didn't have any plans.

Or at least, he *hadn't* had any plans. Until he entered a one-month film competition.

He glanced at the time on his phone. If he left within the next five minutes, he could make it there in time for service. Good thing Buttercup woke him up so early today.

**Ryan:** I'll be there :)

He raced for his closet to put on the clothes he would have worn to his usual church service today. Three minutes later, his clothes were on, his teeth and hair had been brushed, and he yanked on his shoes while herding the animals out of the bedroom. "I'm not letting you sleep on my pillow while I'm gone, Balto."

The dog huffed.

Ryan dumped his coffee in a to-go mug and made his usual check of the apartment before leaving. He patted each of his pets on the head. "Be good." Then he dashed out the door.

Two hours of driving later, he brushed out the wrinkles in the front of his shirt before ducking into the large church his parents attended. He found Mom and Dad standing near their usual seat, conversing with a small crowd of people who ebbed and flowed around them.

Ryan held back a sigh and straightened his shoulders. The Torino popularity didn't seem to have diminished.

Mom locked eyes on him and beamed, curls bouncing as she waved him toward them. "Ryan! I'm so glad you're here."

"Hi, Mom." He gave her a gentle hug. "Glad I could make it."

He turned toward his father and attempted to keep his expression neutral. Dad wasn't a fan of what he considered emotional displays. His dad stood a head taller than Ryan, his salt and pepper hair immaculately barbered, every line of his business casual clothing perfectly pressed. Ryan held out a hand. "Dad."

His father took his hand in a firm grasp for a businesslike handshake. Though not scowling, he didn't smile. Vincent Torino offered smiles as often as he offered generous business deals—not unless completely necessary.

"You know who will also be here today?" Mom held Ryan's elbow, smiling up at him.

"Um. Paul? Travis?" He certainly hoped she hadn't invited his brothers as well. Though the likelihood of those two darkening the door of a church was slim.

"Oh, I heard they stopped by to see you recently. But no, not today, I'm afraid." She nodded across the sanctuary. "Over there."

A hard lump beginning to settle in Ryan's gut, he turned to look. His eyes settled on the flashy smile and shock of dark hair as his mother said, "It's Steve, your college friend!"

A group of young men had flocked around Steve, hanging on his every word as he regaled them with what appeared to be a rousing tale. Steve flashed them indulgent smiles and placed a hand on one guy's shoulder, who looked like he might faint from Steve deigning to notice him.

Mom nudged Ryan forward. "Go on. Service will start in five minutes, you need to hurry if you want to say hi."

Ryan took a few hesitant steps forward, just far enough that Mom turned back to chatting with one of her friends.

After what Steve did, Ryan hadn't told anyone. He had no proof, after all, since Steve deleted the files, and his attempts would only seem like he was jealous of Steve's success and trying to drag him down. So, he moved on with his life and never spoke to Steve again.

Ryan attempted to remain out of Steve's line of sight, greeting members of the congregation as he passed. Maybe he could do a quick circle of the sanctuary and Mom would think he had gone to talk to Steve.

As he drew closer, his former friend's voice carried.

"It's good to be visiting my old hometown. You know, I saw this competition and thought, what a good way to return to my Michigander roots. And why not make it extra special by actually shooting *in* Michigan?"

Ryan's blood ran cold. Steve couldn't possibly mean…

"You only have a month to do it, right?" One of the young guys whistled. "That's impressive."

"Well, you get used to some tight deadlines in Hollywood. I'm looking forward to getting some quaint shots in Roseville, really pander to the locals."

Before Steve could spot him, Ryan ducked behind a column holding up the second tier of seats in the sanctuary. He pulled out his phone and navigated to the website for the Roseville Film Festival. Steve had to be talking about this one. The same festival Ryan was entering.

Blood roared in his ears. Steve *had* a life in Hollywood. Why did he have to do this? What did he have to gain from entering a competition that might help burgeoning filmmakers break into the industry and instead taking the prize for himself?

Before he quite knew what he was doing, he saw that his thumbs had taken him to Zinnia's contact information.

**Ryan:** It looks like we have some serious competition for this film festival. I was thinking maybe the whole cast and crew should watch previous winners to get some inspiration.

He'd watched the previous winners over and over, of course, analyzing everything they had done, but it wouldn't hurt to have everyone else do so as well.

He hit send before his mind caught up with him. What was he doing, texting Zinnia on a Sunday morning? Where were his professional boundaries? He was treating her more like…a friend.

The first chords of worship sounded from the stage, and Ryan jolted. He didn't have time to explore those thoughts any more right now. He shuffled through the crowd to join his parents in their row.

As the songs rose from the congregation, Ryan added a prayer of his own.

*Please, Lord. Even if we aren't the film that wins…please don't let Steve crush any more young filmmakers' dreams.*

# Chapter Twelve

"IF I WATCH ONE MORE SAD film, heads are going to roll."

Zinnia clicked pause on her laptop in meeting boardroom 302. She then proceeded to glare at a head of lettuce from her wedge salad she'd partially consumed for lunch.

"I'm talking to you, Mr. Lettuce Head."

"Phew. I'm certainly glad you're not talking about beheading me."

Caroline's voice from the door caused Zinnia to jump in her rolling chair. She gripped the table to balance herself once more. Fluorescent bulbs buzzed overhead, one of the lights winking on and off. Holding up a salad of her own, Caroline gestured at an open seat with her hip.

"Mind if I—?"

"Be my guest."

"You wouldn't be able to make my head roll anyway." Caroline snorted as she collapsed into the chair. She popped off the top of the plastic salad container. "Pretty sure Clark's already done that with how many activities he has me running around to."

Ah yes, Clark, the whole reason Zinnia hid in this room today. Often, Clark forgot that room 302 existed. She couldn't blame him. Thanks to water stains that formed patterns on the ceiling and the buzzing light bulbs that must've migrated straight from a horror movie set…if Zinnia had any other option, she'd "forget" this room too.

Other workers in the office found excuses to dodge Clark's extra Caroline work tasks he doled out to them. Some went as far as to make up dental appointments just to get out of the building.

Caroline drizzled a packet of Italian dressing over piles of spinach. "I feel horrible about him divvying up my workload, you know?"

Piercing a cucumber with her fork, Zinnia nodded.

Once, pneumonia took out Zinnia for a solid week. Guilt gnawed on her gut for a full month, because Caroline picked up the slack on most of her tasks. Like Zinnia, Caroline had a hard time giving up control and allowing someone else to take a fraction of the burden.

"Honestly, Clark needs to hire another employee." Prongs of Caroline's fork speared a cherry tomato. "If he's going to make me a full-time children's writer, he can't force anyone to do two jobs in one. Not without a substantial raise for all the overtime."

Mouth full of lettuce, Zinnia nodded.

She swallowed. "Let's hope HR helps him to see reason."

"So." Caroline folded a paper napkin onto her lap. Today she sported an autumn-orange, long-sleeve top. "What are we watching? Liv has been recommending me a K-drama about a South Korean woman who accidentally ends up in North Korea and falls in love with a soldier there."

Zinnia snapped her fingers. "*Crash Landing on You.* Highly recommend, it will make you cry."

"Duh, it's a K-drama. You know Liv, right?"

"Tall, sings, wears chunky bracelets on her arms. We did a cooking class last summer."

Like the protagonist in *Crash Landing on You*, Liv found herself the perfect romance…with a worship leader that summer, instead of a North Korean soldier. Even though most things in life didn't seem to be smooth sailing for Liv, she made relationships look effortless, easy.

Zinnia thought back to Ryan, and their time at the archery place.

Nothing about the prospect of *anything* with him seemed "easy" per se. Even when he passed her tests—that all the other guys had failed before—what if he didn't manage to succeed in future ones?

What if he yelled and screamed at her when he got angry, like that one boyfriend from her freshman year of college? The minute she got cold feet, he forced her into a two-hour conversation where he swore that she was "just chicken" and needed to give the relationship a longer try.

Or what if he turned out like her boyfriend the first year out of college? How he ghosted her the second he found out about her family situation, because the emotional baggage felt like too much for him to "deal with." If Ryan dug too much into her past, would he like what he saw?

Or what if he acted like Matt, controlling her finances, appearance, activities, everything?

*Hold up, does Matt do that?*

In either case, romance wasn't easy. Some of the most beautiful things in life seldom were.

"Unfortunately"—Zinnia uncapped her water bottle and sipped—"no K-dramas today. I've been watching all the past winners for the film competition our group is entering. Let's just say, these directors need a lot of therapy."

"That bad, huh?"

"Okay, take this one for instance."

Zinnia toggled the timeline for the film and played Caroline a scene from the beginning.

"You see this happy family, Caroline?"

Two parents, wrapped in smiles, chased two children around a perfect green yard. Bubbles trailed from wands. Birds twittered.

"I see them."

"Okay, fast-forward and…" Zinnia played a scene from the end of the film. "See them now?"

"Ah, they are all dead, and a sinkhole ate their house."

Props to the directors of all these winning films on their special effects. If Zinnia squinted enough, she could imagine the crater on screen could've resembled a sinkhole in real life.

Caroline cocked her head. "What's the name of this film, again?"

"*Sinkhole.*"

"Ah, well, we probably should've seen that ending coming."

"Point is." Zinnia tapped the spacebar, and the film paused, just in time to stop the screech of sorrowful violin strings. "Every single one of these movies that won had a really sad ending. Seriously, the happiest ending I've seen so far is that the dog didn't die in the end."

"Aww."

"Everyone he loved did, though."

"Oh." Caroline cleared her throat. "So a *Call of the Wild* knockoff then?"

Zinnia's lips twitched. *Don't even get me started on my Jack London rants, Caroline. I'm already way overtime on my lunch break.*

Zinnia draped her arm over the back of the chair and leaned against the wall, so her face couldn't be seen through the large windows. Even if Clark never stepped in here, he could still peer through the glass.

"I don't know what to do, Caroline. I texted Ryan this morning, when I was skimming the third film. If we want to win, we probably should go with something depressing, right?"

Caroline pursed her lips. She closed the lid on her finished salad.

"Hmm, not sure. My roommate Liv was in a similar situation last year for the music competition she and Elijah entered."

Zinnia had spent time with Elijah and Liv in a cooking class last year. She remembered some of their stories about that music competition.

"How did that go for them again?"

"Elijah and Liv listened to all the winning songs in past years, and let's say…" Caroline winced, face puckering, as if she'd swallowed a lime whole. "There were no Beethovens among them."

"Oof."

"Yeah, really campy songs that said a whole load of nothing. Liv and Elijah were tempted to compromise their song. Then they decided not to."

Shutting her laptop lid, Zinnia mused.

Could their film win with the upbeat ending? Because Ryan hadn't decided on how the movie would begin or end—they'd only filmed portions of the middle—they could still choose the direction of the story now.

Ryan did mention that the film could conclude one of two ways.

One, the girl continued on her path to Hollywood, having seen a future where she could possibly earn a part of her dreams.

Or, two, she could go through another door and end up in a job that made watching paint dry seem like a trip to an amusement park. Forever lonely, forever sad, but forever secure in a well-paying gig.

*My gut wants to do the Hollywood ending.* Would that compromise their chances of winning, though?

Caroline appeared to read Zinnia's expression. "Of course, music and film are two very different things. I don't want to overstep here. All I'm saying is, it's worth a thought."

With that, Caroline shoved her seat back and scooped her trash into her palms.

"If it's any consolation, Zin, there's a whole lot of sad in the world. If you can do anything to make it a little happier, a little brighter, a little more full of hope—it's worth it."

She dumped her finished lunch into the garbage bin and disappeared from the door.

Doors. Zinnia always liked the symbolism of those. They always led to somewhere—sometimes terrifying places, other times, right onto the set of a certain filmmaker with beautiful dark eyes.

As Zinnia picked at a corn muffin, made by Joy, a hard knock pounded the door. She glanced up and her blood iced.

Clark loomed at the entrance. Great, he'd found her.

"Zinnia, Caroline left for another off-site task."

Zinnia shrunk into her gray suit. Shoulder pads threatened to consume her ears as she formed herself into a turtle shell.

"Yes, sir?"

"I have some of Caroline's copy assignments I need you to edit. It'll be in your inbox."

"Yes, sir."

Much as Zinnia wanted to help, the more tasks Clark assigned her, the more he wouldn't see a need to contact HR about hiring someone new.

If she said no, however, that could get her a one-way ticket to the ground floor, holding a box that contained all the contents of her cubicle.

After she tossed the remains of her meal into the garbage, she hugged her laptop to her chest and stared at the entrance to the boardroom. Clark had long since evacuated, likely scavenging the office for another worker to take on more of Caroline's tasks.

Although Zinnia liked the idea of doors—

She stepped out of the boardroom and headed toward her cubicle.

—something about walking through the door of room 302 and into the office sent shivers down her spine. Almost as if she'd just ambled into some sort of trap.

"These directors need to seek professional help."

Ryan read the message from Zinnia out loud to Buttercup and chuckled. "They are pretty depressing. With some, ah, interesting ideas of what constitutes a plot twist. Looking at you, *Sinkhole*."

Buttercup blinked at him before jumping down from his lap and wandering into the other room, where an annoying owner wouldn't bother her with his ruminations.

Ryan returned his attention to the desktop screen and the photos he had been editing. He'd had a mostly productive day, despite occasionally staring into space, agonizing over the direction of the film project.

Sad ending, or happy ending?

He knew what Steve would do. Ever since stealing Ryan's story in college, Steve had created a reputation for ironic, tragic endings.

Yet, if Steve was their competition, they needed to stand out from him. The most un-Steve thing to do would be to craft a happy ending.

Ryan heaved a gigantic sigh and ran a hand through his hair. Productivity had waned over the past half hour. Time for a break. He grabbed Balto's leash, pulled on his coat, and followed the prancing husky outside.

While Balto sniffed what appeared to be the most interesting scent known to dogkind on the same tree he sniffed every day, Ryan typed back a reply to Zinnia.

**Ryan:** Creative types often do, I hear. But the judges seem to like it. Maybe we can go for something somewhere in the middle.

As he hit send, his phone began ringing. Caller ID lit up the screen.

For a moment, he debated ignoring the call. He was still technically in the middle of a workday. But, since he had planned on walking Balto for at least twenty minutes anyway, he might as well multitask.

He tapped the screen to accept and held the phone to his ear. "Hi, Mom. What's up?"

"Ryan, it's so good to hear your voice."

He raised a brow and herded Balto away from the tree, onward to the rest of the walk. "We just saw each other yesterday."

"And I'm glad we did, but I can still be excited to hear from you." He could hear the frown in her voice.

"Of course. It's always good to hear from you too, Mom." *Kind of.*

"I was talking to some local families at lunch after church, and you know what I learned? Steve isn't the only one back in town."

From the barely contained excitement tingeing her words, Ryan had a feeling he knew exactly where this was going. "Oh?"

"You remember Kharis Youngtree? She just finished her MBA and returned to town. Her mother said she's single."

"Mom."

"Your dad and Bob Youngtree have worked together, you know. They're good people."

"Yes, I'm sure they are." A gust of wind whipped an orange leaf past his nose. "I don't think that concerns me here in Roseville, though."

"It's only a couple hours. Hardly long distance. You two were friends in middle school, right? Maybe you could give her a call."

Not only did he not possess the phone number of a person he vaguely knew fifteen years ago, he also didn't think an MBA with a life of her own would take kindly to a random call from a stranger. Let alone the fact that he had no desire to talk to any other women.

Wait. Other? *Brain, what do you mean "other"?*

"I appreciate you trying to help, Mom, but I'm not actively looking to date anyone right now. I'm focusing on work and my friends."

She sighed. "I suppose. It just makes me sad knowing you're alone. I wish you would at least give it a try."

Balto snuffled through a pile of leaves, and Ryan wished he and the dog could switch places for a moment so he didn't have to have this conversation.

"I've gone on dates with a lot of people. I even tried a couple dating apps. I haven't found the right person."

"Well, don't give up too soon, you know? And it may be someone you aren't expecting."

"Yeah. I'll keep that in mind."

"I saw Steve talking to Kharis. Maybe—"

Ryan tuned out as much as possible while Mom updated him on Steve's romantic prospects, the last topic he felt a desire to hear about.

He had indeed gone on more dates than he could count. Usually, he knew within the first ten minutes that they wouldn't work out, and he didn't want to enter a relationship just for the sake of being in a relationship. That didn't benefit anyone involved.

After giving his mother time to tell him about the latest church gossip, he broke in during the briefest of pauses. "I'm sorry, Mom, I'm almost back home from taking Balto out, and I have a lot to do, so I need to let you go."

Thankfully, she didn't take too long with goodbyes, and Ryan returned to his work, trying to think about Steve and film endings as little as possible.

Instead, he continued messaging Zinnia.

**Zinnia:** Something in the middle, huh? Maybe only half the cast falls in a sinkhole, and the other half survives.

Ryan snorted aloud. As the two of them shot messages back and forth, punctuated by some stretches of silence due to work tasks, his pensive mood lifted. He may not know how the film would end, but they had plenty of work to do still before the final scenes. They could focus on making those the best they could be.

He arrived early at the "set" that evening, a clearing surrounded by trees filled with vibrant fall leaves in every hue of yellow, orange, and red. He intended to truly make the colors pop, maybe get a few shots of leaves drifting toward the ground on the breeze.

*But Steve said he's taking inspiration from Michigan scenery too.*

He shook away that thought.

As he began unloading equipment, he heard leaves crunching. He looked up to see Zinnia headed his way, shaking her hair out of a bun, a blazer slung over one arm and a tote-sized bag over the other.

"Hey." He set down a duffel full of cords, a smile blooming. "You're early."

"I didn't have time to head home between work and shooting, so I figured I would come straight here." She set her bag down nearby, then reached in, pulled out a sweater, and exchanged it for the blazer. "Sorry, still getting into costume a bit."

"No worries, we have plenty of time." He popped open a tripod. "Did you bring a shovel?"

She paused, frowning. "A shovel?"

"Yeah. For the sinkhole."

She snorted, and her eye roll made him grin.

The ringing of a bike bell turned his attention in the other direction. Tristan rode toward them on a blue bicycle, waving with one hand. "May I present, something blue!"

One of the requirements for the film festival—a blue object that was important to the plot. In this case, Ryan had decided two important characters would meet when Zinnia's character got "run over" by the bike.

Zinnia hiked one brow, looking the bike over as Tristan rolled to a stop. "That's a nice bike. Did you get it just for this scene?"

"Nah, it belongs to someone in my dorm. He let me borrow it." Tristan rang the bell again. "Its name is Madame Blueberry."

"College students name bikes now." Ryan unwound a cable. "Good to know."

Soon, the rest of the cast and crew arrived. They ran through the scene a few times without the bike, practicing blocking before adding wheels. No one wanted the actors to *actually* collide. Zinnia's slow-motion dives and rolls prompted laughter, and from the smile on her face, she seemed to be enjoying herself too.

Maybe he wasn't quite sure how this film would end yet, but in the meantime, being on set…

Well, it reminded him of why he fell in love with film in the first place.

They mastered the bicycle scene in only three takes. "That's the one," Ryan called. He strode onto the set and offered Zinnia a hand up. "Nice work everyone."

She took his arm, and he pulled her to her feet. A leaf stuck in her hair, and without thinking, he plucked it away.

Her eyes tracked the leaf as he dropped it. He felt his ears redden. But why? Embarrassed about a leaf?

He turned toward Mariana. "You got that secondary shot?"

She gave a thumbs up from behind the camera. "You got it, boss. Looks good. Do you want to come check?"

He took a deep breath. He could do this. "I trust your judgment, Mariana." He looked back toward Zinnia. "If there's anything a little off, we can fix it in post."

Zinnia's eyes widened a little, then she smiled.

With that smile, the last of his anxiety melted away. Before he could think better of it, he brushed her fingers in a silent thank you.

Then he scurried back to the camera before his ears burned even redder.

# Chapter Thirteen

"YOU LOOK LIKE YOU'RE IN DESPERATE need of some apple cider."

Zinnia peered up from her cubicle at the squat woman at the entrance. A new hire, one whose name Zinnia hadn't quite figured out—maybe Susan? "Maybe Susan" had wound her graying hair into a tight bun today. The short woman sported a gray suit jacket and slacks.

"Apple cider?"

Zinnia's head had gone dizzy from staring at her computer too long this Thursday afternoon. Much as she enjoyed filming with Ryan…really, *really* enjoyed it…full workdays and movie stuff right after had taken a toll on the body.

"Yes, it's a family recipe." Maybe Susan leaned on her hip. "Secret ingredient is some grapefruit slices, to add a little sourness."

A gurgle sounded from Zinnia's insides. She checked the clock, hoisted above one of the conference rooms. Already two o' clock, had she skipped lunch?

"Well." Zinnia rubbed her fingers on her own pair of slacks. The thin fabric provided little warmth against the October chill when she walked outdoors. She'd have to take a tip from some of the office interns and wear wool-lined leggings, paired with a dress, more often. "Apple cider does sound lovely."

"Follow me."

Zinnia lifted herself from her rolling chair and trailed Maybe Susan to the break room. Empty, hours before the small room tended to burst with life. It was often full of coworkers microwaving meals and stirring forks into egg salads.

Maybe Susan reached for a ladle in a crock pot. Cinnamon sticks floated to the top of the mixture.

Apple scents sent Zinnia's head bobbing again. She vowed to

crack into the slice of string cheese she had in the break room fridge, to prevent herself from passing out.

Steam wisped off the Styrofoam cup that Maybe Susan handed to her.

"Thanks." Zinnia blew on the rim and sipped. Oh, heavenly…she collapsed into a chair. Warm liquid in her insides embraced her like a warm, autumn hug.

"Pretty good, eh?" Maybe Susan leaned against the counter and drew in a long drink from her own cup. "Figured you could use a pick-me-up. Been hunched over that computer for several hours straight."

Had she?

When Zinnia got into "the zone" at Helping Hope, she could tune out almost any noise or distraction. Plus, Maybe Susan worked in a different department, so they seldom crossed paths. She must've been one of those employees to take breaks by walking around the office.

"Yeah, there's a lot going on, I suppose."

"With Clark divvying up Caroline's tasks, no wonder."

Yes, that, but Zinnia couldn't tally on all of her fingers the number of stressors in her life right now. At the end of the last filming session with Ryan, he'd brushed her hand. By accident? Or maybe on purpose?

Zinnia couldn't tell, but something about the action sent butterflies exploding in her stomach. It scared her and excited her. That something so beautiful, and so out of her control, could be unfolding.

At the same time, though, when he did that, images of Matt surfaced. Why? She'd tried not to dedicate any space in her brain to him.

"I know that look." Maybe Susan's gruff voice broke up her thoughts. "Tell me about the boy."

Heat filled her face. In a sheepish motion, Zinnia buckled her chin toward her neck.

"Well, I don't really want to bore you with the details…"

"Zinnia, I have spreadsheet upon spreadsheet to look forward to when I get back to my desk. Please 'bore' me"—Maybe Susan tossed up air quotes—"with the details."

Zinnia did.

In fact, for a solid ten minutes, she recounted the hand brushes, the not-date dates, the laughter shared over bagels. Twinkles filled Maybe Susan's eyes. Then, Zinnia stopped short. Once again, the image of Matt burned into her brain.

"I don't know, maybe it won't work out."

The woman cleared her throat after she drained the rest of her cider. By now Zinnia's had gone cold. "Why would you say that? Are you nervous?"

"I—" Zinnia could feel the heat as scarlet crept up her neck. "I keep thinking of my sister's husband. Which I know is weird. But long story short, I dated the guy, and my sister scooped him up. I don't know why *he's* the one popping into my head. It's not like I'm attracted to him."

Well, not anymore.

"Hmm." Maybe Susan thumbed her chin after she tossed her cup into a trash bin. "For the longest time I wanted to go into counseling. Even got a psychology degree. Ended up in finance, but maybe I can flex some of those skills. Tell me a little about your sister and her husband."

"Okay, so he's the total package, and she gushes about him all the time. No wonder, because her life is absolutely perfect—" Zinnia sucked on her teeth and explained about the modeling career.

"Hold on."

Maybe Susan tossed up a hand with chewed fingernails. "You mean to tell me that he paid for her to change herself and made her get into a new hobby, rather than dance?"

"No—I, er."

Come to think of it, Georgia never did say she wanted to go into modeling.

"I could just be reading into it." Maybe Susan fiddled with one of the buttons on her suit. "Modeling really isn't something you can keep up with your whole life. I do know some women in their forties who do it, so maybe times are changing, but do they ever plan on settling down and having a family?"

"Oh, well, Georgia did want kids, but…" Zinnia chewed on her lip. "I guess Matt didn't want them, so, no family."

Maybe Susan's bushy brows narrowed.

"That…doesn't sound healthy, Zinnia."

"It doesn't?"

How come Georgia would gush about Matt nonstop then?

"Yes, it sounds like Georgia is probably unhappy in her marriage, and that you dodged a bullet when he chose her over you." She aimed a pointer finger at Zinnia.

"S-she seems so happy though."

All air had released from Zinnia's lungs, like someone punched her in the gut.

"Resentment is building. I promise you. Maybe the reason you think of Matt—when it comes to this Ryan guy—is because you're being cautious. You don't want to end up in the same situation as Georgia. From what I've heard about Ryan, though." Maybe Susan winked. "I don't think you have to worry."

As Maybe Susan exited the break room, Clark popped into the doorframe seconds later.

"Have a minute, Preston?"

Zinnia bolted from her seat. "Sure, sir. I can meet in your office."

"Here's fine. Busy day, too busy to walk back to a different room."

Ah, so the break room would become a work room. Maybe Zinnia needed to talk with Joy about how to approach boundaries with Clark.

Clark slid into a chair and plucked a stir stick out of a Styrofoam cup. His fingers rubbed the edges of the wood.

"Zinnia, I must say that I've always been impressed by your work ethic."

As she sank back into her chair, her spine straightened. "Thank you, sir."

"Which is why I'm offering you to take over Caroline's role."

Oxygen sucked out of the room. It took Zinnia several moments to breathe again, and when she did, she blinked several times.

"Oh, I, er." Speech wouldn't work.

"Caroline is going to be transitioning into a full-time writing role for us. As you can imagine, she has large shoes to fill. The position would come with a pay raise but would require some additional hours to ensure that all the tasks would be completed, as you would be carrying out your same responsibilities."

Needing something to do to occupy her buzzing thoughts, Zinnia, too, grabbed a stir stick. She kept her gaze pressed on it, so she could avoid eye contact with her boss.

"Of course, you don't have to make the decision now. Think about it for a couple of weeks and get back to me. You'll have a memo in your inbox, detailing what all is involved in the role, salary, and any other information you'd need to know."

Clark patted the table twice and left the room.

It took Zinnia several minutes to relax her shoulders and to unclench her jaw.

"Oh goodness." If the film thing didn't work out, she'd have to say goodbye to all future acting opportunities. After all, Clark might fire her if she said no to the opportunity. Maybe he'd promote some grateful intern into the role.

The stir stick snapped in half in her fingertips.

She collected the pieces and tossed them in the bin. The moment she did so her pocket buzzed. Zinnia dug out the phone and read the text. This time, Aunt Millie sent an individual message to Zinnia, instead of a group message to her and her sister.


**Aunt Millie:** Just realized I have a few more boxes for you to go through. Any chance you can stop by after work?

Memories of her previous time in Aunt Millie's basement burned her skull. She typed back a reply.

**Zinnia:** Will Georgia be there? I'm not sure if I want to do it while she's at your house.

Aunt Millie responded moments later.

**Aunt Millie:** Why not???
**Zinnia:** Because—

Zinnia paused and remembered her conversation with Maybe Susan, moments before. Then she typed out the rest of her response.

**Zinnia:** Because Georgia seems unhappy about some things Matt is doing, and I feel like she's taking it out on me.

Before she sent the message, she evaluated it. Was that true? Had Georgia built up some resentment that she'd deflected onto Zinnia? Certainly felt like it.

Vindication swelled in Zinnia's chest as she clicked send.

Moments later, dread pooled in her stomach. Something about texting that message felt like she'd just written her own death sentence.

One of the actresses tipped her head back, using a dropper to deposit artificial tears in her eyes. She slapped her cheeks a few times, reddening them, then nodded. "Ready."

Ryan gave Tristan the thumbs up, and the PD raised the clapper.

In the scene, Zinnia and the actress were both supposed to be teary-eyed. Though Zinnia evidently could cry on command—a skill Ryan admired and definitely did not possess, along with any other acting skills—the other actress required a little help to achieve that watery-eyed look.

Four takes later, Ryan took a deep breath in, held it, and let it out. *That was a good take. You can fix that little lighting issue in post.* "Looks great, good job everyone. Let's move on to the next scene."

Zinnia met his eyes and gave a small, comforting smile, as if to say, *The take was good. You're doing the right thing.*

The anxious feeling in his chest calmed, just a little.

Filming seemed to float by as they prepared each shot, went through takes, and made adjustments. As cast and crew worked around one another almost seamlessly, Ryan's heart swelled with pride in his little team.

Finally, they reached the last scene of the day. In it, one of the male actors needed to use the word "plethora" in his dialogue in order to fulfill the festival's requirements.

"What is a…" Tristan squinted at a copy of the script. "A 'plee-THOR-ah'?"

Martell tried to cover up a snicker, but with his hands full of sound equipment, he failed. He muttered under his breath, "Pleethe sir, what is a pleethorah?"

Water spewed from Mariana's mouth, directly onto Tristan.

"Oy!" Tristan reeled back, eyes wide. Pages of the script flew through the air, fluttering to the ground.

As Martell and the male actor roared with laughter, Mariana coughed, hiding a plastic water bottle behind her back. "It's not what it looks like, director," she choked out between laughs and coughs. "I…definitely don't have liquid on set."

Tristan wiped his dripping face. "Yeah, I have evidence that's a lie, director."

Ryan couldn't maintain any sort of stern expression, especially once Zinnia burst into giggles, bent in half with laughter. Her mirth broke his resolve, and he guffawed. "Everyone take five, and someone explain to Tristan what a plethora is."

As the cast and crew dispersed, most still chuckling, Ryan headed toward Zinnia as she wiped tears from her eyes. That wide smile…maybe having a more relaxed set wasn't so bad.

She sucked in a deep breath, still half giggling. She dabbed at her eyes with a tissue. "I'm going to have to touch up my makeup, aren't I?"

"You look perfect." His thoughts froze. Oh no. "I mean. The makeup. It's not messed up. Uh. Waterproof mascara, am I right? Miracle stuff."

She chuckled. "Didn't know you were a makeup connoisseur."

*Thank goodness. I didn't make it weird.* He took a step back in mock offense. "You didn't notice my eyeshadow today?"

"Whoops, sorry. You blended it so seamlessly. Such a natural look." Before she could say anything else, a loud rumbling emitted from her abdomen. Her cheeks reddened. "Excuse my stomach. I didn't get a chance to eat between work and filming."

"No dinner?" Helping Hope worked her too hard. "Hey, I only had a snack myself. Want to grab some food after we finish this scene?"

Shoot. Would she think he was asking her out? He didn't want to scare her. He just wanted to make sure she actually got some decent food. But *was* he asking her out?

*Stop. Stop overthinking.*

"Sure." She hesitated. "Are you a fan of poke? There's a poke and boba place I've been wanting to try."

His brothers would make fun of him for eating "Japanese rabbit food." He could almost hear them laughing. *"Don't you want a burger or something? A steak?"*

"I love poke. It's a plan."

They wrapped up filming within the next half hour. Tristan used his newly learned word as many times as he could in every sentence. "I'm just going to clear up this *plethora* of cords. I think we had a *plethora* of good takes today. There is a *plethora* of water on me from Mariana."

"You're giving me a plethora of reasons to want to smack you," Mariana retorted. She handed him a tripod. "And that last one wasn't used correctly."

Soon enough, Ryan found himself walking toward the parking lot with Zinnia. His phone emitted a ding, and he checked it. "Ah. Must have forgotten to silence email notifications. Another client looking for family photos. Fall is a busy time for those." He turned off the volume and stuck the phone back in his pocket.

Zinnia regarded him with a thoughtful expression. "You stay pretty busy, don't you?"

He shrugged. "I try to keep my schedule reasonable, but I have been known to go overboard from time to time. Work-life balance and all."

"Hmm." She said the next words under her breath, as if more to herself than to him. "I think I had you pegged all wrong." Before he could ask questions, she pointed toward her car. "That's me. I'll see you there."

The entire drive to the poke restaurant, Ryan hummed a jaunty tune. In the parking lot, he waved toward Zinnia, who had beat him there.

In that moment of distraction, his car stalled out, and his engine revved as he pulled into a parking spot. *Great. She'll think you can't drive.*

He emerged from the car sheepishly, meeting Zinnia on the sidewalk in front of the small establishment. Her brow wrinkled as she gazed toward his car. "Do you drive a stick shift?"

"Yeah." He rubbed the back of his neck. "Sometimes it's a little…unruly."

Her expression cleared, and she huffed a laugh. "It really has caused you some problems." Without explaining her cryptic words, she hooked her arm through his and headed for the door. "Let's eat."

His ears heated at the gesture. He followed obediently.

Once they sat down with their food, Ryan dug his fork into a delicious medley of rice, tofu, seaweed, and a variety of greens. His brothers could say what they wanted—they were missing out on a lot of things with their snobbery.

Across from him, Zinnia sipped her popping boba, eyes lighting as the spheres burst. "Love this stuff." She set down her drink and reached for chopsticks. "By the way, filming has been great lately. I think everyone is really enjoying how you're running things while still giving people agency to put their own spin on things."

"I think that's more your doing than mine. I have a lot to thank you for in this process." He poked at a piece of cucumber with his fork. "To be honest, I've had some pretty bad experiences in the past with crew members taking advantage of anything I didn't directly oversee. But this project…it feels different."

Zinnia raised her boba tea. "To the cast and crew."

He raised his own. "To giving up control."

They laughed and chatted over their food, swapping stories of everything from Helping Hope to crazy college tales to sibling stories. By the time the restaurant was nearing close, the thought crossed Ryan's mind, *This might not actually be a date, but it's better than any date I've ever had.*

He walked Zinnia to her car. "I guess I'll see you bright and early tomorrow morning."

"Nine thirty is bright and early?" She raised a brow.

"For our college students? On a Saturday? Tristan is going to show up with an energy drink in each hand, I guarantee it."

She laughed and opened her car door. "See you at the crack of dawn, then."

Ryan moseyed toward his own vehicle, feet light as air. A great day of filming, spending time with Zinnia…nothing could bring down his mood this evening.

"Ryan, my man!"

He froze mid-stride, then slowly turned to face the voice.

Steve strode toward him down the sidewalk in front of the stretch of shops, two young groupies trailing him. "Did I hear you're entering the film festival?"

Ryan gritted his teeth. Steve had the audacity to greet him so casually? After what he'd done? "That is correct."

"Wow, it's great to see you." Steve grabbed Ryan's hand and shook it while looking over his shoulder at the two younger guys. "We knew each other in college."

Knew each other? Worked together. Lived together. Dreamed together.

One of the guys adjusted his glasses. "So you knew Steve before he was famous. Were you a film student?"

Famous? A stretch. "Yes."

"Why don't you tell Ryan here what we've been working on, Robbie?" Steve slapped the young man's shoulder. "Not too many spoilers, of course. Just the little pitch we've been giving everyone who asks."

"Oh. Well, uh, Steve's script is really good. It's about this woman who…"

As Robbie rattled off a somewhat convoluted summary of Steve's project, Ryan felt the blood drain from his face.

Steve's script sounded a lot like his. Right down to a bicycle collision.

But how? Were their brains really so similar? Had Ryan taken too much inspiration from what worked for Steve?

Regardless, he couldn't have anyone thinking he had copied Steve.

"Thanks, Robbie," Ryan interrupted. "Steve. I have to go. I have lots of work to do."

He spun on his heel and power-walked for his car, heart pounding in his ears.

Tonight might be an all-nighter.

# Chapter Fourteen

ZINNIA PRESTON MADE IT A RULE not to check her work email on the weekends. Especially after last night, where she felt that the last of autumn's fireflies exploded in her chest.

Time with Ryan indeed proved to quell her stress of all things work. Because despite what Clark said in the office on Thursday, he hadn't emailed her the memo for the new position.

Yet.

Every part of her hoped Clark had forgotten about giving her Caroline's job.

As she sat on a couch in front of the theater on Saturday morning, however, instinct took over. She tapped on her inbox, and regret pooled in her stomach moments later.

*Zinnia,*

*I'd left this deal memo in my drafts. Apologies for not sending this sooner, as promised on Thursday. Please see the attachment below and have an answer back to me within two weeks.*

"Within two weeks." That meant by October 22, she'd need to have an answer to him about her future.

Her eyes swam back and forth as she scanned the deal memo attachment. Although nothing compared with corporate salaries, the memo did include quite the increase in her current paycheck.

Grandma would call her a fool for turning down such an opportunity.

"You look like you want to destroy your phone."

Zinnia glanced up and spotted Mariana sashaying toward the couch, a basket handle looped around her arm. If it hadn't been a chilly autumn morning, bordering close to the upper thirties in temperature, Zinnia would've guessed that Mariana would soon venture off on a picnic.

"Your phone." Mariana set the wooden basket onto the coffee table near the couches. Then she collapsed into a cushy chair near the stairs that led up to the theater. "Did it do something mean to you?"

Zinnia chuckled and slid the device into her pants pocket. "No, just some work things. Probably shouldn't be checking email anyway, not with us filming in the next half hour or so." She needed to focus on her work as an actress and put all the Helping Hope stuff on the back burner of her mind.

"Speaking of film." Mariana leaned back into the chair, until the cushy head of the seat threatened to swallow her neck whole. "Where's Ryan? I peeked inside the set. Everything's set up, but he's not there."

"Think he had to go print something off."

This morning, when Zinnia arrived, she caught Ryan rushing down the hall and muttering to himself. She decided to stow her greeting until he looked perkier. Sometimes it took Ryan a few minutes to load in the early hours.

"I've been really proud of him lately." Mariana leaned forward and popped the lid off of the vintage basket. Zinnia wondered if she was the type of person to peruse older items at flea markets and antique shops. "Muffin?"

"Proud? How so?"

Mariana held out a plastic-wrapped treat. Zinnia accepted it from her and chuckled inwardly at the thought of them bringing the breakfast pastries onto set. Ryan would have a conniption after what happened during what he now called, "The Spill Incident."

"He's been way more chill." Mariana unwrapped her own muffin. Chocolate chips poked out of the top. "Like, he started us off by calling 'cut' every two seconds. And now, the lighting doesn't have to be perfect, and the sound doesn't have to be pristine. I think someone must've talked some sense into him."

She arched a brow at Zinnia.

Zinnia's chin buckled. She forced her focus onto her muffin and unpeeled the wrapper. As she bit into the pastry, she mm'd at the mixture of cinnamon, pumpkin, and chocolate.

"Wow, Mariana, you're amazing at baking muffins."

"Miracle, really. Considering two hundred of us in my dorm share *one* oven. An old one at that."

Zinnia brushed a crumb off her lap. "Really? Is that even legal?"

Mariana shrugged. "It's college. Universities can get away with a lot, you know."

Alas, Zinnia *did* know. Her own college over-promised and under-delivered to the students and took thousands of dollars away from her bank account in the process.

"Back to Ryan." Wow, Mariana wouldn't give up on him, would she?

Zinnia wondered why she balked talking about him. Maybe because when they did so, her face would grow all hot. Wings would flutter in her stomach. Firecrackers exploded in her chest.

Ryan made her feel warm and vulnerable, all at the same time. Like a campfire on a brisk October night. Sadly, the thing about fires was, if you didn't exercise enough caution around them, they'd burn you to a crisp.

How close could she get to him before he hurt her? Like all the other guys who came before him?

Mariana's voice broke up her thoughts. "Why do you think our director was so crazy at the beginning? I'm glad he's cooled down a little, but he was really nitpicky during the first few days on set."

"It's a control thing." Zinnia set her muffin down and popped open the lid of her water bottle. She drank in a long sip. "From what I could tell from some of our conversation last night, he's had some bad experiences with other crew members on film sets. So if he's in charge, he can make sure everything *he* wants to happen will happen."

"Life doesn't work like that though."

Zinnia cocked her head as Mariana removed a tea bag from her magenta-pink thermos water bottle. She set it on a paper plate that she must've also packed in the vintage picnic basket.

"What do you mean, Mariana?"

"I mean that the more you try to control life, the more it will control you. Take my roommate for instance. She's blocked off her entire schedule in five-minute chunks. Theater major, so her life is insane. She's even sectioned off time for 'have a mental breakdown.'"

Yikes, Zinnia remembered those days, and didn't miss college at all.

Cinnamon and apple scents trailed from Mariana's thermos. Zinnia could really go for some warm tea or cider right now.

"My roommate's in *Tarzan* too, so the mental breakdowns happen a lot. I guess the choreography's really complicated. One girl already twisted her ankle and—"

"Mariana, is there a point to all of this?"

"—yeah, sorry, rabbit trail. Point is, even though my roommate is really trying to control her schedule, things go wrong. Homework assignments take her longer than planned. Calls with her boyfriend go for several hours, instead of the one hour she blocked off. She's learning that even though she tries to micromanage every minute of her life, life tends to have other plans."

Guilt panged Zinnia's chest.

Didn't she often try to do that? Sure, she didn't decide her life minute-by-minute, but if she didn't get her morning workout in or water her plants on time, anxiety would gnaw at her insides for the rest of the day.

Did Ryan's brain work like that?

If so, she had to applaud him for relinquishing any control on the film set. She imagined it would take all of his strength to do that.

"Have you tried talking with your roommate about this stuff, Mariana?"

Mariana leaned her elbow on the armrest of the chair. "Tried, but she's not the kind of person to listen, really. I do get it. I used to be a lot like that in high school. Then I met with a counselor, and there was something she said that I can't forget. Ever."

The girl took in one more swig of her tea.

"She said, 'There's beauty in letting go. In knowing that Someone else has control of the situation, even when you don't.' She's a Christian counselor, you see."

A cross necklace, hidden in the folds of Mariana's sweater, blinked in the light. Zinnia hadn't realized that she and Mariana shared the same beliefs.

*Have I been doing that? Trying to control my life when Someone else has a much better idea of what's going on?*

She tossed up a quick prayer that God could provide answers soon about work, about Georgia, about Ryan.

Normally she would've been concerned about the lack of replies via text. However, her aunt had a tendency to drop conversations before they ended.

Zinnia watched as Ryan rushed down the hallway and about jumped when he spotted the two of them on the couches.

"Oh, good, Zinnia. Glad you could come early."

"Sure thing, Director." She hated how far the smile spread on her face when she took him in. "Any lines in particular you need us to go over?"

"Actually, all of them."

By now, Ryan had reached the coffee table. One of his hands held a bundle of stapled papers. The other ran through his hair. Dark circles plagued his eyes this morning. Did he get any sleep last night?

He dropped the stacks of papers onto the lid of the picnic basket. Zinnia picked up one of the scripts from the top of the pile and scanned the lines.

She stopped short.

None of this looked familiar.

"Ryan, did you change…the entire script?"

"Scrapped half of it. Try and learn what you can. We're going over scene three today. Hopefully our other actors will show up soon."

Before anyone, particularly Zinnia, could protest, Ryan darted off again.

Zinnia leaned back into her seat and massaged the incoming headache at the center of her forehead. On top of all the stressors from her life, she didn't need this.

Mariana sucked in air from between her teeth. "I take back what I said about Ryan. Looks like he still has a lot to learn."

"Okay, I think we can wrap it up for today."

Ryan pinched above the bridge of his nose, staving off pain that had begun to pierce his temples. Or maybe that burning sensation stemmed from the glares his cast and crew had been shooting in his direction all day.

He couldn't help it. Their film *had* to be different from Steve's. No judge would believe Ryan hadn't ripped off Steve's ideas.

As soon as he called wrap, the crew silently began tearing down. Tristan had been sulking like a scolded puppy ever since Ryan snapped at him about energy drinks on set—again. Mariana's jaw was clenched, probably because of all the times Ryan had called for a scene to be shot again. Were the takes actually worse today, or were his nerves getting to him?

Zinnia walked toward him and placed a tired hand on his shoulder, patting once before continuing her trajectory, as if she couldn't even muster words.

He had messed up. Big time.

He turned toward her. "Zinnia."

She stopped, looking back over her shoulder.

He hesitated. What could he even say? "I'm sorry" didn't seem good enough. He *was* sorry. But changing the script...he hadn't had a choice.

"Have a good weekend," he finished lamely.

She turned away with half a wave.

Several minutes later, he sat in his car, staring at the steering wheel. *Well. That's over. What else could go wrong today?*

He pulled his phone out of his pocket. He'd had notifications silenced while filming to keep his attention on set. He expected a few messages, but when he saw four texts and three missed calls from Andy, his stomach dropped.

*Oh, no. The engagement shoot.*

**Andy:** Hey man, we still good for later today?

**Andy:** I'm heading to the location.

**Andy:** Hey dude, I just gave you a call. You okay?

**Andy:** I'm going to go ahead with the proposal. I hope you're okay, dude. Shoot me a message when you can.

The voicemail Andy left was much kinder than Ryan deserved. "Hey, Ryan. I'm about to get to the location, and I just wanted to make sure we're still on. I should have checked in yesterday, but I got caught up in other things. Text me if you get this? Thanks, man."

A rock in his gut, Ryan called Andy back. As the phone rang, he swallowed, trying to come up with the words to say.

"Ryan!" Relief tinged Andy's voice. "Are you okay, dude? Had me worried."

Guilt hit Ryan even harder. Andy had been worried about his wellbeing. He didn't sound angry. Would that change once he learned the truth?

If so, Ryan deserved it. He'd dropped the ball on one of the most important moments in the couple's life.

"Hey, Andy." His mouth felt dry. "I'm so sorry. I'm fine. Nothing is wrong. I just…well. I have no excuse. I let you down. I was filming and completely forgot that I planned to end early so I could head to the shoot."

"Oh." A beat of silence followed. "I get it, man. Things happen." Energy infused his voice. "The important thing is, I proposed, and she said yes."

"Congratulations." Ryan took a deep breath. "I don't know how I can begin to apologize, dude. I can't believe I forgot." He tapped his fingers on the steering wheel, trying to think of any way he could make this situation even the smallest bit better. "I'm happy to do a post-engagement shoot with you two and the ring, although I know it isn't the same as the moment of. It will be completely on me, of course. Any location. More than one, if you want." He coughed. Why was his throat so dry?

"You know what, I bet Caroline will like that even more." Andy chuckled. "She'll probably color coordinate our outfits. We can talk later and set up a time."

"Yeah. Absolutely. Thank you."

After hanging up, Ryan let out a long breath. He had let down his cast and crew, Andy…and Zinnia.

She'd worked so hard to help him overcome his tendency toward the control freak side of things. Their dinner last night had been perfect. Until Steve, once again, ruined everything.

No. Until *Ryan* ruined everything. He didn't have anyone to blame but himself for what happened on set today.

Ryan started his car, lost in thought. After what Steve had done, Ryan had felt the need to control everything. But Zinnia showed him that people—the right people—could be trusted. Ryan had chosen to let Steve get to him again. He'd let Steve win.

Was that why Steve had talked to him in the first place? To rattle him?

Once home, Ryan fed a very hungry Buttercup and Balto and took the dog for a much-needed walk. By the time he returned to his apartment, he had a message in mind.

He plopped on his couch and began typing a text to Zinnia.

**Ryan:** I messed up today. I was really controlling and nitpicking. I had an encounter with our competition that got in my head, but that's no excuse. If you have a chance, I'd like to apologize in person. Maybe over coffee? Drinks on me at She Brews? I'll be bringing something for everyone on Monday, but I owe you an apology most of all.

With that message sent, he drafted an email to his cast and crew.

*Hey, everyone,*

*I've been honored to work with such a talented team on this film. You all have given so much to this project, and I threw you a curveball today by switching up the script at the last minute. I need to apologize for how I went about it. I think the changes were necessary, but I should have listened to more input from all of you and been less micromanaging.*

*We only have a couple days left of shooting, and I look forward to working with all of you to pull this film together—with your input and ideas.*

*Best,*

*Ryan*

*P.S. I'll be providing pizza on Monday, so let me know if you have any food allergies.*

A pizza bribe might be a little low, but who could resist pizza?

His phone buzzed right after he sent the email. He opened his text messages.

**Zinnia:** You hit my weakness with a bribe of coffee. Today wasn't great, but I appreciate the apology, and I'm up for talking in person. Tomorrow?

Ryan's breath whooshed from his lungs. That felt like a promising response. He checked his calendar. He'd agreed to help out with some media at church tomorrow after service, but after that…

**Ryan:** I'm tied up at church during the day, but how does evening sound? If it's too late in the day for coffee, Griffith told me She Brews has some new fall drinks and hot apple cider.

Her answer came swiftly.

**Zinnia:** I do love hot apple cider.

As they coordinated a time, tension began to release from Ryan's shoulders. Tomorrow, he would tell Zinnia everything.

And hopefully, if he was lucky, she could forgive him.

# Chapter Fifteen

Zinnia never expected to go to a plant for relationship advice, and yet, here she was.

"What do you think, Peter? Do you think Ryan is going to break my heart?"

To no one's surprise, Peter Parker the spider plant didn't answer.

Fresh from church, today Zinnia wore a gray sweater dress coupled with black leggings. She sighed and clutched Peter's pot as she paced back and forth down the hallway that led to the front door.

"I don't know, Peter. He was acting pretty micromanaging yesterday. If I wanted to get with him, would we have to deal with him controlling the entire relationship?"

Zinnia's socks skidded up and down the tile floor. She cradled Peter close. One fall could make him crack on the hard flooring.

A knock at the door juddered her senses.

"Must be Joy."

At church, Joy had mentioned experimenting with a new Bear Claw recipe. Maybe she'd finished the pastry early.

Weird, though… From what Zinnia could remember from the screenshot of the recipe Joy showed to her, the bake time would take at least an hour.

They returned from church twenty minutes ago.

Cradling Peter in one hand, Zinnia rushed to the door and twisted the knob with the other one.

Georgia stood at the entrance, fist raised, face sheet-white.

"Georgia." Zinnia stumbled back a few feet, dazed by the unexpected visitor. "What a surprise, I—"

"Save it." Georgia stormed across the threshold and slammed the door behind her. "I know what you've been saying about me."

Ice spiked Zinnia's veins. Did she accidentally dial Georgia during one of her rants to Joy? She scanned her memories for any traces of anything she wouldn't say to Georgia's face.

*That would be everything, wouldn't it?*

After all, Georgia took offense to anything that even seemed like a slight.

"Georgia, I'm afraid I don't know what you're talking—"

"Don't start. Aunt Millie told me that you think I'm unhappy in my marriage and that I'm somehow 'taking it out on you.'" She sneered as she tossed up the air quotes. Zinnia didn't realize, until seconds later, that Georgia had advanced toward her in a slow, stalking manner. "Oh, please. *You're* the one who's a bully, Zin, and now you're acting like a victim. Trying to turn people against me."

Did Zinnia *ever* bully Georgia?

Sure, in their childhood, they'd get into lots of spats. Their grandma encouraged their gladiatorial verbal assaults. Said it would build character and a thick skin.

Past high school, though, Zinnia always tried to placate Georgia. Maybe Georgia had perceived some of Zinnia's actions through a vicious lens.

Zinnia gripped the wall for support. Above her, a cross stitch of a bundle of thorny roses hung from a nail in the wall. "Georgia, listen, there's probably a misunderstanding—"

"What do you even know about relationships anyway? *You* haven't found a guy, and I think at this point, it should be obvious why."

This stopped Zinnia short. Her heart hammered in her eardrums.

Did she just hear Georgia say that right? Ragged breaths trailed from her lips and her chest grew tight. Every part of her wished she could warn Georgia of the impending panic attack, but Georgia would blow it off as "playing the anxiety card to get out of this conversation."

"I—what did you say?"

Georgia halted, but she cocked her head and lifted a brow. She had the high ground. "Come on, Zin, I thought even you would've gotten it by now. You're loud, a workaholic, and honestly, very hard to love. If you had been doing the right things, you could've probably married right out of college. Since you clearly are still single, you must be doing something wrong."

Itchiness stung Zinnia's eyes. She gathered all the oxygen, and thoughts, she could muster and let out a deep breath.

"Georgia," she said coolly, "that's pretty hurtful."

"It's the truth, and honestly, I feel at peace for telling you. Someone *had* to, since everyone's been thinking it all these years. I'm the only one who had the guts to say anything, apparently. Now—"

She reached forward and snatched Peter out of Zinnia's arms. By now, all of Zinnia's limbs numbed, unable to prevent Georgia from doing anything.

"Why don't you mind the plank in your own eye, Zin, before worrying about the specks in other people's?"

Right then, Georgia flattened her palm. Peter Parker sailed to the floor, and his pot cracked. Georgia spun around, flounced through the door, and slammed it. Zinnia sank to the floor and tried to scoop the dirt into a mound. Her hands shook and breaths rattled her throat. Spots covered her vision. She'd been breathing too fast. Tingles filled her arms and she slackened against the wall. It took several minutes for the panic attack to pass.

As it finished, another knock sounded from the door.

*Please, God, no.*

She couldn't handle another Georgia confrontation. She could've sworn she heard tires ripping up the asphalt as Georgia made her grand exit. But maybe, in the midst of the heavy breaths, she didn't hear her sister return.

Tears pricked Zinnia's eyes. With whatever strength she had left, she lifted herself and padded to the door. A fresh headache pounded her temples. She twisted the knob and a beaming, but flushed, Joy stood at the entrance.

"Hey, Zin, so sorry to bother you. I'm sure you don't have any sliced almonds, but just wanted to check to make—"

Joy halted, eyes darting back and forth, scanning Zinnia's no-doubt swollen face. Her neighbor held up a finger.

"One moment, please."

Then Joy rushed off, into her house. She returned moments later, key fob in hand.

"Ben says he can watch the kids for the afternoon." Joy clicked a button on the key, and her car in her driveway beeped. "Get in the car, Zinnia."

Zinnia sponged the tears on her cheek with the fabric from the sweater dress. "Wh-what?"

"Get in the car. There's a harvest festival downtown, and I'm buying you whatever you want." Joy gestured at the vehicle. "In."

Stunned, Zinnia stumbled forward, locked her front door, and slid into the passenger seat. For the next hour, Joy didn't ask Zinnia what happened. The two of them gawked at glassblowers creating miniature swans and had a fun taste test at the apple butter churning station.

They perched on a picnic table and picked away at a large bag of sweet kettle corn. Salt danced on Zinnia's tongue.

"Okay, Zin." Joy crunched on a handful of kettle corn. "Tell me who did this to you. Because Ben and I recently went to a Renaissance Faire, and I bought a dagger, so if you need me to stab anyone—"

Zinnia drew her knees up to her chest.

"No, that's okay, Joy. Maybe she was right. She said she was telling the truth, and apparently everyone thinks I'm a horrible person. Maybe they're right."

Much as Zinnia enjoyed perusing booths of wooden roses and local artists' paintings the whole afternoon, her mind raced back to Georgia's words.

*"You're loud."*

*"You're a workaholic."*

*"You're hard to love."*

Did everyone believe this about her? Insecurities buzzed in her skull like a swarm of wasps, angry that the coming winter would take out their hive.

After Joy pressed her, Zinnia recounted what happened. She finished with, "Maybe Georgia had good intentions. She was telling the truth, after all."

"No." This came out through gritted teeth. "No, Zinnia, she wasn't."

Kids hovered around the apple butter churn.

"What do you mean? I *am* loud. I do work a lot, and—"

"No, Zinnia. Something you may not know is I worked at the school newspaper back in the day. We were always focused on the truth. To tell the right story, to tell the facts. Let me tell you about truth."

Joy clasped her hands in her lap.

"Truth is objective. Yes, sometimes it can sting, but the truth is not meant to be a weapon. The second someone uses words to manipulate, to bludgeon, to cut down, it no longer becomes truth. It becomes something far more sinister. Your sister knew which words would injure you the most, and she used them. That's not loving, Zin."

Zinnia's lip quivered. She bit it to stop it from tremoring. "Then, what is the truth? About me?"

Every part of her worried that Georgia spoke true. That everyone, deep down, believed Zinnia didn't deserve love.

"The truth is that you are beautiful, hardworking, loyal, giving, and—" She raised a brow. "Very, very easy to love. The truth is Georgia probably hates herself, or at least, her very trapped situation with her husband. She's deflected it on you, and I'm sorry she did that to you."

Joy banded an arm around Zinnia's shoulder.

Tears blurred Zinnia's vision. "What should I do about Georgia then?"

"Heal, forgive when you feel ready, and leave it to God to show her what truth really is."

Warmth spread throughout Zinnia's stomach, and for the rest of the afternoon, she almost forgot about Georgia's words. Almost.

Ryan still hadn't recovered from Friday night's all-nighter. After an early morning and long day helping out at church, he might go for coffee despite the relatively late hour.

He had claimed a pair of cushy chairs in She Brews, perfect for chatting. He wiped sweaty palms on his jeans. He would hate to ruin his friendship with Zinnia over his own neuroticism.

The bell over the door jangled. He stood as a figure in a gray sweater dress entered.

Zinnia's cheeks were pinked and kissed with a touch of sun as if she'd spent the day outside, her hair a bit windblown, unusual for her. As Ryan approached, he thought her eyes might look a bit puffy, but they sparkled as she turned her gaze toward him. "Hey, sorry if I'm a little late. I was with my friend Joy."

"No worries. I think I'm early." Ryan nodded toward the counter. "Can I get you something?"

After they placed their orders, they carried their cider back to the chairs Ryan had saved with his coat. He sat, jitters shaking his fingers. How to begin?

Before he could say anything, Zinnia spoke. "I'm sorry. You didn't have to do this. I've been hard on you. It's your film, and I've been loud and hard to work with—"

"Whoa, whoa." He held up a hand. "Are you…apologizing to me that I did something I need to apologize for?"

She blinked at his interruption. "Um." She shrugged one shoulder. "Maybe?"

His apology speech he had been rehearsing in the car evaporated like the steam coming off his coffee. "You're not hard to work with at all. In fact, you're probably the reason we've gotten this far. You're honest and keep me accountable—and in a way that's helpful without making me even more stressed."

Where had she gotten the idea that any of this was her fault? Did her sister have anything to do with it?

"Oh," she said softly.

"We're here for *me* to apologize, because after everything you've helped with, instead of being upfront with you, I freaked out and took it out on the cast and crew. I'm sorry, and I want to work to do better with our last couple of days." He straightened. "So if you have any suggestions, lay them on me."

She stared at him, hot cider resting untouched between her palms. "I guess I'm just not used to people taking responsibility for their actions."

Something definitely happened. Between her puffy eyes and the way the words rang of fresh hurt, he would guess whatever hurt her occurred today. "Did your sister do something?" he blurted out, then backtracked, stumbling over his words. "Er, not that it's my business. But if you wanted to talk about it…I don't know, I might be off base, it just seems like you're not quite yourself. Uh, not that you seem…well…I'll stop talking now."

She chuckled, her shoulders relaxing. "I don't know how you could tell, but yeah, I had a bit of a run-in with Georgia."

She briefed Ryan on the situation with her grandmother's belongings, her encounter with her sister, and the painful demise of Peter Parker's pot. "She was pretty upset about what I said to my aunt. And she kind of…said some very hurtful things to me because of it." Her cheeks colored, and she didn't elaborate.

Ryan clenched a fist, brain spinning with stern words he'd like to share with Georgia, some not very nice. Good thing Zinnia had a friend like Joy. *Does Joy need family Christmas photos?* Ryan would do them for free. Anything to show a token of appreciation.

"I hope you know you didn't do anything wrong," he said once she finished. "Georgia was way out of line."

"Yeah." She fiddled with her cup, now half empty, before resting her hand on the arm of the chair. "That's what Joy said. And that Georgia is probably projecting her own pain."

"That sounds right." Ryan hesitated, then placed his hand over hers. "For what it's worth coming from me, if you ever need someone to talk to or just hang out with when it comes to Georgia, I'm happy to reassure you that you aren't crazy. We can even do things that have nothing to do with film. Amazing, I know."

Her cheeks pinked slightly as she glanced down at his hand over hers, but she didn't pull away. The corner of her lips quirked. "You still want to hang out? Even when I've threatened to throw bagels at your camera?"

He laughed, sinking back into his own chair. "Even then."

They chuckled and sipped their drinks. After a moment, Zinnia sobered. "So. You changed half the script. What was that about? You said something happened."

"Well. It's kind of a long story."

She crossed one leg over the other, leaned back in her seat, and looked at him expectantly.

He spilled the story of Steve—how they had once worked together, Steve's betrayal, and now how Steve had entered the film festival with a project too close to Ryan's script for comfort.

"So that's why you changed it," Zinnia said when he finished. She shook her head. "I get it. That Steve guy is a real piece of work. But maybe next time you could give the team an explanation?"

Oh. "Yeah. I guess that would have made more sense. When I freaked out, I guess I kind of just…went into super-control mode."

"After what Steve did, I don't blame you." She sighed. "I try to control a lot of things in my life too, but I think I'm starting to learn that we have to trust other people as well. Just, the right people."

*I think you might be the "right people," Zinnia.* He didn't voice that thought aloud. Instead, he glanced at the time on his phone, and his eyes widened. Sharing their stories with one another had lasted a long time. "It's later than I thought. Do you want to get some food, maybe?

You could even give me thoughts on the script if you wanted to."

Her smile brightened her eyes. "For the sake of the film, of course," she teased.

"Of course." Once this film ended, he would have to come up with new cheesy excuses to hang out with Zinnia.

But that was a thought for later. He didn't need to worry about controlling this process.

# Chapter Sixteen

"UGH, ZINNIA, MY ARM HURTS TOO much. It's so tired."

Caroline leaned against Zinnia's cubicle. Even at ten this morning, Zinnia had developed quite the headache from the number of tasks in her inbox. She'd have to skip lunch just to get out on time, and to the filming today.

"Why's that, Carrie? Did you overdo it on arm day at the gym?"

"Could be that, or it could be from having to hold this guy up."

Zinnia peeled her eyes away from her computer, and gasped. A brilliant diamond ring glittered on Caroline's finger.

"White sapphire, actually." In a sheepish motion, Caroline tucked a loose strand of hair behind her ear. "Everyone's been asking what type of jewel it is, and I figured that diamond mining can be quite a dangerous business so—"

"Oh my gosh!" Zinnia bolted from her seat.

Was Caroline a hugging person? Was *Zinnia* a hugging person?

Zinnia settled for shaking Caroline's non-ring hand. "Congratulations. How did he do it?"

"To be honest, he gave it away before we even got to the national park. He's been nervous this whole week. Not to mention, my roommate is horrible at being subtle, so if Andy hadn't indicated he was proposing, Liv would've told me."

Caroline recounted to Zinnia about the proposal. Zinnia's heart warmed at how much Caroline's eye sparkled as she spoke.

When Caroline finished, she drew in a long sip from her large water bottle.

No doubt, several coworkers at Helping Hope made Caroline tell them the same story. From what Zinnia could recall from her college days, girls in her dorm who got engaged would get peppered with questions like, "so when is the wedding?" "what's the theme and colors?" "when are you getting your wedding dress?"

Caroline set down her water bottle on the ground and triangled her arm on her hip.

"I have two weird favors to ask of you, Zin."

Zinnia's fingers itched to return to her laptop. In her periphery, she spotted two new bolded emails, likely from Clark. He'd decided today, Monday, would be a good time to send her loads of copy assignments he'd forgotten to give to Caroline on Friday.

Even though Zinnia had given no indication about where she stood on the promotion, Clark acted like she already told him yes.

Zinnia forced herself to fold her hands on her lap. "Sure, what do you need from me?"

"First, I was wondering if you would be one of my bridesmaids."

Despite the noises of phones ringing and laptops clacking, all sound deadened in Zinnia's ears. She felt her eyes go wide.

"Oh my goodness, Caroline, I'm honored. I have to admit I didn't think we were all that close."

Especially not after what happened in the spring of the previous year. Maybe Caroline didn't have many female friends. If Zinnia knew anything about other women, they tended to get thrown off by workaholic types.

Even at her own church, several of the ladies would balk when it came to conversing with Zinnia. Most of them had chosen to be stay-at-home moms and didn't think they could talk at length about their children's habits in front of a childless, single woman.

Sadness swelled in Zinnia's gut.

*Georgia was right. There is something wrong with me. Otherwise, I'd have several kids and a husband by now.*

Despite Joy's advice, Zinnia wondered for hours on end if Ryan perceived her to be "loud" and "hard to love." She hadn't told him about that part of her encounter with Georgia. Even though he invited her to coffee, and they had an amazing conversation, she couldn't help but wonder if secretly, he couldn't stand her.

*Probably thinks that I'm more trouble than I'm worth and will never talk to me again after this film.*

"Honestly, Zinnia." Caroline twisted the ring on her finger. "I feel like you and I have gotten a lot closer over the past few months. Plus, much as I love Hadassah and Liv—the other bridesmaids—if I put either of them in charge, my wedding is going to be a disorganized mess. I think you'll be able to control a lot of the fires that come up."

Caroline stepped into the cubicle and squeezed Zinnia's shoulder.

"It's totally fine to say no, if you don't want to—"

"Yes, Caroline, yes. I'm so excited to be part of this."

Indeed she was. No one entrusted her with the role of bridesmaid prior to this. Once, a college friend told her she'd, "almost made the cut, but I'm afraid you'd upstage me." Although the girl likely meant it as a compliment, Zinnia got invited to very few weddings after that.

"That brings us to the second favor." Caroline chewed on her lip and backed toward the entrance of the cubicle.

"Which is what?"

"Andy's mom is in town. She attended a mini party thrown at Andy and Elijah's apartment, after the proposal. Some people from Andy's church were there, and—"

Caroline pinched the bridge of her nose.

"Sorry, rambling. All to say that, I managed to get an appointment at a bridal store nearby. I called them yesterday, and they just so happened to have a cancellation and could fit me in. Andy's mom drives home to Tennessee later today, and I figured she'd want to be part of it."

"A fitting? Today?"

Zinnia's mouth dried.

Another email blinked in bold at the top of her inbox. She'd planned to skip lunch today, not add in a dress fitting appointment that would take well over an hour, or more.

"You don't have to go with me, but Hadassah and Liv are able to make it. I'd love to have the whole bridal party there if possible."

Zinnia's expression softened.

How could she say no to the first person who ever invited her to take a part in a wedding?

"Of course I'll go. When's the appointment?"

"Eleven. We leave in twenty minutes, to beat out the lunch-rush traffic."

Ten minutes later, and only one of twelve tasks done for Clark, Zinnia climbed into Caroline's car. They sped off to the bridal store. When they reached the parking lot, ballgowns and mermaid-style dresses greeted them in the display windows. Hadassah, Andy's mom, and Liv, all bundled in cardigans, waved at them next to the front door. Zinnia observed how Andy's mother sported a winter coat. The temperatures in Tennessee didn't dip this low this time of year, she guessed.

Once they stepped inside, a woman in all-black clothing checked Caroline in. She led the group to a large dressing room, covered in mirrors.

A consultant greeted them and asked Caroline for a wedding date—next October—and what styles of dresses Caroline wanted. Caroline pulled up the Pinterest app and showed the woman several pictures of gowns. Zinnia peered over Liv's shoulder to take in the lacey garments and long sleeves.

"Wonderful. Well, I'll let your group onto the floor." The consultant indicated the several rows of dress racks that covered the length of the store. "Each of you can pick out a dress or two for Caroline to try."

Hadassah raised a hand.

"Yes?" the consultant asked.

"We're allowed to pick out dresses? I always thought the consultant decided everything." Her voice came out timid.

Zinnia, back in the day, binged every episode of *Say Yes to the Dress*. To her recollection, consultants did the majority of the work in that show.

"That happens in some stores, but in ours, we want the bridal party to be as involved as possible. I'll lead you to the racks."

Minutes later, Zinnia found herself swallowed by plastic garment bags. By the sound of it, the others had returned to the room. She took a few more moments to locate a dress with long sleeves and a lacy bodice. Then she joined the others on the bench in the fitting room.

Caroline tried a few of the other ones.

Zinnia didn't know who thought it was a good idea to put the poor girl in a strapless gown, but Caroline, in the kindest voice possible, said, "Hmm, maybe not," and shimmied out of the thing as fast as possible.

After several more gowns, Caroline stepped into Zinnia's pick. Zinnia's heart catapulted into her throat as Caroline tried it on. Caroline's skin glowed when the consultant zipped her up.

She spun around on the circular pedestal at the center of the room and faced the mirror. Her fingertips gripped the lacy layers of the dress.

"Oh my goodness, who picked this one?"

In a timid motion, Zinnia lifted her hand.

"Zin, it's perfect, I—" She clasped her hands to her face and swiveled to the consultant. "I think we have the one."

As Caroline checked out, Zinnia slipped her phone out of her bag. Thank goodness she kept this thing on silent, because several more email notifications blinked on the screen, along with the time—12:46.

By the time they'd get back to Helping Hope, it would be well past one.

For the rest of the day, Zinnia plowed through her work tasks. As soon as she'd finished one, however, four more would appear in the top of her inbox when she clicked refresh.

She finished at 5:36 and shut her laptop.

Even going at the speed of light—or, well, the speed of Zinnia— she couldn't stay on top of everything. In fact, she once had to ask Caroline to bring her some water from the cooler because she couldn't pry herself away from her desk long enough.

*Ryan is going to kill me.*

This answered the question about what would happen if she said yes to taking on Caroline's position in addition to hers.

*I will have to say goodbye to film, if I tell Clark that I'm accepting the promotion.*

Shoving her laptop into her bag, she raced for the door, and prayed Ryan wouldn't freak out too much at her late arrival.

Ryan glanced at the time on his phone. It wasn't like Zinnia to be late. Should he text her and make sure she was okay?

Mariana fiddled with the camera. "We're all ready as soon as Zinnia gets here."

Tristan stretched and yawned. "Does this mean I can go get my energy drink while we wait?"

"No drinks on set," half the cast and crew shouted in unison.

As Tristan grumbled in a tone that seemed only half joking, Ryan spotted Zinnia dashing toward them.

"So sorry," she puffed, shucking off her coat as she ran. "Work kept me…lots of tasks…still behind."

"That's all right." Ryan forced his frantic feelings to subside. Just because they were fifteen minutes behind schedule wasn't a reason to panic. *Relax. Don't be too controlling. It's okay.* He could feel the eyes of his team on him, watching for his reaction. "Take a moment to catch your breath if you need it, and then we can start the scene."

He thought he saw a candy bar exchange hands between Tristan and Martell. Had they been making *bets* on how he would respond?

Zinnia quickly calmed her breathing, smoothed her hair, and slipped into character.

The crew worked together like a well-oiled machine, and even the actors seemed to delve deeper into their characters. Ryan guessed they'd had more time to go over the altered script.

One of the actors tripped over her words on an unintentional tongue twister, sending them laughing and giggling through four takes before she got it right, but Ryan couldn't bring himself to mind with how much mirth the mistake brought his cast and crew.

When Ryan called "cut" for the last shot of the day, he didn't receive a single glare. Especially when he announced, "All right, let's tear down, and then pizza on me."

Tristan whooped, slapping Martell on the back. "Let's go, dude, we gotta hurry up and get pizza." He darted around the set.

Mariana rolled her eyes at him. "You eat pizza at least twice a week."

"And it is a heavenly experience every single time." He placed his hands together as if in prayer.

Ryan made eye contact with Zinnia as she hid a giggle behind her hand.

"I know pizza is usually a safe option," Ryan said under his breath to her, "but I didn't know I was encouraging pizza idolatry."

She snorted. "In good news, I think your apology is very much accepted."

They swarmed a local pizza joint not long afterward, and Ryan ordered multiple pizzas for the table. Martell and Tristan put away slices at an astonishing rate. *Was I that much of a human black hole in college?* His mind went back to several instances of ordering a large pizza as a midnight snack to share with Steve, both of them devouring it within moments. *Yeah, we were like that too.*

Thinking of the way he and Steve had laughed over pizza, chugged energy drinks while working on late-night last-minute projects, challenged one another to video game battles… He never would have guessed Steve would one day betray him.

The pizza turned to cardboard in his mouth.

"Hey." Beside him, Zinnia cocked her head. "Are you all right?"

Had he made a face? How had she sensed the shift in his mood?

He looked around the table, at his smiling and laughing cast and crew.

They had been working hard. Everyone had given their all, working together to produce something they could be proud of. Even if they didn't win…he was glad he'd had a good experience on a set again.

"Yeah. I think I am." He blew out a breath. "I can't believe tomorrow is our last day of shooting."

"It went by so fast." Zinnia took a thoughtful sip of water. "I don't know what I'll do after it's done."

Ryan's phone began to buzz in his pocket, but he ignored it as Zinnia seemed about to speak again.

She hesitated, then added, "My boss wants me to take on a new role."

His phone continued to buzz. Who could be calling? He tried to tune out the noise. "You don't sound excited about that."

"It will be a lot of extra work…" She trailed off. "Do you need to answer that?"

He pulled out the phone and glanced at the caller ID. His dad? Why would his father reach out? They hardly ever talked.

"Uh. I guess maybe I should answer this one."

He shimmied out between the packed chairs in the pizza joint, heading for the door to take the call somewhere a bit quieter, where Dad wouldn't hear the rowdy sounds of a family pizza joint. He didn't think his father would approve of the venue.

The phone had quit ringing by the time he made it outside, but he called back, his heart rate increasing as the line rang. Why would Dad call? Had something happened to Mom?

"Ryan." Dad's voice rumbled through the phone.

"Hey, Dad. Sorry I missed you. I needed to get someplace quieter. Is everything okay?"

"Everything is fine with me." In the brief moment of quiet, Ryan thought he heard the sound of a phone or copier in the background. Was Dad still at work? His father continued, "The question, son, is whether everything is all right with you."

Ryan's eyebrows shot up. He rounded the corner of the building, pulling his light coat closer against the nighttime fall chill. "I…think so."

"Your brothers visited recently. I have an offer for you."

*Oh great.* "Oh?"

"You know I'm opening a branch near you. I want you to help run it. A Torino on the ground."

"I appreciate it, Dad, but—"

"You'll receive the same compensation I would pay anyone in the position." He named a salary more than triple what Ryan currently made a year. "I need you to start in four weeks."

Ryan leaned against the wall. He was used to being reminded by Mom and his brothers that Dad would hire him. But the official offer of a position in Roseville, where he didn't have to leave behind everyone he knew, with a salary he could hardly fathom what to do with…

Balto would love a house with a yard. No one would question what Ryan was "doing with his life." And despite himself, Ryan's mind went to Zinnia. She wanted to be an actress. That had to be difficult while trying to work a full-time job. What if he could help? After all, his own film career was going nowhere.

*Stop. Don't think like that.* "Four weeks? Wow. I didn't realize things were moving so fast."

"Business moves apace."

Less than three weeks from now, Ryan would know the results of the film festival.

Maybe he should take that as a sign—if they won the festival, he would stick with film.

If not, maybe it was time to accept a stable job.

He took a deep breath. "Can I give you an answer on that in two and a half weeks?"

Silence for a moment, until Dad's somewhat disgruntled voice returned. "That's cutting it a bit close, Ryan."

Ryan waited with bated breath.

Dad grunted. "All right. Two and a half weeks. I want an answer by Friday, October 28th."

The day of the festival? "Uh, could Monday wor—"

"The twenty-eighth, Ryan. Have an answer."

The line went dead without a goodbye.

Ryan let out his breath in a whoosh. The day of the festival was shaping up to be perhaps the most nerve-wracking of his life.

# Chapter Seventeen

ZINNIA SHUT THE DOOR AND GAZED out into the void in horror.

"Cut," Ryan called from the camera. "That was amazing, Zinnia. I think that's a wrap, everyone."

The cast and crew, in the classroom, cheered.

Zinnia had just filmed the last take of when she entered "the door." She and Ryan decided they'd film two alternative endings—the scenes of which they'd shot during other days. Her character Phoebe would enter a different door, each one with a different outcome.

Door number one led to a possible career as a film star. But her character, entering through it, had no idea if the dream would pan out or not.

As for the second door, it took her character to a boring job, but a secure one. They'd just filmed that ending, where Phoebe glimpsed the scene before her, horrified, but accepting of her mundane fate.

She grabbed her bag, next to the pile of the crew's belongings, and scanned her emails. Despite it being eight o' clock on a Tuesday, Clark had emailed her several times. The headings for the messages read—

"Checking in on Your Decision"

"More Thoughts on the Merger of Your and Caroline's Position"

"Please Respond: URGENT - Additional Ideas for the Transition"

*What happened to giving me a full two weeks to decide?*

She'd dodged Clark in the office Monday and today, since whenever he ran into her, he'd tap his wristwatch. Indicating he'd like an answer soon.

Would she have to confront him earlier than she thought?

"Since we finished early." Mariana looped her backpack straps over her shoulders. "What's the plan for post? Do you need us, or—?"

"No."

Ryan answered this a little too fast. He pried himself away from the camera and addressed the crew. Everyone bubbled around Ryan in a circle for one final roundup.

"I'll do the edits, but I may talk with some of you about helping out." He cut a glance at Zinnia. "Some of you have had some great suggestions throughout this filming process."

Her heart squeezed.

Of course she'd love to help him. Although she didn't know much about editing, Griffith taught her a thing or two about good storytelling. Perhaps she could give Ryan some direction when it came to that.

Ryan clapped his hands together.

"Before we head off, I just want to thank each and every one of you. I know pizza doesn't really make up for all the hard work you guys have done. I'll try to think of a gift I can give each of you to thank you for your efforts."

"You can thank us by winning that contest for us," Tristan bellowed. This sent giggles throughout the circle.

Ryan's face went sheet-white, but he maintained a smile. "We'll certainly try our best." An awkward pause held the group. "Well, I don't want to keep you guys too long. I'm sure you have homework and such."

"Actually." Mariana's heels bobbed back and forth. "There's a Halloween Open House happening back at my dorm. We were all going to catch the tail end of it if we happened to get out early. Do you guys"—she gestured at Ryan and Zinnia—"want to join us?"

Ryan and Zinnia exchanged a glance.

Zinnia didn't mind Halloween. Although she wouldn't peg herself as a *Nightmare on Elm Street* type, she and Georgia used to watch *It's the Great Pumpkin, Charlie Brown* as an October tradition in their childhood.

"Just how scary are we talking?" Ryan shoved his hands into his pockets. "Because Griffith made me watch a horror movie last year, and

I don't think I can stomach much after that."

Ah yes, Zinnia recalled that.

During Griffith's Christmas play last year, he told Ryan that if Ryan didn't do the light cues correctly, Zinnia would treat him far worse than the villain of that horror movie. Based on how Ryan reacted to her having a bow and arrow in hand, maybe his Zinnia fears had abated.

"They said last year was *Monsters Inc.*-themed," Mariana explained, "so I don't think it's exactly *Texas Chainsaw Massacre.*"

Ryan cut one more glance at Zinnia. Something about his expression said, "I'll go if you go."

Hmm, Ryan had been wanting to spend more time with Zinnia as of late. The archery pick-a-date, the coffee…*what if he does like me?*

Georgia's words echoed in her head.

*No, he couldn't. Not if I'm hard to love.*

Despite the sinking feeling in her gut, she nodded at him. "Sounds like a plan."

The group headed out into the night. Brisk wind nipped at Zinnia's cheeks. She noticed how Ryan dawdled closest to her, perhaps to soak up her body heat.

Clustered together, the cast and crew walked a good half mile and reached the dorm. A man in a Jack Skellington costume tipped his hat to them at the entrance. Pumpkins and LED candles lined the sidewalk that led up to the building.

"Oh, *Nightmare before Christmas.*" Zinnia elbowed Ryan in a playful gesture. "I don't know if you're going to be able to handle something that scary."

He chuckled. "Listen, after you hear the song 'Kidnapping Santa Claus' when you're five years old, you would be scared of that movie too."

Zinnia offered her arm to him. "Well, allow me to lead you through this very frightening open house."

Ryan slipped his arm into hers, and they ventured through the double doors. Costumed college students encouraged them to meander down the halls and slip into suites to play various spooky-themed games.

Halfway down a hallway filled with fake cobwebs and blacklights, Zinnia's phone vibrated in her pocket. She winced. Clark had sent her an email again, or at least, she assumed so.

Ryan peered down at her. "Doing okay?"

She forced a smile and nodded. "Yep, why don't we go into this suite? Looks like they have a fun game."

The game? Pin the beard on Santa Claus.

From what Zinnia could remember about the film, it took themes from both Christmas and Halloween.

A boy dressed as the ghost Oogie Boogie handed Zinnia a blindfold. She slipped it over her eyes, and someone spun her around. "Beard" in hand, she stumbled forward and probed the wall with her fingertips. Once she landed on what she assumed was Santa's face, she slapped the beard onto the poster.

Right as she did so, several girls screamed.

She slipped off the blindfold and peered into pitch darkness.

Blackout.

Suites in the dorms at this college didn't come with windows, and someone must've shut the door to the room by accident.

Zinnia forced her breathing to go steady.

Last time she'd been in pitch darkness, she had to hold back a scream. In Colorado, after a pageant, her grandmother took her and Georgia to The Cave of the Winds. During a portion of the tour, through the stalactites and stalagmites, they shut off all the lights in the cave.

Darkness swallowed them.

Scared of what Georgia would think, Zinnia held back tears and a shriek that day. Her breaths had grown ragged, though. When the cave turned the lights on again, her grandmother found her in a fetal position on the floor.

Her first panic attack, and Georgia never let her forget it.

Back in the dorm, someone slipped their hand into Zinnia's.

"Let's get to the hallway." Ryan's voice came out calm. Zinnia realized how rapid-fire her breaths came out of her mouth. He could probably hear her from across the room.

He tugged her toward the door, and she heard noises of his other hand fumbling to find the knob. When he did, he twisted it, and green light pierced Zinnia's vision.

She let out a long, relieved exhale. The emergency exit signs in the hallway would provide a sliver of light.

When they reached the hallway, the two of them sat against the wall until Zinnia's breathing steadied.

Ryan hadn't let go of her hand.

"Thanks." She fought the urge to lean her head on his shoulder. "Forgot about power outages."

Phone lights from other students illuminated their faces in the hallway.

"I didn't realize you were afraid of the dark." His fingers squeezed hers.

"Yeah, I'm"—her phone buzzed once more—"afraid of a lot of things."

"Like what?"

Wincing, she recounted for him the job offer from Clark—and with some coaxing, the confrontation from Georgia.

"Oh gosh, Zinnia. I'm so sorry. I know you said you had a strained relationship with Georgia, but I didn't realize she'd said something that hurtful to you. That must've been awful."

"It was, I—"

Her bottom lip quivered. Thank goodness for the dark lighting, that he couldn't see her this vulnerable, this shattered.

"—I'm so afraid that she's right. I know my neighbor Joy told me that's not the case, but what if I'm hard to love, Ryan? What if I deserve to be alone because I'm not demure or quiet enough?"

His hand squeezed hers harder, and he pulled her toward him. His other arm wrapped around her in a hug. They sat suspended in that gesture for a long time. Then he released.

"People don't earn love, Zinnia. That's not how love works. If people think they somehow did enough things to get a significant other, they're sorely mistaken."

Zinnia blinked away an itchiness in her eyes. Ryan continued.

"You want to know the true reason why you haven't found someone yet, Zin?"

She nodded. Then realized he probably couldn't see the motion in the lighting. "Yes."

"Some people walk into jewelry stores, see the price tag on the best diamonds there, and walk away. Do you know why?"

"Why?"

"Because they realize how much value those things have, and they realize they can't afford it. Directors get the best cameras, because they know they will produce the best films, but they realize the price is worth it. Maybe the reason why you haven't found someone is because they see your value and it scares them."

"Well, I *am* scary." Zinnia snickered.

Still, the sentiment from Ryan warmed her heart. Maybe someday someone would appreciate her value.

"Ryan, do you—?" She paused. Could she ask this question? She went for it. "Do you think I'm scary?"

"Not anymore."

Right then, lights flooded the hallway. Power returned to the building.

No, Ryan wasn't scared of Zinnia.

But the feelings stirring in his chest when he looked at her…those, he was a little bit scared of.

As lights brightened the halls of the dorm, he looked down and saw her hand still clasped in his. He quickly let go.

Cheers sounded through the dorm from college students sugared up on Halloween candy.

"Dude." Tristan bounded toward them, a plastic pumpkin on his head. "Perfect timing for a Halloween party, right? I thought maybe we might get to experience a real-life horror flick. Don't worry, I'm here to protect the old people." He bounced on his feet in front of them, punching the air.

"Old people? How old do you think we are?" Zinnia stood, then winced as her knees popped upon standing. She looked up toward the sky. "Very funny."

"Well, at least have some respect for your elders and tell me where you got *that*." Ryan pointed to Tristan's "hat" as it wobbled precariously atop his head. "I think it would suit Zinnia."

She elbowed him.

"He *stole* it." Mariana strode toward them and swiped the pumpkin from Tristan's head. "That was part of the decorations, you delinquent."

"My beautiful hat! Come back!"

The two of them ran off bickering.

Zinnia turned to Ryan, her smile uncertain. "I may have had enough Halloween shenanigans for now."

"We could head downstairs to the lobby. I think I smelled some cookies baking in the dorm kitchen."

"You want to steal cookies?" Zinnia raised a brow.

Ryan clasped a hand to his chest in mock offense. "I want to *nicely ask* for cookies that I think they're making for the open house anyway."

Zinnia led the way down the concrete stairs in the dorm's echoing stairwell. At the bottom, they pushed open the fire door and a blast of warm cookie scent wafted over them.

Zinnia inhaled. "Pumpkin chocolate chip. I'm calling it now."

Ryan wasn't one to doubt Zinnia. Sure enough, her nose guessed correctly. In the dorm's cramped kitchen, a group of five residents had laid out sheet after sheet of plump pumpkin chocolate chip cookies across counters, tables, and even a few chairs.

"Do you want some?" A girl with flour smeared on her cheek gestured to the cookies. "*Someone* did the math wrong on how many we needed." She nudged her friend and giggled.

The math culprit belly laughed, holding up a bowl containing even more cookie dough. "I'm an English major, okay? I didn't know quadrupling the recipe would lead to *this*."

"We're going to break the oven at this rate," another student giggled.

Ryan adopted a serious tone. "Whatever we can do to assist. Purely for the sake of being helpful."

The bakers gave them a paper plate loaded with more cookies than the two of them could ever eat and shooed them toward the rest of the lobby. "Spread the word if you can," the English major said. "We need people to eat these cookies."

Ryan and Zinnia found a seat on a lumpy couch Ryan suspected had occupied this lobby since the seventies. He held out the towering plate of cookies. "Bon appétit."

As they munched on the cookies—still warm, the chocolate chips a bit gooey and the pumpkin flavors perfectly balanced—Ryan wondered if he should return to their earlier conversation.

He hated to think Zinnia found herself unlovable, unlikeable. For him especially, nothing could be farther from the truth.

His ears warmed. That last bit…how would she feel if he said it aloud?

Probably better not to. He'd just told her she deserved someone special. Not a struggling filmmaker with OCD and control issues.

"Hey, director. Hey, Zinnia."

Ryan turned to see Martell approaching. "Hey, man." He held up the plate from where he'd set it on the coffee table in front of them. "Want a cookie?"

"Thanks, director." He snagged a treat.

"You don't have to call me that." Formalities had always made him uncomfortable. "Just Ryan is fine. Especially now that filming is a wrap."

"Sorry, man. I kinda got used to it from talking with my mentor. Mind if I…?" He gestured to the seat across from them.

"Be our guest." Zinnia pointed at the plate. "But only if you help us eat these."

Martell grabbed another cookie and plopped into the upholstered chair.

"You mentioned your mentor." Ryan took a second cookie. "Are they a professor?" It seemed odd that a professor would want to be called "director."

"No, he's a guy I met through some local networking. He likes to keep things really professional, but I've learned a lot from him. He's a real pro. I shared our script with him, and he gave pointers for the shots and sound mixing." Martell polished off his dessert and reached for another.

Martell had shared the script without asking? Of course, Ryan hadn't exactly told them to keep it a secret. And why would it matter? Unless Martell shared the script with one of their competitors, no harm could come from additional insight.

Still, unease stirred in Ryan's gut. "Well, I'm glad you were able to find someone in the industry to learn from. That's super helpful."

"Yeah. Especially with his credentials." Martell leaned forward. "I'm not sure if I should share or not, but his first name is Steve. I bet you can fill in the rest."

Ryan's blood froze in his veins. His thoughts went blank, like when the dorm had lost power.

Steve. His nemesis Steve. Had seen his script. Probably even the newest version. And knew everything about it.

Knowing Steve, he would take every tidbit Martell had given him and work them into his own script. No one would believe Ryan had been the one to come up with them. Instead, it would look like Ryan's team had stolen the work of the far better-known filmmaker.

Zinnia's fingers gripped his arm, and she shot him a wide-eyed look. He nodded back slightly. Yes. There was only one Steve who Martell could be talking about.

"Well." Ryan cleared his throat. "That's great, Martell." He stood. "I, uh, think I have some things I need to take care of." He nodded his goodbye to both of them.

Then, leaving behind the plate of cookies, Martell, and Zinnia, he strode out of the dorm, wondering how on earth he could fix this before Steve ruined everything—again.

# Chapter Eighteen

ZINNIA DIDN'T KNOW THAT SOMEONE COULD put a hamburger into soup form, but Joy informed her that "hamburger soup is the hit of Soup Night at church."

By the time she'd arrived at the church, thirty minutes after the event started, a mere puddle of hamburger soup rested at the bottom of a large crock pot. She moved to the next soup, broccoli cheddar, and ladled herself some into a Styrofoam bowl.

A shadow hovered behind her. Zinnia felt the light tap on her shoulder.

She whirled around and almost spattered Joy with globs of cheese. Joy ducked out of the way, with Justice cradled to her hip. Despite his older age, he sometimes liked to be held.

Zinnia thought back to the hallway with Ryan, when he had his arm banded around her.

*Me too, Justice, me too.*

"What took you so long?" Joy set Justice onto the carpeted floor. He screeched like a pterodactyl and ran toward the dessert table. "Traffic?"

Joy nodded at a crowded circular table. She'd reserved an empty seat for Zinnia.

Zinnia plucked two napkins and a plastic spoon. "Clark. He kept sending me tasks at the end of my workday. He's been trying to ease me into the transition of combining my and Caroline's roles."

She slid into her chair.

Women she didn't recognize helped their children spoon the last of their soups. One sawed a knife into cornbread for her little girl. No doubt, even though Zinnia arrived late, the mothers would eat their soup along with her.

With her plastic spoon, Zinnia stirred into the warm mixture. Steam billowed off of her bowl.

She blew into a bite and shoved the gooey goodness into her mouth. Her stomach buckled.

Oh, yeah, if fall could last forever, she'd never have anything to complain about again.

*Makes you wish that soup season happened all year round.*

"I thought you said that you didn't want to take on Caroline's role."

Joy smudged a napkin on Honor's face. The girl had gotten a little *too* into her tomato soup and grilled cheese.

Funds for soup night at their church would go to Helping Hope's at-risk youth program. The church partnered with them and often sent volunteers their way to help with their after-school events.

"I don't." Zinnia dabbed her own lips with a napkin. "Have no idea how I'm going to tell Clark that, though. He's probably going to fire me if I back out now."

If she didn't tell him, though, he'd make her do Caroline's tasks until the cows came home.

"Hmm."

Joy returned to her own seat.

"What?" Zinnia cocked her head.

"From what I can tell of your life, it may be time to confront some people. Clark, Georgia—you did, after all, have no problem confronting Ryan." Joy winked.

Women around the table shared knowing glances. Oh boy, did Joy spill to them about her crush on the film director?

"That was different. Ryan's different. I gave him bagels."

Ryan didn't have the ability to fire her like Clark could.

*On second thought, he could've "fired" me from the set and hired another actor to replace me.* Because he didn't, this proved he listened to her feedback. So much so that he invited her to help him in post.

Okay, but Ryan didn't say soul-crushing words that bothered her to this day, like Georgia had.

*Then again, you told him some of your most vulnerable secrets, and he didn't run away.*

Zinnia's shoulders slumped. "I know I need to go talk to Clark and Georgia. Clark, because I can't keep getting out of work late. And Georgia, because…"

"Because she needs to know you've been hurt."

"Right." Zinnia sighed. "Joy, I don't know how. Clark and Georgia have the ability to really hurt me. One of them already has."

Joy's spoon dug into her orange-colored soup. Maybe a squash of some sort. She set the utensil down and crushed crackers into the dish.

"That's true, Zinnia. I wish I had the answers for you about how to make it as seamless as possible. I would just tell them the truth and do so in a kind way. That way they can't hold anything against you."

Joy meant Georgia more than Clark in that scenario. From what Zinnia picked up from Clark's stories about his time in boxing rings, Clark could certainly take a hit.

The next day, Thursday, brought in low fog and a nippy breeze.

Soon, Zinnia would have to bundle herself in a thermal winter coat.

She stepped out of her car, breath trailing from her lips. After she sucked in a deep inhale, she set off into the building. Her loud footsteps pounded in her ears as she nodded to the woman at the reception desk and marched toward the elevators.

Up the floors, she practiced her speech in her head.

Peter Parker, the spider plant, heard her variations of the talk last night. When Joy and Zinnia set out to the harvest festival, Ben and the kids had picked out a new pot for him at a craft store. They'd decorated it with finger paint and sketches of flowers.

Once she stepped off the elevator, she beelined to Clark's office, before she could have a chance to psych herself out.

When she reached the door, she paused.

This felt familiar. Phoebe also stepped through a door, twice.

Each time held an uncertain or boring future.

Shaky hands reached for the knob, and she twisted it. The glow from Clark's computer highlighted the red underneath his eyes. Did this man ever sleep? A mounted head of some sort, with spiky antlers, stared down at her. She avoided eye contact with it.

"Sir?"

"Huh? Ah, Zinnia." Clark closed his laptop. "Glad you're here. I wanted to talk with you about some more tasks I need done in the next hour, and—"

Zinnia held up a hand.

"Respectfully, sir, I do have something I need to say before we get to that."

Frozen, Clark stared at her. As though Zinnia had petrified him. He snapped out of the stupor and steepled his hands on his desk. "What is it?"

"Truth be told—"

Her fingernails dug into her arm. She avoided locking eyes with her boss.

"—I never formally gave you an answer about the position merger, but to be honest, I don't think I'm in a place where I'm ready to take on something like that."

During the pause, she waited for his protest. It didn't come.

She trained her glance on another taxidermied item, a rabbit.

"Although I want to do all I can at Helping Hope, I'm noticing that I'm spending a lot of overtime in the additional duties. I've been finding myself overwhelmed and skipping my lunch hour, just to get everything done on time. It does come with a pay raise to compensate for that, but I'm finding my work-life balance is being thrown out the window."

Her voice swelled, more confident now.

"For those reasons, I believe, for now, I cannot accept this merger, and hope you understand."

Now, she glimpsed him. He'd sunk into his seat. His fingers

moved up and down a glass paperweight of a tiger on his desk.

"Zinnia, I—" He cleared his throat.

She steeled herself for the termination.

"I apologize."

Blink, blink went her eyelids. Did she hear him right?

"I was unaware that the additional duties were causing you so much stress. You're also right. You never did give me a final decision on this, so it was wrong of me to be sending you all those tasks when you never agreed to them in the first place."

He dropped his hand from the paperweight.

"You see, sometimes I can forget that not everyone is me. I know that I have a tendency to work myself into the ground, but that doesn't mean I should make all the employees here do the same."

The lump in Zinnia's throat softened.

At last, she could swallow, could breathe.

"Thank you, sir, for understanding. I'll continue to give my full effort in my current duties."

Clark waved his hand back and forth, as if to say, no need.

"Zinnia," he barked suddenly, "what are you doing on Monday morning?"

Zinnia's brows furrowed. "Umm, I'm coming here to work, as I usually do."

"No." He jabbed a finger at her. "You're taking the day off. I don't remember you having a vacation anytime in recent years. And don't worry about it being a part of your PTO. This is on Helping Hope, for keeping you overtime so often."

She gasped. "Oh my goodness, thank you, sir."

"Now, get out of my office. Also." He straightened in his seat. "Ignore my last ten or so emails."

Zinnia exited the office, chest swelling.

That confrontation went much better than expected.

A sinking feeling overtook her gut. She didn't imagine the time she had to talk with Georgia would fare all that well.

Ryan knew energy drinks were a bad idea. Especially three within twenty-four hours. Today, though, he was willing to risk a heart attack.

He'd stayed up late after the night of shooting, organizing all of the files on his computer in preparation for editing. On Wednesday, the day after, he'd had so many photoshoots booked and projects to finish that he'd hardly been able to touch the film. But today, Thursday, he was determined.

Steve may know everything about the script. But filmmakers didn't say "we'll fix it in post" for nothing. With some editing magic, a lot of caffeine, and a whole lot of creativity, Ryan could create something Steve would never see coming.

The computer screen blurred in and out before his eyes. He hadn't quite pulled an all-nighter last night trying to finish all of his work so he could focus on the film, but he'd come close. A man could function on three hours of rest, right?

He took off his glasses, rubbed them with a cloth, and put them back on. Nope, the fuzziness was definitely from lack of sleep, not dirty lenses.

His phone buzzed from somewhere nearby, though the sound was muffled. Buttercup made a small noise of protest and leaped off the desk. Ah. She had been sitting on it. She did like to pretend she was a mother duck and his phone was her egg sometimes.

He took a look at the screen and opened the text message.

**Griffith:** Earth to Ryan. It has been 1800 hours since we last heard from your satellite. Have you been claimed by the editorial vortex?

Ryan snorted. After Griffith had heard about Ryan's dilemma, he'd taken it upon himself to make sure Ryan did important things like eat food.

**Ryan:** Ryan to Earth. Not yet claimed by the void. Consumed sustenance at 800 hours.

He set his phone back down, but the space-themed banter gave him an idea.

Steve had always had a realistic style. What if Ryan differentiated his film with bolder techniques? They were supposed to use some special effects for the competition, after all.

He pulled up clips from well-known big budget CGI movies for reference. He'd wanted to show off practical camera effects and angles, but Steve would be doing that too, especially after talking with Martell. So Ryan needed to bring out the big guns.

As he worked, his mind wandered to Dad's proposition. If Steve did make Ryan's film look like a copy, Ryan's career would be done for. Maybe God had brought along Dad's offer for this very reason.

He remembered Ariana, the last woman he had seriously dated. Her words rang in his head. *"Is this all a game to you?"* Maybe he should stop playing the game, grow up, and make a practical decision.

Was that what Zinnia thought of him too? He'd meant what he said about her. She was a diamond, and he certainly wasn't worthy of pursuing her. But if he did muster up the courage…didn't she deserve better than him clinging to an unattainable dream?

*Not helpful right now.* For now, he needed to do everything he could to edit this film into something they could be proud of. He owed his cast and crew that much.

He didn't stop until the light seeping through a crack in the blinds dimmed and his stomach growled so loudly it nearly drowned out the sound effect he'd been editing. He stretched, back cracking. Okay, maybe a break was in order.

As soon as he stood, Balto leaped to his feet, whining. Right, his dog needed a walk. And Buttercup was meowing for food.

He took care of his pets before feeding himself. His hands shook as he slapped together a sandwich. Energy drinks and coffee on an empty stomach had begun to take their toll.

His phone buzzed in his pocket. He pulled it out while taking a gigantic bite of turkey and cheese.

**Zinnia:** How are you holding up?

He glimpsed his reflection in the shiny door of the microwave. Wow. He was looking pretty rough. He rubbed his chin. And he definitely needed a shave.

**Ryan:** Plugging away. Maybe by tomorrow I'll have something coherent. Would you be interested in giving feedback if so?

While waiting for a reply, he rustled through a cupboard for chips. The bag hadn't even been folded and clipped properly. Either Griffith had been snacking, or Ryan was so dead tired these past few days he hadn't been keeping up with his usual immaculate kitchen routines.

Zinnia's response vibrated on the countertop.

**Zinnia:** Sure, just let me know. I'm happy to help.

Would it be weird to invite her over to his editing suite? The processing speed was better there, and they could make easy edits in real time, unlike if he exported files to a laptop. Seeing the film on the large monitors was so much better than squinting at a laptop screen. Was that a bit forward? It was just for the film, right?

In his distraction, he dropped a chip. Balto snatched it up, crunching loudly while bolting from the kitchen with his prize. Buttercup meowed pathetically at the unfairness of Ryan feeding Balto while she starved to death.

*For the film.* It wasn't weird unless he made it weird. Zinnia probably didn't have a clue he might see her as…well. As someone he would like to be more than just a film buddy.

He could invite Griffith over too, since Griffith and Zinnia were friends. He wouldn't want her to feel strange or uncomfortable, so having a third party might make things less awkward.

Maybe he would confirm with Griffith first.

**Ryan:** Thanks, I'll keep you updated. How are things going with your boss?

*Chicken.* But who knew when the edits would be ready to share anyway? He would invite her once the project was close enough to something presentable that he wouldn't die of embarrassment.

As she updated him on her successful talk with Clark, he finished his dinner and headed back to the editing suite, interspersing texts with Zinnia with texts with Griffith.

**Ryan:** Hey, man. Wanna hang out at my place tomorrow while you work?
**Griffith:** I was going to write at She Brews for a while. I've got another play I'm working on.

Ryan spun in his chair. What would entice Griffith?

**Ryan:** I also have coffee. And chips. And you can raid my fridge.

Griffith didn't respond for a bit, so Ryan focused on editing and on congratulating Zinnia for standing up to Clark. Finally, Griffith's message popped up.

**Griffith:** Why are you trying to bribe me?
**Ryan:** Can't I just like hanging out with my bro? As long as you don't mind if Zinnia shows up at one point.

The dots appeared and disappeared.

**Griffith:** You want me there as your wingman, don't you?
**Ryan:** I absolutely do not. I want you there as a witness in case she tries to murder me for bad edits. We're going over the film.
**Griffith:** Okay, okay. I do like the writing vibes at your place. Need me to pick up a bouquet for your date?
**Ryan:** If you do, I will never share my buffalo chicken dip again.
**Griffith:** Now that's uncalled for. See you tomorrow.

Ryan let out a breath. Back to editing. Hopefully he could create something he would be proud to show to Zinnia.

And something Steve couldn't claim he'd copied.

# Chapter Nineteen

On Friday evening, Clark let Caroline and Zinnia out two hours early. He claimed he would post listings for Caroline's job soon, since Zinnia could not manage the workload of two people.

After thanking him several times, Zinnia scheduled a nail appointment for Monday, her day off. Since Ryan wouldn't let them change much about their appearance during their filming, she'd been long overdue for a mani and pedi.

Out early from the office, she followed her GPS to Ryan's apartment, the location of his editing suite. He'd texted her earlier that day that he'd made good progress on editing and was ready for her opinion if she wanted to swing by today.

Along the way, she picked up a dozen apple cider donuts from a harvest festival mid-route.

When she arrived, she rapped her knuckles against the door.

The door swung open.

It wasn't Ryan.

Griffith beamed at her and motioned her in. "Before Buttercup can get out."

"Griffith what are you—?" She stepped inside and set the bag of donuts onto the kitchen table. A ball of fluff rubbed against her legs. Ah, the Buttercup she'd heard so much about.

"Writing a play and find that Ryan's apartment space helps with the creative juices." Griffith returned to his spot on the couch. "My studio feels cramped and doesn't help with getting into the writing zone."

Buttercup meowed at her.

"Hey, there, sweetheart."

Zinnia bent down and stroked the silky fur. She sat on a couch.

Buttercup climbed into her lap and purred.

"Griffith, can you get the door—Oh, hi, Zinnia."

Ryan emerged from one of the rooms. He rubbed the dark circles underneath his eyes. Zinnia prayed that Griffith somehow had the sense to bring the poor director some food. If not, cider donuts would have to do for now.

"Oh my goodness." Ryan's face scrunched at Buttercup. "Of course my cat would like you, but not the one who feeds her."

Zinnia shrugged. "She has good taste, and good judgment."

This made both Ryan and Griffith laugh. Griffith had launched himself from the couch and rummaged through the grocery bag that held the box of donuts.

Balto, a large husky, made a small "boof" sound from underneath the kitchen table. Perhaps he hoped Griffith would drop a morsel of donut by accident. Cinnamon sugar from the pastry littered the table, since Griffith failed to grab a napkin or plate to catch the crumbs. She watched as Ryan's shoulders hiked up to his ears.

Right, he hated messy things.

"Speaking of good judgment." Zinnia figured a subject change could assuage Ryan's anxieties. "Why don't we take a look at the edits you've done so far?"

Ryan's body un-tensed.

"Sure. Follow me to the editing suite."

"Leave that door open, you two." Griffith wagged a finger at the both of them.

Heat filled Zinnia's cheeks. Based on how red Ryan's face turned, he'd been feeling something similar.

"Of course, Griff." Zinnia slapped him on the shoulder, a little hard, a warning not to say more. "We have you as a chaperone, so we'll be good."

In a quick motion, Ryan rushed into the room and waved her in. When she stepped inside, she took in the large computers, enormous desk, and even the foam sound absorbers he'd placed on the walls.

"Impressive."

Ryan ducked his chin. "Right this way to the computer."

He pulled up another rolling chair for Zinnia. She couldn't imagine why he'd have two in here, as he preferred to work alone. Maybe Griffith and Ryan would sometimes work side by side in this room.

"Okay." Ryan's fingers shook as he tapped the mouse and pulled up the video editing program. "Here it goes."

Based on the shakiness of his breath, Zinnia would have to soften any blows she'd give him.

As the movie played, however, she winced.

Ryan needed work on editing.

A few seconds in, she piped up, in the meekest voice she could muster. "Umm, Ryan, was that a screen wipe? To transition into the next scene?"

"Interesting, right? Most people just transition from scene to scene with no wipes whatsoever. This will make us *different*."

Her nose wrinkled. "I'm sorry, but the last time I saw one of those was when I watched the Star Wars prequels."

"Do you like the Star Wars prequels?"

"Joy and I call Episode II *Attack of the Clowns*, because it's so ridiculous."

"Oh."

His shoulders drooped. Pity dug into her stomach. Maybe the video would get better?

It didn't. Halfway through the first scene, the tone of the video turned blue. Everyone's skin paled and her mind couldn't help but race back to a certain film about vampires.

"Umm, Ryan, have you seen the *Twilight* franchise?"

"What? Oh, you mean the blue tones. Well, I'm trying to convey that the scene is sad by the color. It's symbolism, you see. Steve would never think to do something like this, so we'll get ahead of the game by being *unique*."

Steve, again?

Granted, she'd subjected him to plenty of rants about Georgia, so of course he'd have fair game in complaining about the filmmaker Steve. Did he make all of these weird edits to avoid being like his nemesis?

"Oh my gosh." Zinnia smacked her forehead. "Ryan, are those artificial lens flares?"

"Yeah! I was worried someone wouldn't notice those, so I'm glad you did, but I was taking a tip from J.J. Abrams. On the sets of *Star Trek*, he'd have people hold up pieces of glass so lens flares would be showing up in the movie, giving the feel of space."

"Okay, number one—"

Zinnia held up a finger.

"—this film isn't set in space. Number two, J.J. Abrams made legit lens flares. It's very obvious that in this editing software you clicked some button that said 'artificial lens flare.' It makes no sense in this scene to have these, Ryan."

In the dark room, Ryan slumped into his chair. "You hate it, don't you?"

Zinnia chewed on her lip. No, she didn't. The dialogue came through really well on screen, and Ryan *had* made some good editing choices. How could she convey that to him without hurting his feelings?

Grandma didn't train her well for this.

"How about we take a walk, Ryan? Get some fresh air and go leaf hunting?"

"Leaf hunting?"

"We'll see who can find the best leaves. I know that sometimes getting outside can spark some ideas."

Ryan paused for a few seconds. Then shrugged. "I'll take anything at this point. I've been listening to the same clips for hours."

As they stepped outside of the apartment, sunlight pierced Ryan's eyes. He squinted for several minutes until his eyesight adjusted.

"Okay, so." Zinnia bent down and picked up a green leaf, half of it consumed by red. "Why don't you tell me why you did all those weird edits? Because I've seen your stuff before, Ryan, and that's not your usual style."

He sighed and twirled the stem of a yellow leaf in his fingertips. "Steve got a hold of our script. An accident, from one of our crew members spilling too much info to him—you know how he can be. Really has a sway over people."

Zinnia had never run into Steve. From her encounters with Georgia's manipulative words, though, it wouldn't take much of a stretch of the imagination.

"He apparently borrowed several elements from ours, and I'm afraid the judges are going to think we copied him."

Zinnia was pretty sure Ryan explained bits and pieces of this. He'd lost so much sleep that he may have forgotten.

She scooped up a leaf from the crosswalk. This one made her think of a tie-dye t-shirt, with all its yellows, oranges, browns, and greens.

"You're worried history is going to repeat itself? Since he's stolen from you before, and no one would believe you then?"

"Well, I didn't exactly have any proof. No backup files, since he told me to scrap the project. I know better now."

Which was why he acted so meticulous all the time.

As she picked up a red maple leaf, an idea struck her. "Ryan, do you know how many versions of *Cinderella* there are out there?"

He frowned as an acorn dropped from a tree above and plunked against the sidewalk. "At least five."

"Ha. Yes, you're technically correct. There are hundreds, thousands even, spanning centuries. And you know what? People love every variation of the story. You know why?"

His thumbs rubbed the stem of the leaf in his hand. He hadn't let go of this one yet. "No."

"Because they each are a different take on the story. A different angle. Even if you and Steve have some similarities between your movies, you will never have the same film. Because you edit differently, direct differently."

Ryan's face brightened. "You think so?"

"Yes, so why force yourself to make your movie so different, just to avoid being like his? If anything, you should be fully you in your edits. Make something you're proud of."

Ryan considered this for a few moments. Then the leaf fell from his fingertips.

"Okay. I think I have some ideas for changes we can do to the edits." He nodded back at the apartment complex. "Ready to head back?"

"Yes, if—" She raised a finger. "You get some food in you. You look like you're about to fall over."

Six donuts consumed by Ryan later, the two of them headed back to the editing suite.

Since Ryan's film was not about aliens, space ninjas, or teenage vampires, he took out the screen wipes, lens flares, and blue tint while Zinnia kept an eye out for scene continuity.

"The scenes you've edited together, and the raw camerawork in them…" Zinnia tapped her finger on the desk and ran it down a list of requirements for the contest. "Those are fantastic, and you got everything in there. Including 'plethora.'"

He sensed the 'but' coming, and feared he knew exactly where it was going.

"I think when you remove all of the extra bits, the script and camera angles can really shine. And then you can use editing to highlight the good things that are already there." Her smile brightened the dark editing suite. "That's what you have that Steve, I'm guessing, does not. A solid foundation of God-given talent."

Wait, she hadn't pointed out how awful he'd done? Maybe he

hadn't correctly guessed what she was going to say after all. His heart—and the tips of his ears—warmed. "I hope so."

"Well, I hear your lead actress is pretty great." Zinnia smirked and flipped her hair dramatically with a teasing wink. "So the film can't be too bad."

"She is pretty great," Ryan agreed, his tone more serious. "I couldn't have done it without her."

Zinnia looked away and cleared her throat, picking up the paper. "Should we finish what we have so far?"

He clicked Play once again, letting the last thirty seconds of the film run their course, until the clip ended with Zinnia's character reaching to open the door.

Zinnia sat back in the chair Griffith often occupied. She pulled up one leg and rested her chin on her knee, a more relaxed pose than he usually saw from her. She seemed…comfortable. Like she wasn't afraid he would judge her or critique her.

Or maybe he was reading too much into it.

"So." She hugged her leg. "About that ending."

"Yeah." He took a deep breath. "About that."

In college, the films that won the most awards tended to be "thought-provoking" and "deeply moving," which Ryan quickly learned meant "weird" and "sad." He did enjoy a good weird, sad movie. But was that the right call for their film?

"What would you do?" He gestured to the screen. "If you had to make the call?"

She shook her head. "I don't think I'm the person to ask. The part of me that hopes…well, that part wants the happy ending." She lowered her gaze. "It makes me feel like there might be a chance for me, too. Even if that's a bit silly, considering this is just a film, not real life."

His hand drifted across the desk to cover hers. "I don't think that's silly. What else are films for, if not to expand our minds to possibilities and encourage us in our real lives?"

She looked down at their hands, and even in the dim light, he thought he could see a faint blush spill across her cheeks. Oops. He didn't want to be too forward. He removed his hand, reaching for the mouse instead.

"You're right. But that doesn't always mean a happy ending." She sighed and looked up at the ceiling. "I've been praying, but I can't say I've gotten any answers for you."

He drummed his fingers on the desk, frowning at his keyboard. A divine revelation would be nice, but he knew God didn't often work that way. "I'll keep working on the edits leading up to the end and leave it for last. If He gives you any hints, let me know."

"I will. I know I'm not a whole lot of help when it comes to editing, but if you just need someone to bounce ideas off." She shrugged, putting both feet back on the ground as she swiveled in her chair to face him. "I'm here for you."

*I'm here for you.*

What a long way they'd come from Ryan being too afraid of her to even say "hello" properly in a coffee shop. He could hardly remember why he'd been so foolish now.

He might not have any right to say anything to Zinnia…but they sure worked well as a team. He would be happy to spend a lot more Friday evenings side by side in an editing suite.

"I appreciate it, Zinnia. I—"

"Knock knock!" Griffith's voice interrupted him.

Ryan swiveled toward the doorway, where Griffith stood, fist raised as he knocked on the doorframe.

"It's getting late, man. You going to feed your guests?" He rubbed his belly. "If not, I might need to head out for sustenance before I waste away."

Ryan pushed down his annoyance at the interruption—as well as an unexpected wave of embarrassment. It wasn't like Griffith walked in on him actually saying whatever sappy thing had been about to tumble out of his mouth.

In fact, Griffith might have saved him from making a fool of himself.

He rolled his eyes and waved his friend away. "Zinnia already brought us donuts, you black hole."

"Donuts are not dinner." Griffith gestured toward Zinnia. "Are you really going to let a lady starve?"

As if on cue, her stomach emitted a small growling noise. Her hand flew to her abdomen. "Whew. Excuse Mr. Stomach, apparently he has a lot to say."

"Well." Ryan glanced at the time on his desktop. "It is past dinner time." Way past dinner time. Most places would be closed, and he didn't have the groceries to make anything for three people. "Anyone up for delivery Chinese food? Director's treat, of course. Both of you have been amazing on this project." He cocked his head toward Zinnia. "Or is there something else Mr. Stomach would prefer?"

Zinnia laughed, but she looked down at her phone. "I would love to stay, but it's getting pretty late. I think I'd better head home." She pointed an accusing finger at Ryan. "And once you eat, you had better head to bed. You need sleep to do your best editing work."

"Yes, ma'am."

She turned that sharp finger toward Griffith. "You make sure he actually listens."

Griffith put his hands up. "I'll do my best."

After Ryan and Griffith had chowed down on Chinese food and both Zinnia and Griffith left, Ryan stood in the doorway of the editing suite, staring toward the dark monitors.

His father's voice echoed in his mind. *The twenty-eighth, Ryan. Have an answer.*

Hope was a nice thought. A nice feeling. But did hope win awards?

Ryan did not have an answer.

# Chapter Twenty

"I APOLOGIZE IN ADVANCE FOR MY feet."

Zinnia told the receptionist this when she entered the nail spa. The receptionist chuckled and tapped a clipboard holding a sign-in sheet. After Zinnia signed her name, the receptionist gestured at a wall full of shelves. Nail polish bottles lined each row.

"Go ahead and pick your color for your nails and for your toes."

"Will do." Zinnia saluted the small woman. "Also, thank you so much for fitting me in during an unusual time. I'll be back to my normal schedule next month."

Thank goodness they could still set her up with her favorite nail technician today, Heidi.

Zinnia thumbed her chin as she gazed at the colors. Would the sassy Heidi yell at her for choosing fall colors just like everybody else? Zinnia's fingers clasped around two nail polish bottles, one a deep autumnal orange, and the other, a moss green.

Oh well, if Heidi felt snappy today, Zinnia would have to deal. That woman had a precision when it came to cuticles like no other.

Moments later, Heidi approached. Auburn flyaway hairs formed static on her scalp. From what Zinnia could observe at the near-full stations and foot pools, several people had booked last-minute appointments today.

"What gives?" Zinnia asked as Heidi led her to a pedicure pool. "It's not Homecoming today for any schools, is it?"

Heidi shrugged and motioned Zinnia to sit in the cushy chair. "Some days can be unpredictable. You're right about Homecoming, though. This past weekend, we were slammed with appointments."

When Heidi turned on the water, she asked Zinnia to dip her feet in to test the temperature.

"May be a little too hot today, Heidi."

"Not a problem." Heidi flipped a switch to add some cool water to the bath. "You going for your usual? Or you feeling like a treat-yourself kind of day?" Heidi perched a hand on her hip.

Zinnia slipped her feet into the water and rolled up her leggings so her calves could get immersed. Heidi dumped what looked like bath salts into the mixture. A blue light glowed underneath the bubbling water.

"Hmm, I'm not sure."

Heidi switched on the massage settings of the chair. Rollers kneaded Zinnia's back.

"Would you mind showing me the menu? That way I can take a look at the different types of pedicures and decide? We'll do the same manicure as always."

"Not a problem."

A side table perched next to the massage chair. Heidi banged open a drawer and pulled out a laminated slip of paper. Zinnia perused the itcms.

PEDICURE

Includes nail shaping/buffing/trimming, cuticle service, callus exfoliation, lotion massage, hot towel, and your choice of polish.

ZEN PEDICURE

Includes everything included in Pedicure (see above) with sugar scrub, lotion massage, hot towel wrap, and choice of polish.

TRANQUILITY PEDICURE

Includes everything mentioned in the Zen Pedicure (see above) with mud mask for feet and calves.

BLISS PEDICURE

Includes everything mentioned in the Tranquility Pedicure (see above) with a paraffin treatment and lower leg and foot massage with heated rocks.

Prices were listed at the bottom of the menu, with the Bliss being the most expensive.

Zinnia often went for the Tranquility Pedicure. Today, though, hot rocks sounded like pure heaven.

Right as she went to tell Heidi which item she preferred, she spotted a flash of platinum blonde hair.

No…

Georgia gawked at her from the door.

*Does she go to this spa?*

It would amount to a decent drive for Georgia. However, the two of them had visited this place since their teen years. Every Homecoming and prom and pageant necessitated a stop over, and a mani and pedi.

Something about the fact that Georgia still visited this place swelled Zinnia's chest with hope.

Face sheet-white, Georgia spun around and headed out the doors.

Without a moment's hesitation, Zinnia bolted out of the pool and followed behind her younger sister. Brisk breezes froze Zinnia's toes as she raced outside and called after Georgia—who had advanced past the doors of three storefronts.

"Georgia, wait."

"I have nothing to say to you."

Still, Georgia had frozen in place, as if waiting.

"Well, that's probably due to the fact that you showed up to my house, said everything you needed to say, and broke my plant."

In a slow, deliberate motion, Georgia spun around. She arched a brow. "Sorry about the plant."

*Oh my goodness.*

Georgia never apologized. Zinnia's mind reeled for any time in her life when the younger sister ever uttered so much as a "pardon me." Images stopped at the one time Georgia gave Zinnia a bloody nose and said sorry, just so Zinnia wouldn't tell their grandmother what happened.

"And I'm sorry for the fact that you may have felt hurt by

whatever I said. I still feel at peace about that conversation, so if you're holding any grudges, that's a *you* issue." Georgia shoved her hands into the pockets of her peacoat. "Well, I said sorry, so now you have to forgive me for everything that happened that day."

Heat simmered underneath Zinnia's skin.

That didn't count as an apology. Grandma drilled it into them that if someone said something along the lines of, "Well sorry you feel that way," that it was someone trying to get out of uttering a real apology.

Georgia had no idea about how much hurt she'd caused Zinnia. Or about how Zinnia stayed awake an extra hour each night, replaying the conversation over and over. Even if a relationship with Ryan *did* work out, she imagined it would take years to detangle from the lies Georgia told her.

What would Joy tell her to do in this situation? What about Ryan, what would he say?

*They'd probably say to forgive...but also to implement boundaries.*

"Georgia, I—" Zinnia sucked in a breath and blew it out. Cold smoke trailed from her lips. "I forgive you for hurting me—a lot—and for destroying my property."

A snort sounded from Georgia. "What else, Zin?"

Zinnia blinked several times. "What do you mean 'what else'?"

"You insulted my relationship with Matt. I think that more than earned my reaction, and an apology from you."

Roaring filled Zinnia's ears.

*Is she serious?*

Georgia's apology meant nothing then. She justified everything she said before, due to a perceived slight—that Zinnia hadn't even said to her. Aunt Millie conveyed some interpretation of text messages to Georgia, and Georgia flew into a rage without talking through the words with Zinnia in a calm fashion.

Again, what would Joy tell her to do?

*She'd probably say...that the situation is out of my control. That*

*I did everything I could. That I'm blameless in this instance, and I should leave the rest in the Lord's hands.*

Swelling with a newfound confidence, Zinnia's body relaxed. "Georgia, I'm sorry for any words I said that hurt you."

No "buts."

No "you made me feel this way, so I acted out."

No "but that wasn't my intention." Because although it *wasn't* Zinnia's scheme to make her sister suffer, words still hurt nonetheless.

"Hmph."

Georgia upturned her nose. Next to her, a donut shop advertised made-from-scratch pastries. In addition to the pedicure and manicure, Zinnia vowed to stop in there for a treat. After this conversation, she could use any mental boost that she could get.

"I think, Zin, that we really should limit how much conversation we exchange between us. That way you don't hurt me again."

Zinnia's jaw sank.

She clamped her mouth shut. She'd have to pick and choose her battles with her sister, no matter how wrongly Georgia interpreted the situation.

"You know what, Georgia, I think that's a good plan. We could both use a little space from one another and come back when we feel we've healed. In the meantime—"

Zinnia gestured over her shoulder at the nail spa.

"Would you want to join me for a manicure or pedicure? My treat."

This appeared to slacken Georgia's features for a few seconds. She snapped to attention and shook her head.

"I don't take bribes for bad behavior, besides…" She sighed. "I think I need to have a talk with Matt about some things, so even if you weren't being manipulative, Zin, I don't have the time anyway."

Coldness stung Zinnia's eyes. Still, in the midst of her sorrow—perhaps from the loss of a sister she once knew—hope sparked in her chest. Maybe Georgia would confront Matt after all. She just wouldn't admit in person to Zinnia about what she would plan to discuss with her husband.

Zinnia stared down at her toes. They'd turned blue. "Well, suit yourself, Georgia."

She whirled around and re-entered the nail salon. Heidi lingered by the door. The nail technician had backed away a few inches, but Zinnia wondered if she'd listened in on their conversation. If she knew anything about Heidi, the woman loved her gossip.

"Sorry about that." Zinnia's finger wiped moisture off her upper lip. Her nose got a little runny in the cold temperatures. "I'll go back to the pedicure pool now."

As she meandered back, weight lifted off her chest.

Yes, when she got home, she might cry about the conversation with Georgia. For now, though, she felt a million pounds lighter.

"Actually, Heidi." Zinnia returned to her seat and slipped her feet into the pool. Yikes, the water soared in temperature now. "I think I'm going to go with the Bliss Pedicure, the most expensive one."

Heidi cocked her head and pulled a clay mask and sugar scrub out of the drawer. "You sure?"

"Yeah." Zinnia watched Georgia cross the street from the tinted spa windows. "Today feels like a treat-yourself kind of day."

"Okay Andy, now tell Caroline your corniest joke."

Ryan bent his knees, lining up the best camera angle.

Sunlight filtered through bright orange foliage onto the carpet of leaves beneath, where Andy and Caroline posed for engagement photos.

Caroline had received a day off from her boss, so on this Monday, Ryan praised God for the limited number of people frequenting the park in the middle of a work and school day. Fewer people he would have to edit out of the background later.

"Uh, okay." Andy faced Caroline. "What do you call a single kernel of corn?"

Her lips twitched. "What *do* you call a single kernel of corn?"

"A unicorn."

Caroline groaned, and Ryan snapped pictures as Andy chuckled and Caroline made a face at him.

"I've got another one." Andy held up Caroline's hand, so the ring featured prominently in the shot.

The man was a natural. Who knew?

Maybe it was an artist thing. Since Andy was an illustrator, he too had an eye for artistic angles and focal points.

"Ryan has created a monster." But Caroline was smiling. The sort of genuine smile Ryan loved to photograph.

"What did the corn cob say when he received a compliment?"

Caroline giggled. "You realize 'corny joke' doesn't mean it has to be about corn."

"Let the man speak! This is comedy gold." Ryan's shutter clicked. Leaves rustled beneath his feet as he moved to a new angle. "I'm taking notes. Also, can you turn this way a bit?"

The couple did as he asked. "All right." Caroline raised an eyebrow. "What did the corn cob say when it received a compliment, Andy?"

He beamed, already proud of the punchline. "Aw, shucks."

Ryan and Caroline both groaned.

The photo shoot wrapped up with a few more poses, some incorporating leaves or a tree. Ryan liked to give people options. He didn't have to say much to elicit smiles from the happy couple.

His chest panged. One day, he hoped he would be the subject of photos like these, with someone looking at him the way Caroline looked at Andy.

Before he could stop it, his mind filled in Zinnia smiling up at him.

*Whoa, there. Slow your roll, brain.*

Ryan rested the camera on his shoulder. "Anything else you guys would like while we're here? I think we got some good closeups of the ring and some good couple pictures, but we can always add some more poses or angles if you'd like."

"I think those were great." Caroline squeezed Andy's hand. "The ones you showed us look amazing already, and I'm sure the others came out just as well. You're really good at what you do."

His heart swelled with pride. "Well, with subjects like these, you two make it easy."

Andy gestured to Ryan's gear. "Need any help carrying anything?"

"Nah. I'm used to toting everything around." He powered off the camera and screwed on the lens cap. "Besides, wouldn't want to give you an edge in basketball. I see you, trying to lift more weights."

Andy grinned. "I don't need an edge with—"

"No no no." Caroline waved her hands in the air, laughing. "Don't you two get started on the basketball banter. It never ends."

Caroline and Andy waited for Ryan to pack up his equipment and joined him walking back toward the parking lot.

"You're doing that film competition, right?" Andy asked. "How's that going?"

"Oh, yeah. Zinnia's been telling me about that." Caroline's fashion boots kicked through a pile of leaves, and she bounced on her toes. "I'm so glad she's getting to act."

Ryan swallowed. A reminder of how much was riding on this film, not just for him, but for Zinnia as well.

"I think I finished editing last night. It's due tomorrow night, so I'll probably give it one last look before sending it off." Or ten last looks. Either way, he wanted to make sure he turned in their best work.

After that, the crew planned to visit a harvest festival on Friday to celebrate the completion of the project. Ryan looked forward to picking some apples or maybe riding a hayride with a certain actress.

"So you decided on an ending?" At Ryan's look of surprise,

Caroline explained, "Zinnia mentioned there were options."

"Yeah. I think so." He took a deep breath. "I figured I would be realistic." With Dad breathing down his neck, Steve being Steve, Zinnia's issues with her sister…the happy ending felt out of reach. "I chose the melancholy but thought-provoking ending."

Caroline and Andy glanced at each other. Ryan wished he could tell what they were thinking.

"Remember back when Caroline and I had that picture book project," Andy began slowly, "and all of you pitched in?"

"Of course." Ryan had helped them with publicity and getting footage of their launch event.

"I think what really brought people together was the aspect of hope in the book." Andy shrugged. "I don't know a lot about film, though. I'm sure it's different than children's books."

Caroline tapped her lips. "Didn't something similar happen with Liv and Elijah last year when they were entering that music festival? They had to decide between playing what they thought the crowd wanted to hear, and the music on their hearts."

"And everyone loved Griffith's play last winter for its uplifting message," Andy added. "I'm sure a Christmas play is a different thing, though."

"And with every project, each of us has found hope in our own lives." Caroline hugged Andy's arm. "It's amazing the things God can do. The people He can bring into your life when you least expect it."

Ryan's eyes ping ponged between the two of them. "Are you guys trying to say something?"

*Crunch, crunch* went the leaves under Caroline's boots. Ryan got the impression she would be stomping on them if she didn't feel the need to act with at least a little decorum. "Well, I don't think we're in a position to say anything. We don't know film." She fixed him with a penetrating look. "But you do. So I think the real question is, if there were no competition, no critics, nothing riding on this project—what ending would *you* choose?"

Ryan slowed until he realized he'd come to a halt. His ears seemed to ring, as his myriad thoughts narrowed into a single revelation.

*He* was Phoebe, the main character of the film. God had placed two doors in front of him.

Did he trust God enough to choose the one that frightened him?

"I…I would choose the happy ending. The hopeful one."

Andy pointed. "Looks like that's your answer."

"I have a little over twenty-four hours." Ryan's heart rate revved to light speed. "I don't know if I can…well, if I…" He squared his shoulders. "I need to get to work, now."

"Go!" Caroline waved him off. "Run! Don't worry about us or the pictures or anything. We'll tell Griffith to bring you some food later."

"Right. Okay, I—"

"Go!" Caroline laughed.

He would. He would go, and he would trust God.

Camera equipment and all, he ran for his car.

He would pull an all-nighter. He would make this film as close to perfect as he could. He would use his own style, not trying to be anyone else, and use the talent God gave him.

One more thought brought a smile to his face.

He would surprise Zinnia with the happy ending at the film festival. Because whether they won or not, he was putting this in God's hands. Regardless of his own future, he was determined to do whatever it took to make sure Zinnia found the happy ending she deserved.

# Chapter Twenty-One

Zinnia never imagined she'd end up on a hayride with a bunch of Disney princesses. Then again, she had experienced quite a strange autumn.

"Hmm." Zinnia tapped her chin and stared at the two actors, dressed as princesses, across from her. They perched on hay bales. "Elsa and Belle?"

Before Ryan, beside Zinnia, could nod, "Elsa" spoke up.

"For copyright purposes, on the farm, we go by Ice Princess and Rose Princess. Since Belle, I mean Rose Princess, is often seen with a rose in her movie."

The farm—a half hour drive from Roseville—hosted a Pirates and Princesses weekend for families. Actors were paid to reenact some of their favorite roles from popular movies. Before they climbed onto the hayride, Zinnia spotted a Black Beard and Moana.

Activities at the farm included wine tastings, corn mazes, a large slide that sloped down a hill, and, of course, a hayride.

Tangerine glows from the sun highlighted the white in Ice Princess's hair.

"So, Ice Princess." Ryan cleared his throat. "You don't have to act in character around us, by the way. I know you've been doing it for hours on end for the kids."

"Eight hours." Ice Princess massaged her calves. She wore a pair of light blue leggings today. "It's why we're all on the hayride—hi." She waved to some kids as the hayride carts trundled past them. "We all needed a break."

The other princesses, and a lone pirate, murmured their assent.

On the grass below, kids bellowed at Ice Princess to sing some of their favorite songs from the movie. She regaled them with a few notes and then slumped back against the railing of the truck.

"That looks exhausting." Zinnia's fingers rubbed up and down her jeans. Today she'd opted for a light brown sweater that spent most of the year at the top of her closet, untouched. "You both have to be way younger than us to have stamina like that."

Rose Princess laughed into her white-gloved hands. "Oh, hon." Her tongue clicked against the roof of her mouth. "Ice Princess and I are a year apart, right, Ice Princess? Thirty-four and thirty-five?"

This slackened Zinnia's jaw. A cold breeze nipped at her cheeks. She found herself leaning closer to Ryan. To her surprise, he followed suit and pressed his shoulder against hers.

"We started doing this for birthday parties for our daughters." Ice Princess adjusted her sheer cape. Sitting on the hay bale must've made the garment pull hard against her neck. "Then we auditioned for a group that hires out actors to play roles for birthday parties and events like this. We've been doing it ever since."

Grandma and Georgia always spoke of thirty as some sort of harrowing age. That once someone reached it, they would do everything in their power to implement skin care routines, to make themselves forever appear twenty.

"I'm sure you auditioned for it before you reached the age of thirty, though," Zinnia offered.

Possible that the Princess Party agency kept them out of pity.

"Nope." Rose Princess played with a ruffle on her yellow dress. "We auditioned last year. In fact, speaking of auditions, they have been looking for Sleeping Beauty."

Ice Princess lifted a finger. "'Sleeping Princess.'"

"Right, sorry. Anyway, if you added a little curl to your hair, you could be the spitting image of her. Any chance that you act? Our director has been looking for the right one for a while."

Zinnia drew her knees close to her chest.

"I—" Her mind echoed back to the tearoom with Georgia. Her younger sister drilled the importance of skincare routines into her.

"Don't you think I look a little old for that?"

As the cart hit a bump, the two princesses exchanged eyebrow-raised expressions.

Rose Princess plucked a hay straw out of her brown wig. "Do you mind telling us how old you are?"

Zinnia stared at her brown boots. "Twenty-seven."

"Oh, really?" Ice Princess perked up at this and played with a long braid on her shoulder. "I was going to say maybe twenty-two."

"Twenty-one," Rose Princess offered.

Ice Princess let go of the braid. Everyone clung to the railing as the car rolled down a steep hill. "Although, yes, we do have a few princesses who are in their teens or early twenties, most of us are moms or ladies in our thirties. Makeup does wonders, and as long as you sing their favorite songs and make their birthday parties great, kids don't care."

Hope glowed in Zinnia's chest, like the dipping sun behind the cornfields.

"Life doesn't end when you're twenty." Rose Princess's shoulders relaxed when they reached the bottom of the hill. "In fact, I would argue, that's right about when it starts."

The hayride returned to the line. By now, children and families filled the spaces between the stanchions. The princesses waved to Zinnia and Ryan as they dismounted and swept away to join the children in the queue for pictures.

"What was that about?" Ryan stepped off the ride and offered a hand to help Zinnia off.

She took it. Once she reached the grass, they hadn't let their fingers un-twine. Warmth filled her chest.

"Sorry, Ryan." Her hand slackened, but he didn't release. She clasped his hand again. "I'm still detangling from a lot of what Georgia said to me. I apologize if it takes too long, and you don't think it's worth the effort, being around me, and—"

Something pecked her forehead.

Oh.

*Oh!*

Ryan had kissed her hair.

A blush filled his cheeks. His eyes went wide as if he realized what he'd done. "Oh, umm, that was a friendly, comforting gesture?"

Zinnia smirked.

Given all the time they'd spent this past weekend on edits, their conversation had ventured into relationship territory more than once. It had been only a matter of time…

Would she let him continue to venture into the unknown? Even if that meant she would lose some control over the situation?

She squeezed his hand tighter.

"I could use all the comforting gestures I can get."

This sent Ryan laughing. He tugged her toward a corn maze and planted one more kiss on top of her forehead. Maybe in here, they could talk about what exactly they could label the chemistry between them.

"As far as Georgia goes—"

These words from Ryan deadened her spirit. So much for talking about the two of them, instead of her crazy younger sister.

"—things like that take years to recover from. I've had friends who dated narcissists and they blamed themselves for years for what happened in those relationships. How much harder would it be to get back on your feet when a family member exhibits the same behavior?"

A narcissist?

Would Zinnia classify Georgia as that?

With no professional diagnosis, she couldn't exercise certainty. Nevertheless, many of Georgia's behaviors lined up with that. At the very least, Georgia could use a good dose of therapy to work through her issues.

"You're not mad at me then?" Zinnia's voice cracked as their boots sloshed through a muddy patch. Rain turned the ground to mush this time of year. "Because usually this is the part where someone runs away. When they think I'm too much to handle."

"I'm not going anywhere, Zin."

Ryan's footsteps faltered. Zinnia stared at him, then ahead, and discovered why. A man stood amongst a gaggle of fans, and the man's nose wrinkled into a sneer.

"Ryan!"

"Steve," Ryan said through gritted teeth.

"Good to see you." Steve's index finger and thumb ran over a brittle cornstalk leaf. "Did I hear right that you're going to the festival next week?" He elbowed one of the fans closest to him and gestured to Ryan. "This guy used to make the cutest little films back in the day. Good to see him getting his feet wet."

Anger sizzled underneath Zinnia's fingertips on Ryan's behalf.

She watched as his frame buckled underneath Steve's words. Like her with Georgia, it could take Ryan years to unravel from all the knots of doubt Steve placed on him.

Zinnia cleared her throat. "You must be Steve."

"Ah." Steve's spine straightened and he looked her up and down. Must've liked what he saw because he swaggered over to her. Plenty of men in college would act this way around Zinnia when they wanted a date. "You've heard of me."

She cocked her head. "Well, you know, Steve, I've also heard about serial killers, embezzlers, and"—she cocked a brow—"people who steal property that doesn't belong to them. Therefore, I wouldn't get proud about the fact that I've heard of you."

This stunned the group.

One of the boys, in the back, uttered an, "Oooo." Steve cut him a dangerous look that made him shrink and silence at once.

"Also." She tugged Ryan in the opposite direction. "I thought you'd be taller. Have a nice day."

Once they disappeared from the group's view, blocked by several cornstalks, all of Ryan's body relaxed.

"That was amazing, Zinnia."

She shrugged. "The tall comment gets them every time. Boys act so weird when it comes to height."

"I—"

This time Ryan slackened his grip. Zinnia didn't unlace her fingers. He re-tightened his.

"I'm sorry, Zin. I have a feeling that every time I'm around him, I'm going to freeze up like that. No idea when I'm finally going to be able to approach him with confidence."

"Hey, Ryan." She squeezed his hand. Orange sunbeams brightened the corn stalks around them. "I'm not going anywhere."

The film had been due by midnight on Tuesday night, and Ryan had turned it in at eleven p.m. Though he would have liked to keep tweaking until the very last minute, any later and he would have run the risk of the files not downloading fast enough, or the WiFi cutting out, or any other innumerable reasons he could foresee that might cause him to miss the deadline.

He'd pulled an all-nighter Monday night, so after turning in the film Tuesday, he had collapsed into bed and immediately fallen asleep—only to awaken early the next morning with the knowledge that he'd put off several projects to work on the film, and those deadlines were looming.

The rest of the week had faded into such a blur of frenzied work activity that he'd hardly had time to think about the film, let alone catch up on sleep. As a result, the exhaustion still weighed on him today—his eyes had drifted closed a few times on the hayride.

Maybe he *had* in fact fallen asleep in the hay, because he could have sworn he just witnessed Zinnia deliver two devastating zingers in a row to none other than Steve.

And he had kissed Zinnia's forehead—twice. Where did that boldness come from?

It had simply felt right in the moment. Luckily, she didn't seem to mind. Seemed to enjoy it, even.

He looked down at their hands and watched as their fingers wove together while they walked. That wasn't a platonic handhold, right? Why did he feel like an eighteen-year-old kid again, awkward and blushing over something as simple as holding a pretty girl's hand?

"I don't know if this film will go anywhere, Zinnia," he admitted, meeting her eyes. "I want this for you, so much. I want you to be able to act. You're amazing at it. No one deserves a chance more than you."

Her fingers tightened around his. "What about you? You've worked so hard on this. You deserve it just as much, if for no other reason than that Steve needs to take a step down from his high horse."

"Well." He glanced around at the rows of corn. Dusk would be setting in soon, and they hadn't been paying much attention to where the diverging paths led. They should probably head out of the maze and into well-lit areas. "I have…an alternative lined up. My father wants me to run his branch in Roseville."

He cringed. Would she give him that disdainful look, the one that said *you're just a spoiled rich kid*?

Instead, her brow furrowed. "If that's what you feel God calling you to…maybe. But it doesn't seem like you're happy about it."

No, maybe not. But maybe with the job, he would be able to help *her* pursue her dreams.

He couldn't tell her that, though.

"I guess we both have a lot riding on it then." His heart picked up its pace, but he steeled himself to be brave enough to utter the next words. "I'd like to think either way, though, that maybe we could, ah, find a way to still be in one another's lives. Even if we're not working on this film."

Her steps slowed from the already meandering pace they'd been keeping. "Yeah. I mean." Her words came out more hesitantly than usual. "It's always disappointing when you make new friends during a project, and then once it's over, you never see them again."

Ryan's feet stopped moving entirely. Zinnia took one more step before halting and turning to face him.

He glanced at their hands clasped between them, then back up to Zinnia's downcast eyes that didn't quite meet his. "You are an important friend to me, and that won't change. But I was thinking…maybe something in addition to friends?" He cleared his throat. "I understand if you aren't interested in me that way, of course."

She didn't respond for a second, only staring at him with an expression he couldn't quite decipher. Dry corn rustling provided the only sound.

*Now you've done it. Why did you have to say something? Of course you misread this. Why would she be interested in you?*

"I…" She paused and tried again. "After everything you know about me, you would still want that?"

Wait, she thought *he* might not consider *her* good enough?

His chest squeezed. "Of course." He took a step closer, scooping her other hand into his. He could shake Georgia for putting these sorts of fears and insecurities in Zinnia's mind. "Like I told you, I'm not going anywhere."

She had somehow drifted closer, until they were less than a foot apart. Her face tilted toward his, and his breath caught. His gaze drifted to her lips, and, heart beating fast, he started to lean down—

"Aren't corn mazes for kids?" A young male voice rang out through the corn stalks. "How are we *this* lost?"

Ryan stepped away quickly, Zinnia mirroring his action, as a group of three familiar college students came tromping around the bend.

In the lead, Tristan spotted them first. "Thank goodness, real adults."

Martell shook his head. "We've been in here for maybe half an hour. We're not lost."

"Tristan has the attention span of a child, though." Mariana stepped over an especially large mud puddle.

"Hey, guys." Ryan attempted to keep his tone even. The college students had no reason to suspect they'd stumbled into anything, but he knew Tristan especially would be insufferable if he caught wind of potential romantic tension between Ryan and Zinnia. "I can't say we know our way through the maze either, sorry."

"Guess we'll have to team up." Martell gestured past them, toward a fork in the path. "Left or right, people?"

Ryan cast Zinnia an apologetic look, but she simply laughed. "Looks like the crew has one last project. What do you think, director? Left or right?"

"I think we should vote. All in favor of right, say 'aye.'"

As the group shouted their input, Ryan told his pulse to calm down. Now probably wasn't the right time to decide anything with Zinnia anyway.

Not when so many things could change, depending on the results of the competition.

# Chapter Twenty-Two

"FOR THE LAST TIME, ZINNIA, WE'RE not listening to a true crime podcast."

Zinnia chuckled as Ryan gripped the steering wheel of the fourteen-passenger van. In between the week of the hayride and the journey to the film festival, he'd taken a class at the university to get van-certified.

Ten minutes into the drive, Zinnia tried to confiscate his phone so she could choose what music—or podcast—they'd listen to on the expedition.

Zinnia cocked her head and slid her fingers toward the phone again. A GPS told Ryan to take an exit in point-four miles. "Isn't the rule that the person in the passenger seat gets to choose the music?"

In a playful motion, Ryan tapped her hand. "No, pretty sure it's the driver who makes the music selection."

"Yo, I'm pretty sure it's whoever is crammed into the middle seat in the back."

Ryan squinted in the rearview mirror.

"Umm, two things, Tristan. One, you *chose* to sit in the middle seat. We have plenty of room in this van. We don't have fourteen people in our cast and crew."

Behind her, Zinnia heard giggles from the other passengers.

"Two, you've literally been wearing headphones this whole time, listening to music on your own."

Zinnia glanced over the seat to observe Tristan shrug. "Might as well let you all listen to some *good* music."

Ryan frowned and shut off the indie playlist. "There." His tone remained spirited. "Happy?"

Dead silence took over the car.

"Well." Zinnia drummed her fingers on her knees. "Since Ryan has left us in awkward quiet, why doesn't he tell us which ending he picked? Happy or sad?"

"Yes, yes, yes," chanted the people in the back.

Someone tapped in a rhythmic beat on Ryan's seat as he made an exit from one highway and boarded the ramp to the next.

"For the last time." Ryan's engine revved as a car behind them attempted to pass. "It's a surprise. You will all find out which ending I went with when we watch the movie at the festival."

No use. By now, the back seat had begun chorusing, "Ryan, Ryan, Ryan."

As a last-ditch effort to silence them, Ryan tossed his phone at Mariana and jabbed a finger at her. "Don't play anything terrible."

"You got it, boss."

Two seconds later, *VeggieTales* blared through the speakers.

Mariana handed Ryan his phone back for GPS purposes. He did a poor job in masking his groan.

"Oh, come on." Mirth bubbled in Zinnia's stomach. "I think Mariana did a very good job in her song selection."

Ryan's lips twitched. "That so?"

"Why, yes. 'His Cheeseburger' is one of the most romantic songs to ever be composed. What I wouldn't give for a man to compare me to a fast food sandwich."

"Speaking of food." Tristan leaned forward. "When are we going to stop for lunch?"

Ryan sighed. "Tristan, it's barely eleven, and we're only twenty minutes into the drive."

"My stomach disagrees. Says it's been *six* hours."

Those in the back started to shout, "Cheeseburger, cheeseburger," on repeat.

Ryan cut a glance at Zinnia. "Why do I feel like you and I are the Mom and Dad in this situation?"

Seconds later, scarlet filled his face.

For the past few days, Zinnia and Ryan texted a lot. Each spoke of plans to grab another coffee, but work and photoshoots got in the way of any potential dates. She thought back to the near-kiss in the corn maze.

"Er, I mean—it's just they're acting like kids. Were we like that at all when we were their age, Zin?"

"And fries." Tristan started another chant.

"Fries, fries, fries, fries…"

Zinnia's hands clasped onto the knees of her jeans. "I honestly imagine we were much worse."

Minutes later, Ryan relented and pulled off at an exit with a Five Guys. After he double checked to make sure no one had a peanut allergy, they stepped inside. Ryan told Zinnia to order first, and as the server handed her a cup for a drink, he slid his card into the reader.

"What are you—?"

"Whoops." He shrugged. "Sometimes my hands are out of control, and they accidentally pay for other people's food."

"Ooo." Tristan bounced up and down in the line behind them. "Ryan got Zinnia a cheeseburger. Ryan's being romantic."

Before the group could start another chant about "romance," Zinnia slipped over to the Coke machine and selected a drink option. The film cast and crew sat at a circular red table and partook of their meals.

Zinnia decided she'd never tasted a better burger.

As they finished, the cluster discussed which Hollywood elite would make an appearance. The festival website purposely left the details vague. Perhaps in fear that the hopeful filmmakers would swarm the decision-makers who would attend.

"Been scanning through social media from last year." Ryan crumpled his wrapper into a silver ball. "And the years prior. From what I can tell, there will be dozens of people there watching the films. Even if we don't win first place, maybe they'll still be interested in us."

By the way his voice dropped, Zinnia could tell he didn't believe it.

When it came to competitions, everyone remembered who got the gold medal. Silver and bronze always faded into the background.

They piled into the car, and several Silly Songs with Larry later, they arrived at the festival.

Several hundreds, maybe thousands, of chairs littered a lawn in front of a large, sheeted screen.

"It's happening outside?" Zinnia unbuckled her seatbelt. "It's got to be forty degrees out there."

To her knowledge, many film festivals took place indoors.

"Hence why I told you all to bundle up in my email communications." Ryan popped open his door. "We're here a little early, so feel free to grab some concessions, and we'll all sit together as a group."

Zinnia shoved her hands into the pockets of her cardigan and scanned the area for food lines. She spotted a queue for movie popcorn and joined the line that snaked all the way to the seats.

She padded over to the line and paused when a woman in a gray wool coat approached at a similar speed from the opposite direction.

"Sorry." Zinnia gestured in front of her. "You go ahead."

"Thank you."

From the looks of the woman—her smoky eyeshadow and false lashes—everything about her read as a film-starlet hopeful to Zinnia. Good, they had something in common.

Zinnia bounced up and down to generate some heat in her legs. "Are you excited?"

"Hmm?" The woman spun around.

"Are you excited for the festival? It's my first time, so I don't know what to expect."

The woman's expression softened. "Yes, I suppose so. It's always great to meet with people who have a passion for fine arts."

Unease melted in Zinnia's gut. She was just an actress talking with another thespian.

"Right? I mean, it's so cool to connect with people who really *get* it. That there's so much more than just saying lines in front of a camera. There's a whole crew that makes the magic come to life, and it's honestly an honor to participate in an art form that's been around for more than a century."

Two steps forward the line marched.

"What's your name again?" the woman asked.

"Zinnia, sorry." Zinnia shook the woman's gloved hand. "Went right into geeking about film."

"Heather. Are you in one of the films today?"

Zinnia nodded. Heather asked about the premise, and Zinnia started her explanation. A few sentences in, someone tapped her on the shoulder. She whirled around to see Ryan.

He motioned her over.

"In a minute, I'm getting popcorn."

His gestures moved at a rapid pace, more frantic.

"Okay, fine." Zinnia waved at Heather. "Talk soon, nice to meet you."

Ryan and Zinnia paced several yards away from Heather, and Zinnia shoved her hands into her pockets once more. "I hope this is good, Ryan, because you took me away from America's most beloved movie snack, and a nice lady."

"Don't you know who that is?"

Zinnia gave a firm nod. "Heather."

Ryan face-palmed. "Yes, and do you know who Heather is?"

"A nice lady?"

"Yes, a nice lady who happens to be the type of lady who options things for full-length feature films."

Zinnia's veins froze, and she couldn't blame it this time on the brisk wind.

"You mean—"

"Yes, she's one of the *important* people here."

"Isn't that good, though, that I talked with her? She could put names to faces when she watches our film."

Ryan kicked a rock, and it trundled down a grassy hill.

"I guess it's not really your fault. I forgot to mention this to the people in the car, but the festival said we're not supposed to be intermingling with the folks from Hollywood."

Zinnia blinked a glaze out of her eyes, partly due to the breeze. "Oh."

Ryan's expression melted and he clapped a hand on Zinnia's shoulder.

"I'm sure Heather knew you weren't one of *those* people. The festival had to implement the rule because in years past, people would bombard them before and after the screenings. In the hopes that they could force them to do something with their script or film."

Zinnia's tongue clicked against her teeth. "That's awful."

Ryan stiffened. As she turned her head, she saw why. Heather cradled a bucket of popcorn and waved at them.

"Hope all goes well with your film." She winked at them and headed toward one of the seats behind a large table.

On the back of the chair was a label.

"Festival Judge."

Booths sold merch of commemorative shirts, hats, buttons, and more for festivalgoers. Film schools and other organizations peddled their services at their own pop-up tents. Concessions and food trucks sold movie snacks and everything from hot dogs to tacos. But Ryan had eyes only for one thing.

The stage.

Soon, on that enormous screen, their film would play for the crowd currently milling around booths, chatting, laughing, and shaking hands with strangers, industry professionals, and a few C-list actors Ryan recognized. Today, the final day of the three-day festival, not only would their project show, but also the awards would be handed out.

Their slot in the showing order had been fortuitously convenient for driving a van full of people out for one day instead of multiple.

Film buffs and enthusiasts probably composed most of the crowd. Fans gave him enough anxiety. But the Hollywood folks…

The Five Guys they'd had for lunch churned in his stomach.

"Hey." Zinnia gave his arm a squeeze. "We did our best. Now we just need to sit back, watch some films, and see what God has in store." But the lines of worry on her brow belied her words.

"Right." He took a deep breath. "Why don't I go stake out some seats for our group?" He scanned the crowd for their cast and crew. "I think I lost half of them already."

Zinnia pointed at Tristan and Martell toting gigantic fair-style bags of popcorn. "Found two of them. I was going to get popcorn for the group, but I think they beat me to it."

Tristan held up his bag and waved. "We will feast like kings!"

As they approached, Mariana joined their group, holding a stack of plastic cups. "Got these too, so we can share out the popcorn into individual portions." She made a face at Tristan. "I don't want to eat popcorn your grubby fingers have been all over."

He squinted at his hands, as if looking for dirt.

The cast members still seemed to be exploring, so Ryan led the crew—plus Zinnia—toward the chairs. "Let's claim some good ones toward the front if we can. Perks of arriving early."

They wove through clusters of chatting individuals and scooted through the chairs to a row about a third of the way from the front. The students performed the sideways shuffle toward the middle, Zinnia and Ryan after them.

As Ryan sank into his seat, leaving enough open for the rest of the cast, his gaze landed on a familiar form in the second row from the screen, chatting with a known Hollywood figure. He stiffened. Steve. Breaking the rules and hobnobbing with judges.

Zinnia nudged him. "I take it Steve isn't supposed to be talking to that man."

"No. And Steve knows that." Ryan's fist clenched on his knee.

Zinnia placed her hand over his. "I'm sure the judges will see his attempt at cheating for what it is. Steve's gotten away with being slimy for too long. One day, it's going to come back to bite him."

His blood calmed, and he nodded as he looked down at their hands. Gently, he slid his fingers through hers and squeezed.

She didn't let go.

What felt like eons of waiting later, contest directors and other important members of the festival opened the event with announcements, speeches, and a blur of other content that crashed through Ryan's mind and left like a roaring stream, wiping away all thoughts and gone the moment he heard it. Usually, he would enjoy this homage to his favorite art form, but today, his nerves practically vibrated with tension. They couldn't get to their film soon enough.

Film rolled for the first contender. And the next. And the next. Ryan knew some had been eliminated even before this showing, whether for missing required elements, not following guidelines, or being of too low of quality for the festival to show. He hadn't told his cast and crew about that initial round of cuts—he'd been confident they didn't need to worry about those with the quality of their equipment and talent.

Even so, films rolled all afternoon, with few breaks, though viewers came and went in between entries. Ryan's cast and crew finished the popcorn, and still their project had yet to show.

A name on the screen caused Ryan to sit up straight in his seat.

Steve.

Ryan glanced at Zinnia, and she squeezed his hand with a reassuring nod.

The first scene opened. Ryan's eyebrows shot up. The shot was almost exactly the same as an early version of his original script.

As the film continued, the cast and crew around him shifted uncomfortably, tossing each other glances. Martell's eyes widened, and he slid lower and lower in his seat.

"Hey," Ryan whispered to him. "Not your fault. Steve is…just like that." He gave a stiff smile. "Good thing we changed a lot of things since the original, right?"

But as they watched, Ryan realized Steve's film was…

Bad.

The camera work was sloppy. The storyline felt disjointed. Some of the actors seemed confused on what they were saying and what Steve's flowery lines actually meant.

And in the end, the main character…died.

Zinnia snorted, then clapped a hand over her mouth, muttering, "Sorry." She leaned closer to Ryan. "It's just so melodramatic. I can't take it seriously. This isn't considered good film, right? Trying to be edgy for no good reason?"

"I certainly hope not." But who knew? Judges tended to love the tragic stuff.

Tragic. The opposite of his project. He felt as if he might be sick.

Only one film showed after Steve's before the opener of Ryan's team's appeared. His heart kicked into high gear. His fingers tightened around Zinnia's.

At that moment, movement in the corner of his eye distracted him. A well-dressed couple took their seats a few rows away.

His *parents*? What were they doing here? Sure, he needed to give Dad an answer today, but he hadn't thought they would track him down.

He turned his attention back to the screen, currently filled by Zinnia's beautiful, pensive expression. His stress melted away for a moment as he marveled, *She looks so good on the big screen. Like she was made for it.*

As the story neared its end, Ryan felt his team lean forward in anticipation. What ending had he chosen?

On screen, Zinnia opened the door. Looked through.

Beside him, Zinnia audibly gasped and grabbed his arm. He glanced over to see her staring at the stage, mouth open, expression slowly morphing into an enormous grin as she remained otherwise perfectly still, taking in the scene.

End credits. The audience clapped, and the applause seemed more animated than it had for the last several films. Ryan could just make out the judges leaning over, whispering to each other, writing things down. A good sign?

Zinnia squeaked, turned to him, and threw her arms around him. "You chose the happy ending!"

He gave a breathless laugh, not sure his voice would work. "I did." He smiled at the cast and crew, and especially at Zinnia. "I chose hope for the future."

He hoped she knew he meant more than just the film.

# Chapter Twenty-Three

ZINNIA COULDN'T BELIEVE IT. RYAN CHOSE the happy ending.

The awards ceremony would take place in ten minutes. Enough time for people to bolt to the porta-potty stations around the rows of chairs. Zinnia shivered next to the vacant seats as Ryan ventured out to talk with a group of people who Zinnia didn't recognize. Ryan knew far more people in the film circuit than Zinnia. She imagined they all went to the same competitions.

A squeal pierced Zinnia's ears.

She spun around in her seat and spotted Joy, ambling over to her. "Girl."

Joy reached Zinnia's chair and embraced Zinnia in an awkward hug, where Zinnia's head went into Joy's stomach.

"That was amazing, Zinnia. I know I've seen clips of you doing theater before, but that was something else."

Ryan had worked with her through the differences between film and play acting. Even if today didn't end in their favor, at least Zinnia could transfer those skills into future movie gigs she auditioned for.

"Thank you so much for coming." When Joy released, Zinnia glanced behind her neighbor for the usual gaggle of kids who followed Joy around. "Where are Justice and the others?"

"Left them at home with Ben."

Joy held something in her hands, a Styrofoam cup. She blew on the lid and motioned at the drink.

"Hot chocolate. It burned my tongue off the first time I sipped, so I'm waiting for it to cool."

Joy must've grabbed the beverage during a break between films. Twilight crept into the night skies, as they'd turned from orange to purple. Now, bright lights illuminated the rows of chairs.

Zinnia scooted to the side, and Joy transplanted into Ryan's seat. He wouldn't mind. As she glanced over her shoulder, he'd begun an animated discussion with an older woman.

"Although I must say, I don't know how Ben is faring with the little hobbits." Joy ventured a sip. The drink must've cooled enough, because she tipped her head back and drank in a large gulp. "Unfortunately, I can't stick around for the awards ceremony—I'm worried they'll burn the house down if I stay too long—but I wanted to pop by and say hi."

Zinnia gazed at the hot cocoa in envy. Soon, after Joy left, she'd need to get her own to warm her belly.

"I really *do* appreciate you making your way out here."

Joy flicked a droplet of chocolate off of her knit wool scarf. "Do you think you'll do more film stuff after this?"

Zinnia's cold fingers ran up and down her pants.

"I hope so. If not, I apparently have a princess gig I can try out for. You know the actors who come to birthday parties and such?"

Before Zinnia and Ryan left the farm last week, she made sure to get the phone number of Ice Princess. Although all film prospects lay outside of her control, she could try other activities.

Life didn't end at the age of twenty-seven.

"That would be cool." Joy rose from her seat. "Honor's been begging for one of those princesses to come to her party. Although I will say, she may recognize you, so we may not be the best first customers."

"Beats being a dragon or evil queen. I've been trying to convince her for ages that I'm secretly royalty."

The two of them exchanged a hug, and Joy headed toward the parking lot.

Wasting no time, Zinnia joined the snaking queue that led to a hot chocolate and cider station. A few seconds in, someone tapped her shoulder.

"For goodness sake, Ryan, can't I get into a line for refreshments without—?"

She whirled around and froze. Georgia sprawled a timid hand in a gesture of hello. By the way her shoulders scrunched and cheeks pinked, Georgia felt embarrassed. Something Zinnia swore her younger sister had never experienced in her life.

"Oh." Zinnia's throat dried as she swallowed. "Hi."

"Hi."

Georgia's pointed-toe shoes dug themselves into the dirt. She wouldn't make eye contact with Zinnia.

"You did a great job."

"Oh, thanks. I had no idea you were coming."

In Zinnia's periphery, she saw the queue inch forward. She followed along. Georgia didn't move from her place.

"Your neighbor—Joy, is it? She found me on social media and messaged me. Chewed me out in a few voice messages for not treating you well."

Zinnia's blood iced.

Much as she appreciated the gesture from Joy, Georgia would think that Zinnia put her up to it.

Georgia appeared to read Zinnia's expression.

"She mentioned that you had no idea she was doing any of that."

"I didn't."

"Right, so anyway. I still stand by what I said, but I do think I could've delivered the message in a calmer manner."

An understatement. Plant pots didn't tend to shatter in normal conversations.

Zinnia exhaled. As far as apologies went, this would be the best Georgia could offer her for a while. She'd accept what she could and leave the rest of the situation in God's hands.

"I appreciate you acknowledging that, Georgia. Maybe sometime we can talk about how to handle conflict when we get into another fight."

"Right." Georgia smacked her glossed lips. "I didn't come here to talk about that disagreement, though. It's in the past, and I already apologized for it, so let's move on."

Frustration bubbled in Zinnia's gut.

*Let it go for now, girl. Let it go.*

Zinnia planned to get a therapist sometime soon to work through some of the issues between herself and her sister. She hoped a counselor could provide further direction and guidance. And, of course, she planned to pray about the situation plenty too.

"I came to watch you in a film, which you were very good at by the way." Georgia brushed loose hairs that blew into her face out of the way. "Also, I came to tell you that I thought about what Aunt Millie told me."

About how Zinnia thought Georgia experienced some resentment in her marriage?

"Although I think it was *really* not your place to say anything about relationships, since you don't have much experience in those—"

*Easy there, Zinnia. Let's not ball our fist at Georgia. She picks up on all nonverbal cues.*

Zinnia's hand relaxed.

"—it did make me realize that I do miss certain things. Like dance and helping out with kids at church. Matt and I went back and forth a lot on this. Since he's the head of the household, I really have to defer to his judgment, but—"

Georgia's shoes drew a line in the mud.

"He's agreed to let me go to an adult dance class that meets once a week. We perform next year. Next June, to be exact."

*A start.*

When it came to people like Matt and Georgia, Zinnia would take all the allowances she could get.

"That's great, Georgia. I look forward to seeing your recital."

Georgia's lips twitched. A glow kindled in Zinnia's chest. After years of work, perhaps the sisters could re-create the friendship they once shared. For now, though, she'd settle for the amazing pseudo-older sister, Joy.

"Anyway." Georgia's neck snapped up in a straight line. "Really should be getting home. Matt doesn't like when I'm out this long. Lord knows the man doesn't know how to cook. Last time I was out with friends, he ate tuna out of a can."

Neither of them exchanged a hug.

However, as Zinnia waved her goodbye, she thought about all the bullets she had dodged when Matt dumped her and dated her sister instead.

"Hey." Ryan's voice perked her ears.

She spun around and beamed at him.

"You okay, Zin? Saw you talking with Georgia."

Oh, right, she'd shown him plenty of photos of her sister from her social media pages.

"You know what, Ryan?" Zinnia slipped her arm into his. She could get hot cocoa later. "I think I'm better than I have been for a long, long time."

He led her to the row of chairs. The crew and cast returned to their seats. Several of them held various snacks. Mariana offered Zinnia sour gummy worms. She took one and savored the puckering lemon flavor.

"You're sure you're doing okay?" Ryan whispered to her as the MC approached the steps to the stage. "An awards ceremony and an encounter with a sister is a lot to take in for one day."

Zinnia's breath rattled.

Yes, the next two minutes could determine a lot. Plus, Georgia didn't exactly give her full closure when it came to their previous spat. Sometimes wounds took years or a lifetime to heal from.

"I think I'm going to be okay. You know why?"

"Why?"

She laced her fingers into his. Somehow his hands managed to be far icier than hers, but she didn't mind.

"Because, Ryan, I'm completely out of control of this situation."

This caused him to snort. He squeezed her hand. "Is that supposed to be a good thing?"

Zinnia nodded. "It is, and do you know why?"

"I have a feeling you're going to tell me whether I want to hear or not."

"It's because that means Someone else is in control when I'm not."

She glanced heavenward. Ryan followed her gaze, then his eyes roved to the stage.

The MC began announcing the awards.

The speech-making, of course, had to go on forever. Ryan's heart might not be able to take the waiting.

Ryan hadn't been able to catch sight of his parents during the break. He almost wondered whether he'd hallucinated them.

"Third place, director Steve Lebont with *Dying for Stardom*."

Steve's groupies whooped and cheered as Steve strode toward the stage. Yet Steve's posture remained stiff, almost angry.

*Third place not good enough for you, Steve?*

On stage, however, he transformed into the picture of geniality, smiling for the crowd, calling out "friends" in the audience among investors and directors. Notably, he didn't mention his cast and crew.

A filmmaker Ryan hadn't met before took second place. As the woman made her acceptance speech, Ryan's shoulders began to sag. What were the odds his team had won first? He'd hoped to at least place.

As before, movement distracted him. An entire group in motion.

He stared. Andy and Caroline, Griffith and Hadassah, even their friends Liv and Elijah waved from the sidelines, scurrying to take seats along with an older couple, none other than his parents.

*How?* All of their friends must have rushed from work and school to make it here just in time for the awards ceremony.

"No way," Zinnia said, leaning around him to see. "They all came."

Mom gave him a little wave, then pointed at her phone.

He pulled his own phone out of his pocket. A text from Mom read, "Griffith told us we needed to be here today! Also, he brought your friends. Sorry we're late."

Ryan looked up again. At Mom's motion, his father also turned, giving Ryan a slight nod before returning his attention to the front.

*Everyone came—and Griffith organized it.*

His buddy gave a grinning thumbs up.

No matter the result of this competition, with friends like his, he'd already won.

"…directed by Ryan Torino…"

His head snapped toward the stage at the MC's voice saying his name.

"First place in the Roseville Film Festival Thirty Day Filmmakers Challenge."

For a moment, everything seemed to go still.

*Am I dreaming?*

Then Ryan could hear again as the audience cheered. He heard Tristan's distinctive whoop and Zinnia's gasp of delight. She shoved him forward. "Go! You have to go accept the prize."

He stumbled to his feet but possessed enough wherewithal to turn to his team. "No. *We* need to accept the prize." He grinned. "We did this together." He even pointed at Griffith and made a summoning motion. As a co-writer, he needed to be there too.

Ryan didn't care how many brows raised in their direction as his grinning, laughing cast and crew accompanied him onto the stage and crowded around the podium. He looked around at their shining faces, and he knew he only had one thing to say.

"Making a film is a team effort. Every person on set plays an important role, especially in a small indie film like this one. And every person has their own dreams and hopes, none more or less important than another."

He held Zinnia's hand, up on stage in front of everyone. Yup, he had something very important to ask her after this awards ceremony.

"I'm so proud of this team. No matter what the outcome, I'm so glad we all were able to work together. Everyone here has a bright future."

Through the lights, Ryan saw a figure storm away from the second row.

Steve.

For once, Ryan didn't feel even a hint of anger. Instead, he only felt sad for his former friend.

*May you make some realizations, Steve. And may you find some real friends. Like I have.*

The feeling of walking on air followed him through the conclusion of their acceptance, through the congratulations from their friends, through the enormous hug from Mom and the approving handshake from Dad.

"I can't take the job," Ryan said. "I appreciate it. I really do. But..." He glanced toward the stage. "I think I have a different calling."

Dad nodded. "I anticipated as much." A slight smile broke his stoic expression for one moment. "I'm proud of you, son. You made your own way. You're your own man."

Flabbergasted, Ryan could only stare as Dad clapped him on the shoulder and then walked away.

"Hey, Ryan."

He turned at Zinnia's voice.

She stood beside the woman from the popcorn line, smiling. "There's someone who would like to talk to us. Both of us."

Ryan felt like he needed his inhaler once the woman began speaking—speaking about working with them on a feature-length film project she had planned.

"I think you're just the sort of writer and director I need to help me bring this vision to life," she said to Ryan. Then she turned to Zinnia. "And I have a leading role that when I saw you, I knew—it was made for you."

At the end, she gave them both her contact information and the contacts of a few agents she recommended, with promises to be in touch.

After another couple of hours, the festival had finally died down to just a few remaining groups, vendors tearing down, and a crew tearing down the stage.

Ryan glanced around, but their cast and crew seemed to be otherwise occupied, leaving him alone with Zinnia.

"So I guess we might be doing the real thing, huh?" Starlight sparkled in her eyes.

"I guess so." He took a deep breath. "None of us could have done this without you, you know. *I* couldn't have." His mouth lifted in a goofy grin. "I think we make a pretty good team…for a lot of things."

She raised a brow. "A good team, huh?" She sidled a little closer. "Are you trying to suggest something?"

"Maybe we could, ah." He cleared his throat, summoning his courage. "Zinnia, would you be interested in dating, officially?"

Cliché as he knew the sentiment was, he was certain her radiant smile rivaled the moon.

"I officially would."

No college students popped out of the corn maze this time as he leaned down and her arms wrapped around his neck. When their lips met, he couldn't help but feel like he'd stumbled into a movie all his own. Because the way he felt…

It couldn't be considered anything other than a Hollywood-worthy happy ending.

# AUTHOR'S NOTE

As humans, it's a very "human" thing to want to control our situation.

Media tells us that we need to take fate by the reins. That we control our destiny. But if we happen to live in life for about two seconds, we know that so many things happen that we have no control over.

Maybe we tried everything in the dating sphere and "put ourselves out there" in just about every way possible, and we didn't find "the one." Whereas some of our friends had the right guy or girl show up in high school or college.

Maybe we threw ourselves wholeheartedly into our work. We gave up lunches, did unpaid overtime, did everything we could to impress our bosses, and the newest coworker who didn't do all those things got the promotion.

Maybe we tried to be the best friend ever to someone who didn't treat us the best. And maybe we thought that if we were kind enough and did enough nice things that they'd be better to us. And maybe that situation got even worse, to the point where we had to step away from that friendship.

Some of these sound specific? They may or may not have been based on some things that I (Hope) and Alyssa experienced.

But here's the thing. Beauty did spring up from those situations that spiraled out of control.

We had new family members join the ranks through painful divorces. We learned boundaries for ourselves when friends didn't treat us well. We learned that our worth does not come from relationships with romantic interests, but through a relationship with the Most High God.

So much of life happens beyond what we can control. If you're anything like me (Hope), you try to do what you can to "make it happen" for yourself. Then it fails. You realize fast that doors will only open when they are meant to open.

My coauthor and I endured a lot of things that happened outside of our control—in the publishing sphere and outside of it.

Along the way, we discovered that letting go and letting God move is always the best plan.

Life never happens exactly how we want it to happen. But often, it is far more beautiful than we could've personally planned.

So, God, I'm giving You the control. I pray that when I hand over everything to You that You do something very beautiful with what little I have to offer.

www.ingramcontent.com/pod-product-compliance
Lightning Source LLC
Chambersburg PA
CBHW061236210726
48293CB00003B/793